PRAISE FOR Hᴜɴᴛɪɴɢ Jᴜꜱᴛɪᴄᴇ

Sami A. Abrams hit it out of the park as she opened *Hunting Justice* with a powerful punch. This book met every goal that I look for as a reader. It had a sense of mystery, dedication, fear, truth, trust, and finally hope. Five out of five stars for the edge of my seat reading, from the very first page until the very end!

TINA, GOODREADS

I always know to expect a great book when I read one from the Elite Guardians series and this one lives up to that expectation! If you like heart-stopping suspense and action, tons of clues to follow, twists and turns to keep you guessing, and characters that you come to like and "root" for—this is the book for you.

DEBBIE, GOODREADS

This fast-paced, action-packed romantic suspense story has twists and turns. I couldn't put *Hunting Justice* down.

ALLYSON, GOODREADS

The twists and turns and secrets will keep you up, late into the night. Love how Noelle and Jonah found beauty in the dark. I highly recommend this book!

BETH, GOODREADS

HUNTING JUSTICE

ELITE GUARDIANS: SAVANNAH | BOOK TWO

LYNETTE EASON

SAMI A. ABRAMS

sunrise
PUBLISHING

Hunting Justice
Elite Guardians: Savannah, Book 2
Copyright © 2024 Sunrise Media Group LLC
Print ISBN: 978-1-953783-96-7
Large Print: 978-1-953783-98-1
EBOOK: 978-1-953783-99-8

This book is a work of fiction. Names, characters, places, and incidents are
either products of the author's imagination or used fictitiously. Any similarity to
actual people, organizations, and/or events is purely coincidental.

All Scripture quotations, unless otherwise indicated, are taken from the King
James Version.

For more information about the authors, please access their websites at
lynetteeason.com and samiaabrams.com.

Published in the United States of America.
Cover Design: Hannah Linder

I will praise thee; for I am fearfully *and* wonderfully made: marvellous *are* thy works; and *that* my soul knoweth right well.
Psalm 139:14 KJV

ONE

The bodies in the Savannah, Georgia county morgue had nothing on medical examiner Dr. Jonah Harris. Tentacles of fatigue wrapped around him and nearly squeezed the life out of him. Finished for the work day, he dragged himself into his private office and collapsed onto the chair, melting into the cushion. He leaned back and ran his hands over his face. Three autopsies in one day had pushed him to his limit, but the young girl who'd died in her sleep had gutted him.

A vacation sounded better by the minute. Maybe he'd take a day to recharge and gain some perspective again. Taking a tour of historic Savannah, simply relaxing at Forsyth Park with a book, or a stroll down the Riverwalk might do the trick. Anything to get away from the stress.

The office phone, somewhere on his desk, rang.

He lifted a handful of documents and peered beneath the mound of files, searching for the offending noise. A stack of papers slid from the pile and scattered over his desk, knocking his name plaque onto the floor.

1

Jonah sighed. What a mess. He envied people who had the neat gene. He, on the other hand, struggled with ADD, and one of the side effects was the chaos when it came to his organizational skills. Noelle Burton, a member of the Elite Guardians Agency Savannah office, teased him mercilessly. She'd even gone as far as buying him a framed poster for his office that said *A messy desk is a sign of genius.*

He found the phone and snatched the receiver from the cradle. "Dr. Harris."

"Hi, Jonah, this is Ken."

"Ken, how's it going?" Jonah tilted his head and scratched his five-o'clock shadow. Why hadn't his friend, chief medical examiner Dr. Ken Dodson, called his cell phone?

He smacked his forehead.

Holding the receiver between his ear and shoulder, he stood and retrieved his cell phone from his pants pocket. "Sorry. I turned off my cell phone while in autopsy and forgot to turn it on afterward."

"Appears like you've had a long day."

"You could say that, but let's not go there. How's your day off?" He half listened to his friend and mentor while his phone powered on. Several missed calls and text messages popped up.

"Jonah, I need to talk with you."

Ken's serious tone grabbed Jonah's attention. "Sounds ominous."

"I have something rather important to tell you. Can you come over after you finish at work?" Ken's request sent icy fingers crawling up Jonah's spine and onto his scalp.

He mentally ran through what he had to do before he could leave. "I can be there in about thirty minutes. Can you give me a hint?"

Silence met his ears.

"Ken?"

"I've done things I'm not proud of."

"Haven't we all?"

"No, you don't understand. Once this comes out, my professional reputation will be trashed."

Jonah froze. "Ken, you're worrying me here. Give me something?"

A deep sigh filtered across the line. "I'm ashamed to admit it, but I've falsified autopsy records."

Jonah's mind spun, trying to grasp Ken's admission.

"Jonah, please say something."

"I'm not even sure what to say." He clutched the arm of his chair and lowered himself onto the cushion. "Why?"

"Cecile's treatments were expensive. I made a deal with the devil. Now that my wife is gone, I intend to come clean, but I need your help and for you to stay quiet about it."

Jonah ran his hand through his hair. His friend had dropped a bombshell that would have a rippling effect. "You've put me in a tough position. If I keep your secret, then I'm covering up your crime. But if I tell, you'll lose your license and most likely go to jail."

"I would never ask you to commit a crime on my behalf."

"Then what are you asking?"

"I want you to reopen those cases and set the record straight before you take it public. I have my reasons. That's why I want you to come over. I'll give you the files and tell you what to look for."

Jonah sat in stunned silence. His friend had left him little choice in the matter. He blew out a breath. "All right. I'll be there as soon as I wrap up for the day."

"Thank you."

"And Ken..." Jonah swallowed past the lump invading his throat.

"Yes."

"You could have asked me for the money. I would have given it to you." He would have emptied his brokerage account if that's what it took to help the man who'd become like a father to him.

"I realize that now. I'll see you when you get here." The phone clicked off.

Jonah picked up the metal sign that had fallen and shoved it onto his desk. The notes from his last autopsy required his attention before he left for the day.

The dictation complete, he sent it to the medical transcriptionist to type up and glanced at the wall above the file cabinet. The clock mocked him. Jonah should have left fifteen minutes ago. He had to find out what in the world Ken had gotten himself into.

Falsifying autopsy reports? What had the man been thinking? And now he'd dragged Jonah into his crazy. But there was no need to jump to conclusions until he had proof. Maybe Ken had overreacted. Jonah could only hope.

He powered off his computer and tossed the options to Ken's confession around in his mind. Jonah would listen to Ken's explanation and figure out what he was up against, then he'd call his buddy Detective Matt Williams with the Savannah PD and discuss his legal obligations.

Since Ken held the title of chief medical examiner, that left Jonah in charge once Ken revealed his disreputable actions. Not the way Jonah wanted to earn the position. He shook his head.

After quickly glancing around the room and dismissing the idea of tidying the mess, he grabbed his keys. Ken was waiting, and Jonah wanted to get the distasteful business over with.

He slung his messenger bag over his shoulder and waved at one of the techs as he strolled down the hall. He pushed the emergency release bar on the back door and stepped outside.

The May air warmed his skin. Thank heavens the humidity hadn't hit swamp levels yet. Give it another month and sweat would be his friend.

With a sigh, he strode to his SUV. He dropped into the

driver's seat and stared out the front windshield, wishing he'd never received Ken's phone call.

Might as well get it over with. He cranked the engine and pulled from the parking lot.

Phone connected to his vehicle's Bluetooth, he hit the speed dial for Ken. Six rings and the voicemail picked up. "Hey, Ken. Sorry, I'm running late. I'll be there in about ten minutes." Jonah jabbed the End button, disconnecting the call.

He drummed his fingers on the steering wheel. Why hadn't his friend picked up? He maneuvered through the side streets of town, letting his mind ponder the implications of Ken's admission. But until he knew the facts, he had no way of knowing what to do next.

Ten minutes later, he turned down the tree-lined street that Ken lived on. Spanish moss hung from the limbs, dangling high above the ground. Most days he'd find a soothing calmness about the landscape, but today the greenery reminded him of boney fingers from a horror movie, reaching out to grab him. Ominous?—maybe. A product of his dark mood?—most likely.

Jonah parked across from the pale-yellow two-story Victorian-style house that sat away from the others in the neighborhood. He stared at the home he'd visited multiple times on happier occasions. When Ken's wife Cecile had passed away a couple months ago, Ken had acquired hermit-like tendencies.

But Jonah understood. His wife Cara had died in his arms after a car accident. There he was, an ER doctor at the time— one of the best in the nation—and he couldn't save his own wife. Jonah shook off the memories. He had to deal with Ken's problems and not get sucked into the past.

He stepped from his vehicle and shut the door. Exhaling, he crossed the street.

A boom rocked the neighborhood.

Jonah tumbled backward and slammed onto the ground.

Flames erupted from Ken's house. Remnants of boards and furniture flew in multiple directions. Debris rained down, pelting his arms, legs, and torso.

He sucked in a breath and coughed. Pain shot through his chest, and a high-pitched ringing pierced his ears. His head pounded, but he pried his eyes open. The world whirled around him. Jonah blinked away the daze. Forcing himself to move, he rolled and pushed to a standing position.

Heavy smoke hovered above the back exterior of the house and the few standing walls. Flames leaped in the air, destroying the parts of the once-beautiful home that had survived the blast.

"Ken." His vocal cords refused to function. He groaned. Jonah hoped his friend wasn't inside, but deep down he feared Ken had been home when the house blew.

Dizziness almost took Jonah to his knees as he staggered, but he remained upright. He stumbled over broken glass to his SUV and slumped against the front bumper until his head stopped spinning. Once his vision cleared, he'd call 911, assuming his phone still worked. He just needed a moment to gather himself.

Sirens screamed as the emergency vehicles raced toward him. Someone else must have witnessed the blast and called.

His shoulders slumped, and he released a long breath. Closing his eyes, he dropped his chin to his chest.

"Doc!"

He lifted his head.

Detective Matt Williams strode toward him. "Doc, are you okay?"

"I've been better." Jonah had no idea what injuries he'd acquired. His brain hadn't gotten that far. But based on his throbbing head, he'd guess a concussion topped the list.

Matt placed a hand on his shoulder. "No kidding. You look awful."

"Thanks a lot." He touched his forehead, then glanced at his hand. Blood dampened his fingers. He'd shake his head at the injustice, but that would only make him dizzier.

"Come on, let's get you to the ambulance and let the paramedics take a look."

"Ambulance?" Jonah glanced to his right. Fire trucks lined the street. Uh, when had the fire department arrived?

"Never mind. I'll have them come to you. Don't move." Matt hurried off before Jonah responded.

Jonah let his gaze wander over the scene. Pieces of Ken's house lay scattered like a child's Lincoln Logs set, covering his friend's property and the neighbors' yards. But why?

The haze inhabiting his brain made reasoning next to impossible. Either the concussion was worse than he thought, or shock had dug in its claws.

A few moments later, Matt returned with paramedic Aaron Quincy in tow. The twenty-three-year-old medic hefted the black medical duffel higher on his shoulder and ran his gaze over Jonah.

"Hey, Doc. How about we get you seated before you fall down." Aaron cupped his elbow and helped him stand. "Let's use the back of your SUV."

"Sounds like a good idea." Jonah extracted the keys from his pocket and handed them to Matt. He hated to admit that the ability to focus and find the right button on the key fob was beyond his capabilities right now.

Matt chuckled. "Doc, I don't think I'll need those. All the windows of your SUV are blown out."

Before Jonah could register his friend's words, Matt and Aaron assisted him to the back of his SUV and popped the liftgate.

Matt brushed the glass from the interior. "Have a seat."

With his friends' help, he lowered himself onto the hard interior. The weight of what had happened pressed down on him.

"Let's get you checked out." Aaron flashed a penlight into his eyes.

Jonah flinched.

"Sorry about that, Doc." The paramedic continued his exam. "Matt, grab me that blanket."

"What's going on?" Matt asked.

"He's in shock. It's not extreme. At least, not yet."

A blanket was draped over Jonah's shoulders. He listened to the continued exchange going on around him, but the words didn't register in his brain.

The explosion and Ken's confession tumbled in his mind and refused to let go. Were the two linked?

"Doc, look at me. Doc!" Aaron's voice hardened.

Jonah raised his gaze to meet the paramedic's and pulled the blanket tighter. He had to get his act together, or both men would haul him to the hospital without a second thought. "Sorry. What did you say?"

Aaron studied him, then sighed. "I'm sure you've already figured this out, but you have a concussion. I'd advise a trip to the emergency room for a CT scan."

He shook his head and immediately regretted it.

"Doctors make the worst patients," Matt announced like he'd discovered the cure for the plague.

"You don't have to tell me." Aaron slid the blood pressure cuff on Jonah's arm.

"I'm right here, you two." Jonah forced himself to focus. His energy hovered around zero, and the ringing in his ears hadn't stopped. He didn't want to argue with the man, but he had no desire to spend hours at the hospital. "I'll consider it. But for now, the answer is no."

Aaron rolled his eyes and muttered under his breath while continuing to bandage Jonah's scrapes and bruises. "That's not a good idea, Doc."

The antiseptic stung, but Jonah stared at the chunks of wood and parts that used to be a beautiful home. "That may be true, and I'm not stupid. I'll monitor how I feel, but I can't leave—not yet."

Detective Ladecia "Decia" Slaton, mom of the group only because she was a few years older, married, and had three boys, strode toward him. Her somber expression told him all he needed to know.

"Hey, Doc."

"Decia." He swallowed the bile creeping up his throat. "You found Ken?"

She nodded. "The explosion blew his body from the house. He's in the yard. I haven't examined him yet. The firefighters are still working on the blaze."

How had he missed Ken's body? Then again, it didn't take a medical degree to know he was in shock.

"I'm sorry, Doc. He was a great guy." Decia's soft tone squeezed his heart.

Tears burned his eyes. He blinked them away and sucked in a breath. "Thank you."

Decia rested her hand on his arm. "What can we do, Doc?"

He tore his gaze from the devastation. "Catch the person who did this."

Matt placed his boot on the bumper. "Why would you think someone's responsible for the explosion? SFD is speculating a gas leak."

How much should he say? The situation required legal advice, but he had no proof with Ken gone. Jonah glanced at Matt.

His friend raised an eyebrow.

"Let's just say that Ken asked me for help. I left work and headed straight here. Arrived moments before the house blew up. It's a bit of a coincidence, don't you think?"

Decia leaned against the other side of the SUV. "I'd like to hear more about what Ken wanted your help with."

The pounding in Jonah's head chose that moment to increase. He had to figure out the truth before he mentioned specifics to the detectives. He had promised Ken, and he intended to keep that promise. But he had to give them something. "Ken requested that I reevaluate a few autopsies for him."

"Why would he do that?" Matt asked.

"I never got all the details. He died before I found out."

Decia studied him like a bug under a magnifying glass. "Doc, you're a lot of things, but a good liar isn't one of them."

"I'm not lying."

"Maybe so, but you aren't telling us the whole truth." He felt sorry for her three boys when they got in trouble. The woman was tenacious.

The detective reminded Jonah of his grandmother. Not in age or looks, but in how she read people like a human lie detector. "Your boys must not get away with anything."

A cheesy grin graced Decia's face. "Nope. I have a whole police department watching out for them."

Jonah chuckled, then groaned. "Give me time to figure out what's going on. You'll be my first call once I do." But not a minute before. He owed Ken that much. He'd given Decia and Matt the probability the explosion wasn't an accident. He knew the detectives. The information would not go uninvestigated.

"I can live with that...for now." Matt dropped his boot to the ground. Glass crunched under it. "But we still need to take your statement. I'm willing to wait a little while for the shock to wear off and that headache to ease, but it needs to happen sometime tonight."

"I appreciate that." If his head didn't stop pounding, he wasn't sure how much help he'd be.

Aaron packed his medical bag. "I've done all I can do. I hope you change your mind about the hospital."

"If I need it, I'll go." He examined the paramedic's

handywork and signed the *refusal to be transported* paperwork. "Thanks, Aaron."

"Sure thing, Doc." Aaron bade Matt and Decia goodbye, then took off to join his partner.

"Would you like a ride since yours is toast?" Matt gestured to the broken windows of the SUV.

"I...uh...I think I'd like to stay for a bit."

"Does your phone work?" Decia asked.

Jonah pulled the device from his pocket and tapped the screen. It lit up. "Thankfully, yes."

"We'll be around until we can get a look at Ken's body. Let us know if you change your mind about the ride."

"Thanks, Ladecia. I appreciate it."

The two detectives strode down the cordoned-off street.

Jonah sat alone in the back of his SUV, staring at the mess that used to be his friend's home. Fire hoses sprayed the remaining flames while the captain yelled instructions to the firefighters. The stench of charred wood and who knew what else burned his nose.

He toyed with his cell phone, pondering what to do next. Ken was gone, along with the explanation behind the falsified autopsy reports.

The urge to call Noelle had his fingers hovering over the speed dial. If he asked, she'd come. That was the kind of friendship they had.

But at the moment, he wasn't ready to face her—or anyone.

———

Elite Guardian Noelle Burton turned the lock on her three-bedroom craftsman-style house. She pushed the door open, placed her keys on the hook next to the entry, and lugged her duffel bag into her bedroom. Fatigue shrouded her body from the long week of protecting a celebrity model from a stalker while on vacation in Hilton Head.

Earbud in, she called Raven, the administrative assistant at Elite Guardians Agency Savannah, while she unzipped her bag.

"Hello."

She smiled at the chipper greeting. "Hey, Raven."

"Noelle. How'd it go?"

"Everyone's safe." She'd thought her last assignment would end in tragedy, but thankfully it hadn't. Beyond the potential loss of life, it wasn't a blemish she wanted on the new EGA Savannah office that she managed. "Chrissy Logan is doing as well as can be expected, and her stalker is behind bars."

"That's good to hear. Take tomorrow off. You deserve it."

"Maybe." Noelle appreciated the faith Lizzie and the other Guardians had placed in her to make the new branch office a success. She refused to let them down.

"Look, we know who really runs the office."

She chuckled. Raven wasn't wrong. The woman with the penchant for all things goth ran EGA Savannah flawlessly. "When you put it that way...I'll consider it."

"Good. Now get some rest."

The line went dead. Noelle shook her head and unloaded her duffel.

Dirty clothes in the hamper, she added clean clothes and refilled personal items in her go-bag. She placed the duffel in her closet and changed into a tank top. Home—the only place she'd wear the skin-revealing shirt. Her gaze drifted to the picture of her grandmother, a model who'd died of skin cancer a month before Noelle's fifth birthday. Noelle had been devastated, but it was her mother who'd changed. She demanded a model-perfect look, an annoying gift from her grandmother, and developed a new obsession with protection from skin cancer.

"Thanks, Mom, for the self-esteem problem."

She shook off the shame and eyed her bed. A nap sounded good after a week of being on alert, but her mind wouldn't shut down that easily. She retrieved a water bottle from the refrigerator and headed to her home office.

Pictures of homicides dating back fifteen years covered one wall. The set of photos of the faceless victim—her own case—made her stomach clench.

The scars on her upper arm, a gift from a serial killer, itched at the memories. The man had destroyed her sense of security at age seventeen, but she'd worked past her trauma and driven herself to become a detective at the Savannah Police Department.

Noelle's cell phone rang, jerking her from the past. She glanced at the caller ID and smiled. "Hi, Lizzie."

"Hey, girl. How's it going?" Her friend, Lizzie Tremaine Lee, sounded happy. And why shouldn't she be? She'd married her best friend on Christmas Eve. Lizzie was one of the few that knew about Noelle's past and her discontent with her law enforcement career.

"Things are going well. The new agency is busy."

"Are you happy you took the management position Olivia offered you?"

"I am." When Lizzie had approached her about a change in careers, Noelle had known she couldn't pass up the opportunity. Olivia Savage had taken it a step further and offered her the manager job at the EGA Savannah office. "I have a great core team with Alana Flores and Juliette Montgomery. And our admin, Raven, is amazing."

"Bottom line, are you content?" Leave it to Lizzie to cut to the heart of the issue.

Noelle's mind drifted to her job and friends. She *had* found contentment in her life over the past year.

"Noelle?"

"Yeah, I'm here. To answer your question...yes. Being a bodyguard has given me a new perspective."

"I'm glad."

"So, how's married life?"

Lizzie laughed. "With Charlie, it's always an adventure." Her friend got quiet for a moment. "It's more than I ever dreamed it could be."

"Oh, Lizzie." Her friend had lived through one heartbreak after another. "I'm thrilled for you." What Noelle wouldn't give to have someone to share life with. But her lack of experience in the romance department made it difficult to go beyond friendship. Besides, no man would attach themselves to someone as damaged and broken as her. Rubbing the thick white lines that covered her upper arm and extended to her chest and torso, she sighed.

"I have to get going. But remember, I'm here for you if you need to talk...about anything."

"I know. And I appreciate it. Take care, Lizzie."

"You too, my friend."

Noelle stared at the phone, then tucked it into her pocket. Her gaze traveled to the section of recent homicides on the wall of her office, and she lost herself in the cases. The ages of the women didn't match the older kills; however, they all had cuts that matched Noelle's.

A musty odor tickled her nose, and darkness closed in on her. Pain radiated through her upper body.

No. You're not in that room. You're home. Safe. She breathed deeply, struggling to bring herself to the present.

A ringing pulled her from the memory.

Noelle shook off the flashback and fumbled for her phone.

"Hello." Her greeting was breathier than she'd intended.

"Elle, it's Jonah."

She smiled at his nickname for her and pushed the past to the recesses of her mind. "Hi, Jonah. How are you?"

"Um...not so good."

His shaky tone registered. "What's wrong?"

"Ken's gone."

She straightened. "What do you mean? As in, he left town?"

"No, Elle. Ken's dead. Someone blew up his house."

She stumbled to her desk and dropped onto her office chair. "How? Why?"

"That's the thing. He asked me to come over to discuss a..." She heard him exhale. "...problem. I got delayed at work and arrived a few moments before his house exploded."

"Are you hurt? What can I do?" Jonah was a good friend. Probably the closest she'd ever get to a boyfriend. She hated hearing the pain in his voice.

"I have scrapes and bruises plus a mild concussion. But more than anything, I could use a ride. My SUV is damaged. And with the head injury, I shouldn't be driving."

She could relate. A year ago, she'd suffered a concussion that'd sidelined her for weeks. "Where are you?" Noelle hurried to her room and threw on a three-quarter-sleeve blouse over her tank top. She rushed to the entryway and grabbed her keys.

"I'm still at Ken's. I couldn't leave."

"Stay put. I'm on my way." She dashed out the door.

"Thanks, Elle. I hate to admit it, but I'm a bit lost as to what to do."

The fact he'd declared his mental state spoke of the trust he placed in her. If only she could return the sentiment. On most things she had trusted him, but her time in the hands of a serial killer—not so much.

"Hang tough, Jonah. I'll get you through this."

"I'll be waiting." He hung up.

There was more to the story than Jonah had divulged over the phone. She knew it down to the marrow of her bones. And she intended to find out what. Noelle hit the speed dial for Juliette.

"Hi, Noelle. Aren't you supposed to be sleeping?"

"Not happening at the moment. Jonah called. He said he's hurt, and Ken Dodson's house blew up."

"Is Ken okay?"

"He's dead."

Juliette's sharp inhale came over the line. "What do you need from us?"

"Nothing right now, but that might change. I'm headed over to check on Jonah and find out what's up."

"I'm sorry to hear about Ken. But I find it fascinating that Jonah contacted you first."

Noelle knew where that statement was going. "We're just friends."

"Sure, keep telling yourself that. The way he cared for you after he beaned you in the head with the line drive during that softball game—nope, not buying it."

"Friends, Juliette. That's all we'll ever be. I'll let you know what I find out."

"I'll let Alana know. We'll be waiting."

"Thanks." Noelle hung up and focused on getting to Jonah as fast as possible.

Twenty minutes later, she parked at the end of Ken's street. Fire trucks and police cars blocked her from getting closer. Red and blue lights flashed in a steady tempo. Yellow police tape looped the yard, blocking civilians from entering.

She ducked under the ribbon and flashed her special law enforcement credentials at the patrol officer guarding the scene.

He nodded, and she continued her trek toward the smoldering house.

A figure, hunched over in what used to be the manicured front yard of the chief medical examiner, caught her attention. She squinted. Jonah.

Hurrying to his side, she called out. "Jonah."

He straightened.

She glanced down at what had his attention and sucked in a breath. The explosion had thrown Ken into the yard.

The sheet used to cover the man's body had been folded back, exposing his torso. The stench of burnt flesh made her eyes water. But it was the bullet hole in his chest that roiled her stomach.

She stepped closer and held out her hand. Jonah clasped it and squeezed. When his gaze met hers, the pain in his eyes ripped her heart to shreds.

"You don't need to remember him like this." Noelle prayed he'd listen and walk away from the gruesome scene.

He stared at her with a vulnerability she'd never witnessed before. "I failed him."

She tilted her head. "How?"

His shoulders sagged, but he held tight to her hand. "He called me, needing my help. You know how I am. I got caught up with work. Lost track of time. I should've arrived earlier, but I was late. Maybe I could have saved him." Jonah's gaze dropped to Ken.

With her free hand, she not-so-gently gripped his chin and forced him to look at her. "Don't go there. You are not to blame for this." When he didn't attempt to look away, she eased her hold. "Jonah, if you'd left work on time, most likely you'd have been killed too."

"But what if—"

"No. We are not playing the what-if game. It'll get us nowhere." She softened her tone. "I feel bad about what happened to Ken. He was a great guy. But I will not apologize for the fact that I'm glad you didn't walk in on whatever happened. Maybe I'm being selfish, but I refuse to be sorry for feeling relieved that you aren't the one lying there under that sheet."

Tears pooled in his eyes. "Thank you for coming."

"Always." She smiled.

The corner of his mouth lifted for a second, then drooped. He let go, then bent to lift the sheet and cover Ken.

Jonah stood and ran a hand through his hair. "Elle, I need a favor. An investigative one."

"Name it." If the man wanted her help, she'd do whatever was necessary.

"I'll pay you."

She shook her head. "No way."

"But—"

Noelle held her palm out, stopping him. "Are we friends?"

The crease on his forehead deepened. "Yes. But I'm not sure why."

"Excuse me?"

"I beaned you with a softball and gave you a concussion."

"So? To me it was the start of a wonderful friendship. You took care of me. Made sure I had everything I needed. Kept me company when I was bored out of my mind because I couldn't work. You know me better than most."

"Same."

"And let's not forget, you know my quirks." She waggled her eyebrows.

He laughed. A bit forced, but it was a sweet sound.

She turned serious. "You know about my murder board and the cold cases. No one, not even Lizzie, knows that."

Jonah placed his hand over his heart. "And I'm honored." His brown eyes bored into her blue ones. "But I don't know all your secrets."

She sucked back the gasp that threatened to escape. How did he know?

"Elle."

She mentally shook off the panic. "I have to say the same about you. You're holding something back." He opened his mouth, but she put a finger on his lips to stop him. "And that's okay. I don't have to know everything."

He seemed to mull over her words and nodded.

"Now, why don't you give me a hint at what you need my help with."

Jonah ran his fingers through his hair, then glanced around as if to confirm no one would hear him. "Ken did something he wasn't proud of and wanted me to reopen a few of his cases."

Noelle's stomach jumped to her throat. What had Ken gotten himself into? And now he'd put Jonah in danger by bringing him into the mess.

She blew out air between pursed lips. "I think you need to tell me everything."

––––––––

Tucked behind a tree down the street, Jack watched the flurry of activity. Dark-gray smoke danced toward the sky, and a hiss from the water hitting the flames filled the air. When the house had splintered into pieces, a smile had bloomed on his face. Then he'd seen the smoldering body in the yard and wanted to scream.

The explosion should have blown to bits that ungrateful... He gritted his teeth. His blood boiled at the unfairness. The bullet he'd placed in Ken Dodson's heart had solved his problem and given him a sense of satisfaction, but he'd had no intention of leading the cops to his door. A gas leak to eliminate any evidence of his presence had been the perfect plan—until it wasn't.

The rigged natural gas line had ignited as planned and should have destroyed the evidence of his presence in the house, including the cause of Ken's demise. Somehow, he'd messed up, or the universe had conspired against him. Either way, the mistake spelled disaster. He sagged against the tree and thumped the back of his head on it. Stupid. Stupid. Stupid.

The doctor's coworker, Harris, had arrived moments before

the house detonated. Not an odd occurrence for Dodson's friend, but not exactly normal.

Jack scratched his jaw. Why had the man shown up today? The good ol' doctor had hung up the phone when Jack walked in to confront him. Had Dodson told Harris about the agreement?

His heart rate spiked. *No! He wouldn't have. Would he?*

He wiped the sweat from his brow and peeked around the tree, spotting Harris with some lady.

If the chief medical examiner had spilled the blackmail, he had to stop the flow of information. He couldn't risk the truth coming out.

Options flitted through his mind. He nodded. Decision made. Dr. Jonah Harris had to die.

TWO

"Not here." Jonah scanned the fire scene from his position next to Ken's body. He had no idea why icy fingers crawled up the back of his neck, but he'd heed the internal warning. "Let's go somewhere else to talk."

Noelle cocked her head to the side and studied him. "You think your mystery suspect is lurking?"

He ran his fingers through his hair, not bothering to smooth down the mess he made. "Honestly?"

"Of course."

"I have no idea. But I can't shake that creepy feeling of someone watching."

"Okay. I won't question your gut." She gestured down the street. "Why don't we grab a quick bite to eat at Ricky's Café around the corner. You look like you could use something to settle that stomach."

He grimaced. The thought of food made him want to hurl. "Maybe a ginger ale and some toast."

Noelle scowled. "That bad?"

"It's not great." He had to be careful or the woman would toss him in her car and head straight to the nearest hospital. "But it's manageable."

"You'll tell me if it gets worse?" She pinned him with a glare.

"Promise." And he would. He might not like a trip to the emergency department, but he wasn't stupid. Head injuries weren't something to mess around with.

She nodded. "Then let's go."

Jonah took a step and swayed.

Noelle's hand shot out and grabbed his arm. "Easy there, cowboy."

He snorted. "As if. I'm a city boy through and through."

A chuckle escaped her lips. "Leave it to you to take me literally."

"Full disclosure, that's all." He shrugged and took a few more steps. "I think I'm good now."

"Seems like it," Noelle responded, but she never let go of his arm while they walked in silence to Ricky's.

He appreciated her support—literally. His legs hadn't felt this wobbly since the one and only time he'd gone bungee jumping. He used to thrive on the intensity of the emergency department, but now he coveted the relaxed atmosphere of the morgue. At least he didn't face life-and-death situations anymore.

The last hour had proved his craving for adrenaline rushes had disappeared. He supposed that's what happened when you couldn't save the woman you loved more than life itself. A lot of good being the top ER doctor in the region had done. He'd failed his wife Cara in the worst possible way.

They strode from the residential street and turned onto the business-lined main street.

Pedestrians hurried down the sidewalk, rushing to get who knew where. Cars zipped by as the tail end of rush hour faded. Life went on.

The events of the day caught up with him, and his pace slowed. Either Noelle didn't notice, or she chose not to say anything.

Jonah's scrapes and cuts burned, and his head pounded from the exertion. He wanted to laugh. Since when had two blocks become exercise?

The sight of the small diner next to Belinda's Bookstore made him want to cheer. The window's red script lettering, Ricky's Café, called to him. Jonah hated to admit how badly his injuries were affecting him, but sitting down had become his goal.

Noelle opened the door to the café. The bell dinged, and she gestured for him to enter.

He plodded to a booth next to the window and dropped his aching body onto the seat. He rested his head on the cushioned back and closed his eyes. His mind blocked out the noises around him. The murmur of voices in the eating establishment faded.

How could Ken be dead? A lump sat like a boulder in his throat. What a waste.

"Jonah?" Noelle's subtle Southern drawl shook him from this musing.

By sheer will, he opened his eyes and stared into the brightest blue irises he'd ever seen. How had he not noticed the fascinating color before? He tilted his head and studied her. Her blonde hair that parted on the side fell over one side of her face. Jonah's fingers itched to touch it, to see if it was as silky as it appeared.

"Did you hear me?"

He blinked. "I'm sorry, what did you say?"

"That's what I thought." She tucked the stray strand of hair behind her ear. "What just ran through that head of yours?"

No way he'd admit his wayward thoughts. She was way too

important to confess his sudden attraction. *Sudden? Liar.* "Not important."

A glass of water sat on the table in front of him. Condensation dribbled down the mason jar that held the ice-cold drink. When had the waitress come by? Man, he needed to get his head in the game.

"By the way, I ordered for you."

His gaze jerked to hers. "What?"

Noelle chuckled. "You were a bit out of it. I figured I'd give you time to pull yourself together and not disturb you for a minute or two."

"Thanks, I think." Jonah slumped in his seat. He'd always struggled with the inability to stay focused due to attention deficit disorder. In fact, he had no idea how he'd made it through medical school. But his current state zoomed off the charts even for him.

"How's the head?" Noelle took a sip of her iced tea.

He came close to brushing off her question, but they'd made a pact over the summer, when he'd monitored her concussion, to be honest about injuries.

"My head is throbbing, and I don't expect that to heal overnight." He shrugged. "That's not unexpected after a bomb went off that close and sent me flying. The cuts and scrapes on my hands, knees, and cheek sting, but in a few days, I won't know they're there. Now, the bruise on my thigh—that might take a little longer."

She raised a brow and smirked.

Jonah gently shook his head. "Too much honesty?"

She lowered her glass to the table. "No, not at all. I expected that I'd have to pry the truth from you."

"You almost did." He raised a shoulder.

Hands full of plates and bowls, the waitress bustled to their table. She placed steaming bowls of chicken noodle soup and fresh individual loaves of bread in front of them. Steam rose from the food, carrying the mouthwatering aroma with it. "Anything else?"

"No. I think we're good." The waitress ambled away and Noelle picked up her spoon. "Eat."

"Yes, ma'am." The corner of his mouth lifted, but he couldn't muster a full smile.

She rolled her eyes, then pointed her spoon at his bowl and took a mouthful of her own. "Mmm. I just love Ricky's chicken noodle. I wonder what he puts in it to make it so flavorful."

"Oregano." Jonah scooped another spoonful into his mouth.

"Excuse me?" She scrunched her nose in the cutest way.

"Oregano. I overhead him one day grumping at his new cook, saying he'd skimped on the oregano."

Noelle ducked her head, and her gaze shifted from one end of the café to the other. "Your secret is safe with me."

He laughed at her ridiculousness, then put his fingers against his forehead. "Stop being a doofus. You're making my head throb."

"Admit it. Even though it hurt, you needed the laugh."

She wasn't wrong. The day held a heaviness that threatened to smother him. His time with her had lifted the heavy blanket of confusion. "You know me well."

Her shoulder lifted and fell. "Enough, I guess."

The truth of her statement hung between them. They'd paved the way to a great relationship, but both had untold secrets lingering in the background, neither of them willing to reveal the darkness of the past.

They sat in silence until their meals disappeared.

What was it about chicken noodle soup that had a healing effect—whether physical or emotional?

"I needed that." Jonah wiped his mouth and dropped his napkin on the table. He stretched his back, relieving the ache settling deep in his muscles.

Noelle neatly stacked her plate and bowl, then his, and

moved them to the side. She clasped her hands and rested them on the table. "Are you ready to tell me what's going on? Or are we going to sit here and pretend nothing's wrong?"

That was the problem. He had no idea what he'd stepped into. "Well, there was this bomb." He gave her a cheesy grin that lacked enthusiasm.

She glared at him with her classic *you're an idiot* look.

"Okay, fine. I had finished my last autopsy for the day and went to my office to work on the report." Jonah ran his finger around the mouth of his glass and released a long breath. "Ken called and told me he wanted to speak with me. That he needed my help."

"Did he tell you exactly what it was about?"

"I'll say," Jonah mumbled under his breath. He shuffled through his options. He planned to keep his promise to Ken and stay quiet, wait until he had proof before he told the detectives. But he couldn't do this alone. Mind made up, he steeled his spine. He had to tell Noelle. He rested his elbows on the table. "Ken dropped the proverbial bombshell that he'd falsified autopsy reports."

Noelle's eyes widened. "As in plural?"

Jonah nodded. "He said he had the original reports and wanted me to reexamine the cases."

"What did you tell him?" She flattened her palms on the table and leaned forward.

"Not much. I was trying to get my mind wrapped around what he'd said. He invited me over to discuss it." Jonah rubbed his temple. "And you saw what happened. I never spoke with him again." Jonah stared out the window, wondering, not for the first time, whether he could have stopped Ken's attacker if he'd been on time.

"Don't."

He scrunched his forehead. "What?"

"At the risk of sounding like a broken record, you had no way of knowing. If you'd arrived on time, you'd probably be dead right along with Ken."

Her insight into his mind was spooky. He folded his arms over his chest. "So, now you're a mind reader?"

"Pssh. You, my dear friend, aren't that hard to figure out."

Now it was his turn to raise an eyebrow.

She chuckled. "Jonah, you're an incredible doctor. Even though you choose not to use your talents in that capacity anymore, there's no way you'd stand by and let someone get hurt. It's ingrained in you to do whatever's in your power to fix people."

"Yeah, maybe." He gripped the edge of the table to ground himself.

"There's no *maybe* to it." Noelle covered his hand with hers. "You've got a big heart, Doctor Jonah Harris."

Her words sank in and lit the dark places within him. "I'll keep that in mind."

"You do that." Her gaze held his.

"And being a broken record might not be a bad thing. I might need to hear that I couldn't have stopped this more than once."

"I can do that. And I'll help you look into Ken's claims."

"I appreciate your willingness. I don't see how I have much of a choice. It was Ken's last request."

Jonah's phone rang. He fished it out of his pocket and answered. "Doctor Harris."

"Doc. It's Matt."

"Hey, man. What can I do for you?" He mouthed *Matt* to Noelle and she nodded.

"I'd like to get your statement about the explosion, if you're up to it. I can wait a bit longer if you need me to, but I need it soon."

"It's fine. Noelle and I are at Ricky's Café. We're finished. It won't take long to walk back. We'll head your way in a few minutes. Does that sound okay to you?"

"Great. Thanks, Doc. See you soon." Matt hung up.

"I'm guessing he wants to grill you," Noelle said with a wicked look.

"Ha. Ha. Very funny."

She rolled her eyes and scooted from the booth. "Come on, *Doc.*"

He couldn't keep the silly grin off his face. Unlike the others in his life, Noelle rarely called him Doc. She reserved it for teasing moments or those times when they worked on the same case in a professional capacity.

Hands on the seat, Jonah pushed up to slide from the bench and groaned. His muscles had stiffened.

Noelle grabbed the check. "I'll go pay while you try to get your body moving again."

"Thanks. I'll meet you outside." *I hope.*

He heard her chuckle as she walked away.

"Okay, Jonah. You can do this." Great. Now he was talking to himself. He took a deep breath and hauled himself from the booth.

With a quick wave at Ricky through the kitchen server window, Jonah pushed open the diner door and stepped into the warm Savannah air.

Dirty brown puffy tendrils snaked in the sky and lingered in the air—evidence of destruction from Ken's house a couple blocks away.

Jonah stood at the curb and arched his back, stretching out the kinks.

A car horn blared, and an engine revved.

He flipped his attention to the noise. He squinted, processing what he saw.

His eyes widened, but his feet refused to move.

A black SUV headed straight for him.

———

"Jonah!" Noelle sprinted toward him. A black monster of an SUV jumped the curb and aimed itself at them. Her arm wrapped his waist, and her momentum sent them into the middle of the street. She pulled him to herself, twisted, and braced for the impact of the road.

She hit the pavement—hard—taking Jonah's body weight. The impact knocked the wind from her.

Tires screeched. An engine revved. And a vehicle sped away.

Black dots danced behind her eyelids. "Jonah?" The lack of oxygen stole her ability to speak.

A car door slammed and shoes hit the blacktop. Noelle prayed no one hit them, because all she could focus on was getting air into her lungs.

Jonah rolled from her grip, easing the pressure. "Elle, are you okay?" His hand cupped her cheek.

She forced her eyes open.

"Cough."

What in the world? How to breathe had escaped her, and he wanted her to cough?

"Do it." His tone held a no-argument edge to it.

She coughed. Or at least tried.

"Again."

This time when she coughed, her lungs filled with air. She took in a couple of shallow breaths, then a deeper one. Noelle remained on the ground, letting the precious oxygen work through her system. "Thanks."

Jonah's smile melted her heart. "You're welcome."

She'd never realized how handsome he was. His short-cut beard begged for her to touch it, and his chocolate-brown eyes did funny things to her insides. And why was she noticing this now? Okay, so maybe she'd thought about it before, but for the love of everything, they'd almost died. She pushed aside the inappropriate response.

"Hey! Are you two all right? That SUV came out of nowhere

and veered onto the sidewalk. It aimed right at you." One of the drivers had left his car and now stood beside her and Jonah.

Another driver hurried toward them. "I called 911."

Noelle pushed to a seated position. "I think I better call Matt and Decia." She pulled her phone from her pocket, praying the fall hadn't damaged it.

"What do you say we get out of the middle of the street, huh?" Jonah crouched beside her.

"Nah, I like the possibility of getting run over." She rolled her eyes, and he chuckled. Refusing to add to the pain of his injuries, she stood without his help and dialed Decia's number.

"Detective Slaton."

"Hey, Decia. It's Noelle. We have a situation." Noelle scanned the small crowd around them as she and Jonah made their way to the sidewalk.

"What happened?"

"Let's just say you'll want to come down to Ricky's Café. And bring Matt with you." She had no desire to air her concerns about the driver of the SUV targeting Jonah and her suspicion of why. But the detectives had to know. At least part of it.

When Noelle didn't elaborate, Decia sighed. "Hang tight. We'll be there in a few minutes."

"We aren't going anywhere." Noelle hung up, stuffed the phone into her pocket, and faced Jonah.

"Are you okay?" Jonah placed his hand on the small of her back.

The warmth of his touch made her want things she couldn't have. A relationship. A future. What was wrong with her? They'd almost died. She shoved away the absurd thoughts.

"Mostly." She wouldn't lie about her scrapes and bruises, but overall, no serious injuries.

The crease between his eyes, which marred his features, concerned Noelle. "Your head is killing you, isn't it?"

He grimaced. "That obvious?"

"To me." She'd spent a lot of time with Jonah and had learned his expressions. "Did I hurt you when I tackled you?"

He let out a humorless laugh. "I'm just happy to be alive." He lowered his voice. "I owe you a huge thank you for saving my life."

"Jonah. You don't owe me anything." Shocked at the emotion clogging her throat, she swallowed. "Please, answer my question. Did I hurt you?"

His fingers brushed her upper arm where her hidden scars lay. She fought the instinct to jerk away. The white lines had no feelings of pain, but his touch brought back memories of how she'd gotten them. A time in her life she'd like to forget, but the experience had been so horrible it would stay with her forever.

He narrowed his gaze and studied her before he spoke. "A few more bruises, but you protected my head. That's the important thing. I'd prefer not to have scrambled eggs for a brain."

"Good. I'm glad." She squirmed under his scrutinizing stare. Maybe she hadn't hidden her reaction as well as she'd thought.

Blue lights strobed around them, and officers worked to control the small crowd that had gathered.

"Noelle. Jonah." A woman called out.

Noelle turned to the familiar voice. Decia and Matt strode toward her and Jonah. "Uh-oh, here comes Mom and Dad."

Jonah choked on his laugh.

Stressful situations always had her sarcastic side making its presence known—something she'd developed out of desperation as a teen during the worst time of her life. Being abducted by a serial killer did not-so-funny things to a person.

She tugged on her shirt sleeves, making sure to keep the proof of her nightmare hidden, and returned her attention to the two detectives closing the distance.

A patrol officer headed in their direction, but Matt held up his badge and dismissed the young man. Once Matt stood in front of them, he looked them over head to toe. "What happened?"

Noelle opened her stance and crossed her arms. "Someone tried to run Jonah over."

Jonah grimaced.

Okay, so maybe she should've toned down her response, but now that the shock had worn off, her irritation had taken over. No one messed with one of her friends—especially Jonah. He'd stayed by her side while she recovered from her concussion last summer. But more than anything, he'd witnessed her obsession with the cold cases and never—not once—told her she should let it go.

"Accident?" Decia placed her hands on her hips, matching Noelle's intensity.

"Of course."

"I don't think so." Jonah and Noelle responded on top of each other.

Noelle met Jonah's gaze. "That SUV did not 'accidently' rev its engine and then jump the curb." She used air quotes around the word *accidently*.

Jonah tilted his head. "Why would someone try to kill me?"

She raised a brow. The confused expression on his face had her biting the inside of her cheek to hide a smile. "Don't tell me you've already forgotten our conversation."

Despair washed over his features. "You think?"

She shrugged. "I think it's a good possibility."

Arms crossed, Matt stared at them. "Want to tell us what's going on?"

She waited for Jonah to answer, but he stayed quiet. She had a decision to make, and she needed to make it quick. His earlier words tumbled in her brain.

Decia's gaze drifted from Jonah to her. "Noelle?"

How she handled this would affect her and Jonah's relationship. He'd trusted her. The only thing that helped her conscience was the fact that she, along with her coworkers at EGA Savannah, had law enforcement privileges and were experts at investigations. True, her words would stretch the meaning, but Jonah had confided in her.

"Have Jonah give you his statement about the explosion and about the SUV that almost hit him." She sighed. "As for my statement, I walked out of the café after paying and saw Jonah standing at the curb. An SUV picked up speed and jumped the curb, heading straight for him. I tackled him out of the way, and the vehicle sped off. I did get the license plate number." She rattled it off, and Matt wrote it down. "The only thing I ask right now is that you investigate the owner of that SUV."

Decia scowled.

"I know, Decia. But please trust me on this." She held her friend's gaze.

The woman seemed to study her, then nodded. "For now." Decia returned her focus to Jonah. "Doc, you look like you could use a place to sit down. Since there isn't a great place to wait while we take a few witness statements, why don't you go back into Ricky's. After we're finished up with these folks, we'll meet you there, and then you can give us your statements."

Noelle jerked her gaze to Jonah. Why had Decia suggested he sit down? She sucked in a breath. His pallor concerned her, but it was the way he swayed on his feet that sent her heart racing.

She grabbed his elbow. "Come on." Once inside, she steered him back to the booth they'd vacated a little while ago. She scooted in next to him and leaned in before Decia and Matt finished the witness statements and joined them. "Why didn't you tell me?"

His gaze dropped to his lap. "About what? That I hurt and I'm ready to drop? That I'm scared you're right and Ken's fraudulent actions have put me in the middle of danger?"

"Yes, to all of that." She gently nudged him. "Jonah, please don't shut me out."

"Truth?" His head lifted.

"Always."

"Elle, you're amazing. You've been through a terrible event in your past. Even though you've never told me what happened, and I wish you would, I can tell it was horrible. Yet you've pushed through the trauma, and now you're this amazing bodyguard." His shoulders drooped. "I don't want you to see me as weak."

Her jaw dropped. "I'd never see you that way. You're *Doc*. I know that doesn't explain it." How did she make him understand? "To your friends, you're larger than life. You're not weak. You're the man that shows up and does whatever it takes to help the people around you. Why do you think Ken called you?"

He shook his head. "I have no idea."

The man's lack of confidence shocked her. In all the time they'd spent together, she'd never seen this side of him. "Because Ken knew you'd help without judging him. He knew he could trust you—that you'd keep your promise, and you'd do your best to set the records straight."

"Maybe." His dejected tone not only hurt to hear but made her angry on his behalf.

"There is no *maybe* to it." She inhaled. "Look, we know all the general things about each other and then some. No, we haven't shared our deepest, darkest secrets. Like you said to me, I'd like to hear what's caused you to be down on yourself. But know this: until that happens, I'm here for you."

After a silent moment, Jonah placed his hand on the table and shifted to face her. "Thank you for not outing Ken. The man is—was—like a father to me. Losing him is like losing a piece of myself. After everything he's done to help me, I owe it to him to keep my promise and figure it out first. I understand we have to tell Matt and Decia, but I'd like to see what my friend got himself into before I mention it to them. It's not like Ken's here to explain or defend himself. And with the bullet-hole evidence, it's not like they don't know the explosion was intentional. They'll continue to investigate."

"As long as you realize that it's only temporary." She squeezed his hand. "We'll figure this out."

She had no intention of letting Jonah go this road alone.

He didn't know it yet, but once she talked with Alana and Juliette, he'd have a personal bodyguard twenty-four seven. He'd become an important part of her life. No way she'd allow anyone to hurt him—ever.

Whoever had tried to kill Jonah had made a big mistake.

THREE

The explosion and Ken's final words played on repeat in Jonah's head, along with his own brush with death. The *why* eluded him. But that might be his aches and pains talking.

He opened the passenger door of Noelle's car and pulled to a standing position. He bit back a groan, feeling as stiff as one of the corpses at a crime scene. Willing his body to move, he shut the car door and ambled up the walkway to his house.

He'd bought the place after his wife died. Their home had plagued him with an all-consuming depression, and he couldn't take the heartache of living with the memories. The new house had been his turning point. Since then, the grief had subsided and he'd moved on. He'd even dated a time or two. But the guilt, no matter how hard he tried, had never disappeared.

"You know, this is the first time I've been here." Noelle walked alongside him a bit closer than normal, almost as if ready to catch him if he fell.

Wow, did he look that bad? "Well, there might be a reason for that."

She arched a brow.

"You'll see." Thankful Matt had retrieved the keys from his damaged SUV, he slid the house key into the lock and glanced over his shoulder at Noelle. This was a bad idea. Sure, the woman already knew his quirks, but she'd never seen the inside of his home. He'd spent time at hers while taking care of her when she had the concussion, and later for relaxing evenings watching movies, but he'd never invited her to his place. They'd always spent time at hers.

He sighed and accepted the inevitable. "Don't judge."

Noelle glared at him. "You know very well that I wouldn't do that."

"So you think," he muttered. He wasn't proud of his messy tendencies, but for the life of him, he couldn't figure out how to be normal. Whatever normal was.

She rested her hand on his shoulder. "Jonah, I've seen your office. Did you forget who gave you that poster?" She grinned. "Yes, I tease you, but I've never looked down on you about your habits. I wouldn't do that to you. Besides, I have my own idiosyncrasies with neatness."

He snorted. "That's one way to put it."

"See what I mean? Your lack of...shall we say *neatness*, is who you are."

"Such a diplomatic way of putting it." A smile curved his lips.

"That's me. Politically correct all the time. As if." She rolled her eyes. "Come on. Let's get you inside and seated before you collapse."

Jonah had delayed long enough. Why he was embarrassed in front of Noelle, he had no idea. They'd cultivated a close friendship over the past ten months. He trusted her more than anyone else in his life.

"Fine. Just remember, I warned you." He unlocked the door and welcomed her into his home.

"Go on. I'll lock the door behind me. Find me a first-aid kit so I can take care of your injuries." She motioned him to enter.

"You don't have to do that."

"Yes, I do. Now, quit arguing with me." She gave him a gentle shove.

"I'll grab the supplies and meet you in the kitchen." He pointed to the kitchen on his left, then ambled to the laundry room on his right, where he kept his first-aid kit. His jeans had saved him from the debris, but they were toast. His shirt hadn't fared much better. He retrieved a pair of shorts from his clean clothes pile and changed.

Samson, his cat, moseyed into the room. "Hey there, buddy. How ya doin'?" The cat meowed and wove between his legs. Jonah eased down and ran a hand over Samson's silky fur. "Be on your best behavior. We have company." He straightened and tossed his tattered jeans and shirt into the garbage. On his way out, he grabbed a new T-shirt and slipped it on.

He returned with Samson following. Noelle eased him onto a chair.

"Aren't you a sweetheart?" Noelle greeted Samson with a scratch on the head, then turned her attention to Jonah and examined him from head to toe. It was weird having a woman *check him out*. Not that she had anything on her mind other than treating his wounds, but still.

"Like what you see?" As soon as the words left his mouth, he cringed. Yup, he tended to be awkward when his nerves got the best of him. He hadn't had a woman look at him with such tenderness since his wife, and it had short-circuited his brain.

She smirked but held her tongue—for which he was grateful. Friends. That's where their relationship started and ended. They both had secrets, and neither wanted anything more than a friendship—with anyone. So why had his heart rate kicked up a notch when he caught the direction of her gaze?

"If you're referring to your cuts and bruises, then no, I don't like what I see." She clicked open the container of medical supplies.

He closed his eyes and exhaled. Crisis averted. "Thanks for helping me."

She tilted her head. "Of course. Have you forgotten the weeks you played doctor while I was confined to the couch?"

He froze.

Her neck and cheeks flamed bright red, indicating she realized her faux pas.

To save her from embarrassment, he brushed her comment aside. "How could I forget your concussion, since I'm the one who gave it to you?"

Noelle closed her eyes for a moment and chuckled. "There is that. But seriously, you didn't have to spend all those hours with me. I never blamed you."

"I know you didn't, but I felt bad." She'd hit the dirt, and his stomach had sunk. The memory of her motionless body still made him sick.

"Make no mistake, though. I appreciated your kindness—and our friendship that came from it."

"Me too. The friendship, that is."

"Okay, quit stalling. The shorts help to treat your legs, but you need to lose the shirt so I can clean your cuts and scrapes."

He raised a brow. "Bossy much?"

"Um, yes." She laughed.

Jonah raised the shirt over his head and tossed it aside. His muscles chose that moment to complain. He let out a low moan as he lowered his arms.

"First things first." Noelle dropped three ibuprofens into his hand. "Take those." She found two bottles of water in the refrigerator and handed him one.

As if he'd refuse pain meds at this point. He thanked her and took the pills.

She dropped two in her hand and swallowed them dry before reaching for her water.

He grimaced. "How do you do that?"

The bottle paused next to her lips as the creases in her forehead deepened. "Do what?"

"Take those without something to drink."

She shrugged, then took a sip and set the water on the table. "When you're desperate, you'll take medicine however you can. It's a habit, I guess." Without another word, she retrieved the first-aid supplies and dabbed a square of hydrogen peroxide-soaked gauze on his shallow lacerations.

He sucked in a breath through his teeth at the cold solution on his bare arms and chest. Her gentle touch surprised him. Almost as if she knew how uncomfortable the multiple cuts were.

After she'd finished cleaning and treating his wounds with a triple antibiotic cream, she tossed the used supplies in the trash and washed her hands.

Jonah eased the clean shirt over his head and down his torso, careful not to let the material scrape the injuries. "Thank you."

"You're welcome. Now, how about we get you over to the couch so you're more comfortable."

He stood and pointed to the chair. "Nope. It's your turn."

"Excuse me?"

He gestured to the road rash that required cleaning. The abrasions ran up her forearm and under her shirt sleeve.

She shook her head. "I'm good."

"Elle. You hit the ground hard when you tackled me." The hurt in her eyes...or was it fear?...tugged at his heart and confused him at the same time. "I want to make sure you're all right."

"I'm fine. Really."

"Look." He folded his arms across his chest. "I know I'm not the big bad bodyguard you are. And I mean that in a good way. But I'm a doctor, and I used to be a great one. Let me help you."

"I know you are."

"My patients don't complain."

Her wide eyes made him laugh. "Jonah. Your patients are dead."

"There is that." He gave her a lopsided smile.

She shook her head. "You're a dork. I can wash my arms in the sink." She patted his cheek, then moved to the sink to wash up.

Her touch sent a jolt of electricity through him as if he'd grabbed hold of live wires with his bare hands. He stood stunned at the realization, unable to put a coherent sentence together.

"See? All done." She dried her arms with a paper towel and tossed it in the trash. "I'll put the first-aid kit away if you tell me where it goes."

"Just leave it. I'll get it later."

She bit her lip, trying to hide her grin.

He scanned his kitchen. "I know. I know. I'm a mess."

She shook her head and helped him to the couch.

He lowered himself onto the seat and sank into the cushions. The aches and pains from his close calls barked at him. His headache had dulled but hadn't disappeared. Overall, he'd escaped with minor injuries. He'd take it.

"Join me." He patted the cushion next to him. Samson chose that moment to jump onto his lap and curl up.

Noelle continued to stand. Her gaze roamed the living room, taking in the state of his home. Now that she'd treated his wounds, he held his breath that she wouldn't go running and screaming from his house. He mindlessly stroked Samson's fur as his gaze tracked to where she focused her attention.

Books lay on the floor next to the bookshelf. Magazines

littered his coffee table. Two mugs with the remains of coffee sat on the end table next to him. He'd left shoes and socks strewn across the room. Not to mention the dishes piled in one side of the sink in his kitchen, or the state of his bedroom. All in all, his house was a shambles.

"I'm sorry."

She spun to face him. "About what?"

He gestured to the disaster that was his home. "This. I know it's probably giving you the willies to stand here with such disorganization around you."

"Maybe a bit, but, Jonah, this is your home. You deserve to be comfortable in your living space."

"But yours is so…"

"Spotless. Over-the-top. Meticulous." She chuckled. "We both know that I have OCD tendencies. But unlike the actual diagnosis, I can look past the way others live. It's only my world that must stay insanely organized."

"I've noticed." He still didn't like her dealing with his chaos. He dragged his hand down his face. "I grew up with my parents scolding me about the mess I left in my wake. But I had little control over my actions. Most of the time I felt like Pig Pen from the *Peanuts* cartoon. Not with dirt but with clutter from my lack of organizational skills. My mom and dad never understood how I lived like that. And I had no clue how not to be that way."

Noelle eased onto the couch and sank her fingers into Samson's fur. "That must have been hard."

"Over the years, I figured out how to make life work for me, but I continually chased ideas like trying to keep feral kittens on a blanket. The only place I achieved calmness was at work—whether in the ER or in autopsy. There, my mind settled, and I hyperfocused on my job." He had a hard time describing the dichotomy between the orderliness of his work space, and his office, car, and home.

How did he explain the chaos of his thoughts under normal circumstances? The best description he'd ever heard was from the classic meme that it mimicked having a hundred tabs open on a computer and not knowing where the music was coming from. And for him, that was a mild portrayal.

"My parents refused to put me on medication." He got it. He really did. As a doctor, he hated that solution for many reasons. However, for him, it seemed to be the only answer. "During college, I started taking meds for ADD, but they made me feel wonky. After trial and error, I found the correct prescription and dosage. Life became enjoyable. Just don't ask me to have a clutter-free space." He no longer suffered to exist in the world around him. Oh, he continued to deal with the effects from his attention deficit disorder, but he could live in his skin now.

"That makes your...habits...understandable." Noelle stood and wandered to the fireplace mantel. She pointed to a picture. "Is this your wife?"

The air left Jonah's lungs, and he struggled to catch his breath. Sure, he missed Cara, but he'd moved past the deep ache of losing her. It was the guilt that continued to have a stranglehold on him.

"I'm sorry. I know it's a painful topic for you."

He blinked. When had he given her that idea? He hadn't told her the details about the night of the accident. "Yes. That's Cara."

Noelle raised a brow, waiting for him to continue, but he refused to go there. If he admitted his guilt in her death, the truth of his failure would come out.

When he didn't elaborate, she placed the photo back on the mantel and turned to face him. The softness in her features had vanished, replaced by something akin to a mask that hid her emotions. "I'll let you get some rest. I'll pick you up in the morning and drop you off at work. Matt said he'd take care of your SUV. That'll give you time to get a rental." She paused and pinned him with her gaze. "But remember, you have a mild concussion. Don't drive before you're ready. You have friends to help you."

He'd hurt her by not responding to her previous comment, but he couldn't go there. Not yet. So he nodded.

She walked out the front door without another word.

He wanted to call her back. Explain how he'd messed up so badly with his wife's accident. About the guilt that ate at him every day.

"I messed up big time, didn't I, Samson?"

The cat meowed.

Jonah sighed. More than anything, he wanted Noelle to see him as a competent doctor and not the failure he was.

———

Noelle hated leaving Jonah at work. The bodyguard in her wanted to hover. But she'd lost the battle before it had even begun. Now she got the privilege of worrying about him all day long.

She leaned against the wall of Bitty and Beau's coffee shop, waiting for her order. Remembering her argument with Jonah about him staying home and resting, she shook her head. The stubborn man had threatened to Uber to work. So, after insisting that he promise to take it easy and call if his headache got worse, she'd dropped him off at his office. And since she'd called her friends and coworkers at EGA Savannah for an early meeting to discuss yesterday's happenings, she owed them a jolt of caffeine.

She, Alana, and Juliette loved Bitty and Beau's. All the employees except the managers had Down syndrome, and their sweetness started the patrons' mornings off with a smile. But if she chose a favorite, it would have to be Emma Grace. The young girl could coax a smile out of the grumpiest person.

"Noelle."

When Emma Grace called her name, she pushed off the wall and strode to the small counter to collect the four coffees she'd ordered. "Thanks, Emmy."

The girl smiled. "I wrote something special on your cup, Miss Noelle."

"You did?" Noelle lifted her cup and read what Emmy had written. *"You are awesome.* Aw, thanks. I needed that today."

Emmy beamed. "See you tomorrow?"

"That's the plan." Noelle grabbed the drink carrier and headed for the door. On the way out, she gave the store manager, Brendan, a chin lift. He acknowledged her with a wave before she left the shop.

She strode to her car and balanced the tray on one hand while extracting her keys from her front jeans pocket with the other. Once inside her vehicle, she checked the time. Ugh. Late again. No doubt Raven would give her grief. She sighed and headed toward the office.

The three-story historical home owned by her coworker Juliette Montgomery housed the new branch office that Noelle managed. Juliette lived in the ground floor apartment and rented out the top two floors to EGA. The main office and general meeting room for clients occupied the second floor, and the third held their personal offices and the company conference room.

Noelle loved the Montgomery family stories behind the old home, but her favorite part of the new office was the historical architecture. Two white columns greeted clients. The beige exterior trimmed in white with black shutters gave the overall appearance a stunning effect. But the best part: the balconies with hanging ferns on the second and third levels provided a nice getaway when things got tough.

She pulled into the courtyard parking lot behind the building and made her way to the main office.

"You're late." Raven sat behind her desk with pursed lips and a raised eyebrow.

"Good morning to you too, Raven." She placed the admin's cup on her desk. "Here's your cotton candy frappé." Noelle mock shuddered.

Raven snatched the cup and spun it to see the message from Emmy. *"You're special."* The smile that graced Raven's face made the trip to the coffee shop worth it.

Noelle bit her lip to keep from laughing. Raven was definitely special. "Emmy knows you." Raven embraced her goth side, but she was the happiest, if not snarkiest, person Noelle knew, and she loved the young woman dearly.

Raven pinned her with a playful glare. "Are you insinuating something?"

"Would I do that?" Noelle smiled and headed for the stairs to the conference room. "By the way, I like your outfit." The black jeans paired with a tasteful and modest black corset-style top along with the new color in the admin's black hair looked fantastic. "And the hot pink hair extensions are great."

"The coffee and compliments do *not* negate you being late. But thanks, and you're forgiven."

Noelle couldn't contain the smile that spread across her face. Typical Raven.

The conference room door stood open, and Alana and Juliette sat around the oval table, chatting.

"Good morning." Noelle entered and placed the coffee carrier in front of them before removing her cup. She sat and took a sip, allowing the caffeine to infuse her body.

Alana lifted her cup. "Thanks for this."

"Ditto." Juliette retrieved her drink, took a sip, and sighed. "Perfect as always."

"Face it, Emmy loves us."

Noelle chuckled at Alana's declaration.

Juliette leaned forward and placed her forearms on the table. "How's Doc today?"

Sinking into the comfortable office chair, Noelle exhaled. "Sore. Upset about Ken. Confused."

"Are we talking about *our* Doc? How'd you get all that out of him?" Alana asked.

Everyone except Noelle referred to Jonah as Doc. After the weeks they'd spent together last summer, he'd become Jonah to her, and she hadn't used his nickname since, except in teasing. "It's not that Jonah said all those things, but I could tell."

"You two have become close over the past year." Juliette smirked.

She shrugged. No use in denying it. "We have."

After a moment of silence, Alana spoke up. "What can we do to help?"

Noelle had sent a text to the other bodyguards giving them the basics, but she hadn't elaborated. Time to remedy that problem.

"Yesterday, at the end of Jonah's work day, Dr. Ken Dodson called him and asked him to come over. He confessed to falsifying autopsy reports and wanted to come clean."

"If he wanted to confess, why tell Doc and not call the police?" Juliette asked.

"Ken wanted Jonah to reopen the cases and fix the false information. According to Jonah, after his brief conversation with Ken, Ken planned to tell the authorities but wanted the truth on record first. He went as far as making Jonah promise not to tell until he'd completed the task."

Alana narrowed her gaze at Noelle. "You think whoever asked Ken to change the causes of death on those cases killed him."

Juliette tapped her lower lip. "And since he came to Jonah first and requested him not to tell, whoever Ken risked his career for could have a long reach and have the ability to cover up the truth before he could make things right."

"It's possible." She nodded. "And if my assumption is correct and the bad guys know Ken talked with Jonah, Jonah could be in big trouble."

"Any word on the attempted hit-and-run?" Juliette leaned back in her seat and swung her chair side to side.

Noelle took a sip of her coffee and set the cup on the table. "Only that they can't ignore the possibility that it might have been an accident."

Alana snorted. "Right. I drive on the sidewalks all the time."

Noelle's cell phone rang. "Hold on." She answered and put it on speaker. "Hey, Matt. You're on speaker with Alana and Juliette."

"Hey, ladies." Without further niceties, he continued. "I ran the license plate from the SUV. It was stolen."

"Figures." Noelle had expected as much.

"Patrol found it early this morning, abandoned near some old warehouses. The crime scene techs are working on it, but I doubt they'll find anything. They've already reported that whoever stole it wiped the surfaces clean, validating your initial conclusion, Noelle."

"Of course they did." Alana rolled her eyes.

"I'll keep digging, but I think this is a dead end, since it was sanitized."

Noelle absorbed the implications of Matt's report. "Thanks. I'll let Jonah know."

"'Preciate it. Gotta go." Matt clicked off before they said goodbye.

She hit the End button and stared at her phone. "I don't like it."

"Me either."

"Neither do I." Alana and Juliette agreed in unison.

Noelle retrieved a pad of paper from the stack at the center of the table and prepared to jot down her thoughts. "I'd like to do a little digging into Ken's background. He was a highly respected medical examiner. Why on earth throw that away?"

Juliette twirled a pen between her fingers. "Doc once said Ken's wife had cancer and the experimental treatments were expensive."

"Maybe so, but doing something criminal?" Alana asked.

Noelle struggled with the question. Would her family have ignored the law to save her? "I guess you never know what you'll do if it's someone you love."

Both women nodded but appeared lost in their own thoughts.

Alana rested her elbows on the table. "The real question is, does the person who torched Ken's house think Doc knows everything and can ID him?"

"Based on the attempted hit-and-run, I'd say it's a real possibility." Noelle pinched the bridge of her nose. Until she and Jonah discovered the extent of Ken's crime, they were working in the dark on the identity of Ken's killer.

Juliette tapped her pen on her bottom lip. "Either that or he's not taking any chances, since Doc showed up right before the house blew."

"Guys, I have a bad feeling about all this." Noelle couldn't ignore the churning in her gut. "Jonah might not agree, but at this point, I really don't care. I'd like to give him our protection."

"Twenty-four hour?" There wasn't a hint of disagreement in Juliette's tone, just a simple question for clarification.

Noelle shook her head. "He'd never go for it. Not yet, anyway. We need proof that the danger is real. I'm thinking more like escorting him to and from work. His mild concussion will work in our favor. Plus, he and I hang out in the evenings a couple times a week, so it shouldn't be difficult to convince him to add a few more days."

"I know you're the boss—"

She held up a hand, stopping Alana from continuing. "I only manage the business side. We're all equals in the bodyguard aspect."

Alana nodded. "With that in mind, Juliette and I will take care of the other cases and make sure they're covered, unless you need us full time. You focus on Doc and the research behind Ken. We'll help where we can, so keep us in the loop."

"Thank you." Noelle released a long breath. She should have known these ladies would have her back on this.

Juliette stood and placed a hand on Noelle's shoulder. "You're really worried about Doc, aren't you?"

"More than you know." The man had snuck his way into her life over the past ten months. Their friendship meant everything to her. But the knot of worry in her belly that wormed its way to her heart consumed her more than she wanted to admit.

Her coworker patted her back. "We're here if you need us. We can always bring in contract bodyguards if needed."

"Thanks. I'll keep you informed as to what I find."

Alana gently gripped Noelle's arm. "Sounds like a plan. I'll go have Raven shift our jobs around and let her know what's going on."

After her two coworkers strode out, leaving her alone in the conference room, her cell phone rang.

The caller ID showed a number but no name. She tapped the Accept button and answered the call. "Burton."

"Hey, Elle."

Recognizing Jonah's voice, she leaned back in her seat and smiled. "Hi, Jonah. How's it going this morning?"

"I only have a slight headache, and the Tylenol has kicked in, so I'm not as sore as when I left the house this morning."

"That's a relief."

"Listen, I'm about ready to go into an autopsy, but I had to call first."

Hearing the tension in his voice, she sat up straight. "What's going on?"

"I'm sitting in Ken's office. I was hoping to find his planner, but it isn't in its normal spot. So until I have more time to look, I pulled his docket for today." He hesitated.

"And?"

"He only has two autopsies scheduled. I'm planning to check out both of them, see if I can find anything weird."

"To confirm if what he said is true?"

Jonah sighed. "That's the problem. He didn't say much, so who knows? I'm probably just paranoid."

"I wish he'd told you more about what's going on." Since Jonah was on an office phone, they both skirted around the fact that Ken had admitted to falsifying reports.

"Me too." Jonah paused. "I'm going to take a cursory look in a bit, but I have my own work to do."

She stacked the six notepads in the center of the table and flipped all the pens in the jar ballpoint down. Satisfied the table had order, she threw away her empty coffee cup. "Please call if you find anything."

"I will. And Elle..."

She dropped into the chair she'd vacated a moment ago. "Yeah?"

"Thanks."

She didn't have to ask why. He meant the world to her too. "I'll pick you up after work."

"I'll be ready."

Noelle chuckled. The man was rarely on time. "See you soon, Jonah."

She clicked the phone off and slouched in her seat. She couldn't shake the uneasy feeling that Jonah had landed in the biggest mess of his life.

Noelle pulled the three-quarter sleeve of her shirt up,

exposing the scars on her upper arm. Scars that reminded her every day how quickly life could change.

She didn't want that for Jonah. He had his own scars, although she suspected they were emotional ones and not physical. But the fact remained, he had secrets that caused him pain. And she wanted to protect him from further harm.

Besides, the idea of losing her best friend made her want to throw up.

FOUR

So, his puppet, Dr. Ken Dodson, had talked to someone about the women he'd killed.

He'd dubbed himself Jack after Jack the Ripper, but unlike his idol, he didn't have the stomach for the abdominal mutilation. But taunting and torturing, yes. He loved to hear them scream when he wielded his knife.

Jack placed the earpiece on his desk and folded his hands in front of him. The bug he'd installed on Dodson's phone had come in handy today. Dr. Jonah Harris knew more than Jack was comfortable with, but apparently Dodson hadn't elaborated.

Maybe if he snuck into the medical examiner's office and destroyed the evidence on the body, no one would be the wiser. A small spill of muriatic acid to damage the body of his latest victim might keep the cops from landing on his doorstep. Oh, sure, it'd bring in an investigation, but Jack knew how to stay under the radar. But without Dodson, the body in the morgue had the potential to ruin everything.

With a quick check of his schedule, he decided if he took an early lunch, he'd solve his problem and be back before anyone missed him.

Jack stood, grabbed the keys from his desk, and exited the building. He kept a change of clothes in his car for those occasions that required his special attention.

He'd get in and get out, destroying evidence his goal—not his normal crusade of teaching an immoral girl a lesson.

He slipped into his car and pulled out of the parking lot.

On the way to the ME's office, he finalized his plan.

Find his latest victim, eliminate the proof of murder and his special gift to his girls, then set fire to the room. Making it look like an accident would be challenging. He doubted he'd have that opportunity. So why not go for it and make a statement? After a quick stop to acquire muriatic acid and a bottle of lighter fluid, he'd destroy the evidence and light the bodies on fire for good measure.

And maybe, if the situation allowed, take care of Dr. Harris at the same time.

———

After a straightforward autopsy, Jonah collapsed in his office chair and pulled a file from the messy stack to his right. The office's administrative assistant, Bonnie, had already railed on him for his lack of organization when she'd attempted to find the document earlier that morning. The truth of the matter—he knew the location of everything on his desk. Or at least which pile. His office only looked like chaos to others.

He flipped open the file and scanned the report, confirming he'd grabbed the correct one.

"Did you find it, Doc?" Bonnie asked from the doorway.

"Yup. Here you go." He held out the report.

"I have no idea how you know where anything is in here."

She accepted the file and tapped it on the doorframe before she hurried down the hall.

He ran a hand over his head and glanced around the messy room. Maybe he should ask Noelle to help him get it organized. A smile tugged on his lips. The disaster he called his office would drive her nuts. She'd probably go running and screaming at the idea of trying to dig through it all.

Pushing the thought away, he sat and opened the bottom drawer on his desk. After last night, his instincts had told him to hide the information he'd procured from Ken's office. He had no clue what details his boss had planned to tell him, but Jonah figured he'd start with the man's current cases and see if anything aroused his curiosity.

Papers in hand, he noted the names, identification numbers, and the basics about the cases. Nothing jumped out at him, but his inquisitive side nudged him to continue investigating his hunch.

His focus never leaving the documents, he retrieved his cell phone from his pocket and tapped the corner of it against his chin. Another set of eyes might help. Someone who had a police background and looked at deaths and crimes from a different angle. Matt and Decia were out of the question since he hadn't come clean with them—yet. He trusted them but wanted solid proof before accusing a well-respected man—a man he considered a father figure and who had mentored him when he'd made the switch to the medical examiner's department—of hiding evidence. Even if Ken *had* admitted it.

His thumb swiped the phone screen, and he hit speed dial for Noelle.

"Burton."

"Hey, Elle."

"Jonah. Is everything okay?" Concern laced her tone.

He wanted to smack himself. He hadn't thought about her

worrying about his call. "A little stiff, but I'm still doing okay. That's not why I called."

"What can I do for you?"

"I'm going to pull the two bodies from the cold storage cabinets and take them into autopsy two. I want to examine the bodies." He let the unsaid reason hang in the air, unwilling to chance someone listening.

"That sounds like a reasonable plan."

"I'd like you to join me. Give me your opinion." And working beside her wouldn't be a hardship either. He shook his head. Wonderful. Now his brain was making up more ways to spend time with her. "You know, from a law enforcement point of view."

"Got it."

Man, speaking in vague sentences killed him, but he had no intention of saying his concerns out loud. "Will you come?"

"Of course. I'll be there in about fifteen minutes." He heard the shuffling of papers, then the jingle of keys in the background. "Let Bonnie know so she'll let me in, then I'll find you."

"Thanks, Elle."

"Anytime." She clicked off the phone.

He called Bonnie, approved Noelle's visit, then leaned back in his chair and closed his eyes. Never in his wildest dreams had he ever imagined his friend and boss would so blatantly disregard his oath.

Why, Ken? Why?

Jonah let out a long breath. Time to get it over with and pull the bodies noted on Ken's docket. He memorized the case numbers and tucked the files in his bottom desk drawer, which held his protein bars and other snacks. With the documents hidden under the mess, he pushed from his office chair and headed down the hall.

He opened the door to the cold storage room. Several

metal tables occupied the middle of the room. Stainless-steel cold drawers lined the wall to his left. An exterior exit sat on the far wall, and floor-to-ceiling supply cabinets filled the area to his right. If he wanted a cursory view, he'd stay in this room, but he wanted to visually examine both bodies, so he'd wheel them into autopsy two, where he'd told Noelle to meet him.

The latch popped on the first drawer. He slid the body from the middle drawer and scooted it onto a rolling table without lowering the sheet that covered the person's face. Then he retrieved a second rolling table and did the same for the body in the lower drawer. He pushed the table toward the middle of the room, next to the first one, and returned to close the storage door.

A cord wrapped around his throat, closing off his airway. He clawed at the cable, attempting to get his fingers underneath. The breath of the person strangling him hissed in his ear. Jonah wasn't a small man. He was muscular, but being taken by surprise had left him defenseless. Refusing to go down without a fight, he kicked out. His shoe clanged against the metal drawer, knocking him off-balance. The cord tightened on his neck. Jonah twisted and flailed to no avail.

If he didn't get air soon, he'd die from asphyxiation. He struggled against the tightening ligature. He fell forward, causing the cord to press harder against his neck. With his head tipped down, he took the opportunity and slammed back into his attacker's face. The man grunted and loosened his grip slightly, enabling Jonah to get a sip of air, but it wasn't enough.

The assailant recovered and yanked the cable tighter.

God, are You still there? If so, I really need Your help.

"Jonah." Noelle's voice floated down a long tunnel.

I'm here. He tried to call out, but black dots whirled in his vision and pushed him toward the abyss.

Seconds later, his body went limp.

The cold, hard surface of the storage drawer broke his fall, and the world fell away.

———

A disinfectant smell reached Noelle's nose. She released the air from her lungs, thankful the odor of a decomposing body hadn't greeted her. She hated autopsy rooms, but she'd sacrifice her comfort for Jonah. She peeked into autopsy two and called out a second time, then moved inside and scanned the empty space. Her days as a detective with the Savannah Police Department came roaring back. Her hands fisted. When she'd worked in law enforcement, witnessing autopsies had ranked high on her *dislike with a passion* list. It brought back too many memories of how close she'd come to lying on the cold metal table.

A shiver snaked up her spine at the stillness surrounding her. She moved to the hallway. "Jonah, where are you? I thought you said autopsy two."

A clunk from two doors down had her moving in that direction. "Jonah?"

A faint odor of smoke mixed with an accelerant drifted in the air. She halted and tilted her head, searching for the source and a clue as to what had her on edge.

The slam of a door jerked her from her thoughts. She drew her weapon from the holster on her hip and sprinted to the cold storage room.

Gun at the ready, she eased the door open and stood stunned at the sight before her.

Two bodies lay on roller tables, their skin eaten away, and the sheets that had once covered them were on the floor, engulfed in flames.

"What in the world?"

Noelle did a quick visual sweep of the room, then shoved her Glock into the holster. She rushed to the fire extinguisher on the wall and released it from the holder. With the nozzle aimed at the flames, she squeezed the trigger on the extinguisher. White foam sprayed the red-and-orange fingers flickering near the bodies.

Whoever had set the blaze hadn't done it that long ago. The sprinkler system hadn't kicked on yet. Was the arsonist still around?

Satisfied she'd smothered the fire, she placed the canister on the floor, then raced to the back exit and propped open the door. The smoke hanging in the air dissipated. With the ventilation complete, she withdrew her cell phone from her pocket and made the first of several calls.

"Detective Slaton."

"Decia, this is Noelle." She wiped the sweat from her forehead while she gave a quick rundown of what had happened. "The weird thing is I have no idea where Jonah is."

"Hang tight. Matt and I are on our way."

"Thanks." Noelle hung up and moved to the desk in the corner of the room to call the building's security. She lifted the receiver on the phone and stared at the lack of cord attached to the headset.

She jumped at a thump behind her and dropped the phone. It clattered to the floor. On instinct, she yanked her Glock from the holster.

A loud bang came from inside one of the cold storage drawers where they kept the dead bodies. Palms sweating, she aimed her weapon at the bottom drawer. Her heart pounded.

Dead people did not make noise. She inhaled, steadying her breathing, and pushed away the ridiculous thoughts.

Glock aimed with one hand and fingers of the other wrapped around the handle, she yanked opened the drawer.

A gasp sent her pulse skyrocketing.

"Jonah?" His hand shot up, and she grabbed it. "I've got you."

"He s-surprised me. I c-couldn't fight him off." His teeth chattered.

"Someone attacked you?" She holstered her weapon and wrapped an arm around him, helping him to a seated position.

"No, I take naps in the cold storage all the time." The words came out as a whisper. He folded his arms across his chest, shivering.

"Not funny." She took in the scene around her. Acid-burnt bodies, a fire, Jonah locked inside a drawer, the missing phone cord next to him. "Wait. Jonah, look at me."

He lifted his gaze to her.

There. On his neck. Red marks in the slightly curved pattern of a stretched telephone cord. The sight made her sick. "He tried to strangle you."

Jonah nodded and winced.

"Hold on." She made sure he didn't topple over, then hurried to the desk. She grabbed the office chair and rolled it to him. "Let's get you out of that drawer. Then I'll find you a blanket and call the paramedics."

Noelle assisted him onto the chair and moved him away from the cold storage. "Decia and Matt will be here soon. I'm sure they'll want to hear what happened, as do I. But first, let's get you warmed up."

"I like that last part."

She cringed, knowing the reason for the raspiness in his voice.

Noelle scanned the room, looking for anything to chase away his chill. She hurried to the opposite side and grabbed two lab coats hanging next to the supply cabinets. "Here. It's not perfect, but it'll do until I can find a blanket." She draped them over his shoulders.

He pulled them tight, tucking his chin into the material. "Thanks."

"Once you're given the medical okay, I'm taking you to my

place." Noelle rubbed his arms to help increase the blood flow. "Jonah, we need to talk."

Before he responded, Matt and Decia, along with Bonnie, ran into the room.

Bonnie took one look at Jonah and her eyes widened for a split second. "I'm notifying security to lock this place down. Then I'm getting you the biggest cup of coffee possible, Doc."

"I'd appreciate that."

The admin gave him a quick chin nod and rushed from the room.

Matt hung up his cell phone. "The paramedics are on the way."

"I don't—"

Matt held up his hand and crouched beside Jonah. "Look, Doc. I know you don't want the attention, but do me a favor. Let me look out for my friend."

Jonah's shoulders drooped. "Okay."

His quick acquiesce had Noelle snapping her gaze to him. She hadn't noticed earlier, and in her defense, her full attention had been focused on getting him out of that drawer, but fear clung to him like a second skin.

She knelt beside him, opposite Matt. "Jonah, we"—she gestured to Matt and Decia—"will protect you. That maniac will not get away with hurting you again."

The tension eased from his features.

Bonnie hurried in. "I found this in the staff room." She handed a wool blanket to Noelle, who exchanged it for the lab coats. "Doc, here's that coffee I promised." The woman held out the mug.

Jonah wrapped his hands around the cup and held the steaming liquid under his chin. "Thanks, Bonnie."

"I'll go keep an eye out for the paramedics." The admin rushed out the door.

"Feel like answering some questions? Or do you need a few more minutes?" Decia asked.

Jonah swallowed a sip of coffee and grimaced. "I'm good."

Noelle glared at him. "Quit downplaying it."

"I'm serious. I'm cold from my time in the refrigerator, but I wasn't in there long enough to do damage. My throat is sore inside and out, but I don't have serious injuries." He pinned her with his intense gaze. "As I said. I'm good."

At times, she wanted to clock her friend. Jonah tended to take care of others but not himself. She'd seen it when he'd cared for her last summer. He'd taken a week off, then when he finally went back to work, he'd work his shift, go home to feed his cat Samson, and within thirty minutes, he'd arrive at her house and stay until midnight with her. Then he'd do it all again the next day.

"You can talk all you want, but the paramedics *will* take a look at you, then I'm escorting you to the EGA office to talk with Alana and Juliette before taking you home." She folded her arms, daring him to challenge her.

Matt choked on a laugh. "She told you."

Decia elbowed her partner in the ribs. "You're not helping." The detective focused on Jonah. "Tell us what happened. And Noelle, jump in when you can."

Noelle nodded and waited for Jonah to speak.

Jonah took another sip of the hot coffee and lowered the mug. "I pulled two bodies for a visual examination. I'd placed them on the roller tables and turned to close the drawer when a guy wrapped something around my neck and proceeded to strangle me. I fought back, but he'd surprised me, and I didn't have time to react. Right before I passed out, I heard Noelle call my name. Then I fell and don't remember anything until I woke up inside the drawer." His gaze drifted to the cold storage. "Can't say I ever want to do that again."

"I don't blame you." Decia turned to Noelle and raised an eyebrow.

Noelle wanted to kick herself for not trusting her instincts. She'd known something wasn't right. But she'd pushed it aside, and Jonah had paid the price for her not acting on that gut feeling. "Jonah called me a little while ago, asking for an investigative eye on the two cases he's referring to. I agreed to come down and got here soon after he called. I went straight to autopsy two, where he said to meet him, but the room was empty. So I called out. When he didn't respond, I continued down the hallway and came in here. The two bodies on the table were mangled, and the sheets were on fire, but the smoke had yet to fill the room. I grabbed the fire extinguisher and put out the flames. That's when I heard Jonah pounding on the inside of the drawer."

Decia finished jotting down her notes. "I bet that was a bit disconcerting."

Noelle snorted. "Ya think?" The look on Jonah's face when she opened the drawer might haunt her for years to come. "Anyway, that's how I found him."

"Anything else?" Decia asked.

She shook her head. "Not that I can think of. Jonah?"

He stared at the floor. "No. Nothing."

Decia glanced at Matt and back to Jonah. "Why did you pull those bodies?"

Jonah jerked his attention to the detectives. "I...um..."

Noelle scrambled to come up with an answer. She knew he didn't want to reveal Ken's secret—yet. Decia and Matt would have to put it into a report, and the information might leak. If Juliette's theory about an insider was correct, they'd tip off Ken's killer. "He's helping with a case."

"Riiiiight." Matt scowled. "Want to try again?"

"Not especially." Determined not to expose the falsified reports without evidence, she'd do what she hated. Beg. "Decia.

Matt. I appreciate you have a job to do. But please, trust me—us—on this. At minimum, give me a little more time."

Decia snapped her small notebook closed. "I know you have law enforcement privileges, but that doesn't mean you're above the law." The detective appeared more concerned than irritated.

"Believe me. I'm well aware." So far, all they had was hearsay. Confessions of a dead man. Once they had evidence, then she'd have to bring them in on the investigation. Noelle rested a hand on the detective's arm. "I won't do anything to make you regret my request."

"Good enough," Decia said as the paramedics entered the room. "We'll get out of your way and send in the crime scene techs. But Noelle, I expect a call."

"You'll get one." And she would. As soon as she and Jonah confirmed Ken's confession.

Matt patted Jonah on the shoulder. "Take care, Doc."

"Thanks." Jonah shifted his attention to the paramedics and consented to the examination.

While the medics got busy treating his injuries, the crime scene crew arrived and snapped pictures and dusted for fingerprints. Noelle used her cell phone and took a few pictures of her own.

She glanced at Jonah and winced at the red marks on his neck. She tapped the speed dial for the EGA office to call an emergency meeting. Jonah didn't know it yet, but he'd just gained full-time bodyguards.

FIVE

The paramedics argued with Jonah before accepting his refusal of further treatment. He sat on the office chair in the cold storage room, wrestling with his thoughts while the crime scene techs scurried around collecting evidence. A hint of smoke lingered in the room, and the chill from his time in the refrigerated drawer had eased. But the bruising on his throat throbbed with a vengeance. Not to mention the terror from the flashbacks of his attack.

"Is there anything you want before we leave?"

Jonah jolted at Noelle's question.

"Sorry. I didn't mean to startle you." She rested her hand on his forearm. "What can I do?"

He shrugged. He had no idea what he needed. Over the last twenty-four hours, his world had collapsed and his life had turned upside down. A glance at the disfigured bodies had his mind pinging from one thought to another that included things nightmares were made from. "Drop me off at home so I can forget any of this ever happened."

"You really think I'm going to leave you alone?" Noelle made a sweeping motion with her hand that encompassed the room.

"Right." A multitude of snarky remarks came to mind, but he clamped his mouth shut. "I have a change of clothes in my office. The crime scene techs took mine and left me with these scrubs." He pulled the front of his shirt out to make his point. "Plus, I want to search Ken's office for his planner. I don't know where else it might be. There has to be something in there that explains his actions."

"Let's get your things. The girls are meeting us at the EGA office to discuss your case."

His gaze met hers. "My case?"

She tilted her head and arched a brow, as if daring him to challenge her.

"Fine." Jonah pushed from the seat. His knees threatened to buckle, causing him to sway.

Noelle's hand shot out and grasped his elbow, steadying him. "Easy."

"Just the fade of adrenaline."

She snorted. "Keep telling yourself that."

"I don't need you—"

"All I'm saying is, your body requires a little downtime to recover. You're a doctor. You know this stuff."

"Yeah, I do."

Once he gained his balance, she released his arm and gestured toward the door.

He strode out of the room and down the hall to his office. His attitude had everything to do with the day's events. Claustrophobia hadn't been an issue in the past, but Jonah had a feeling tight spaces and restrictive shirts around his neck had become his kryptonite.

He pushed open his office door and stepped in. Noelle followed on his heels. Why did he suddenly feel self-conscious about the disaster he called his office? She knew his faults. Most of them, anyway. *But she doesn't know you failed your wife.*

"It'll only take me a minute to gather my things. I have a duffel bag with a change of clothes and basic shave kit." He motioned to the small closet on the far wall.

"Take your time. No need to hurry." She moved to his "me" wall and examined his diplomas and certificates.

A lot of good those had done him when he'd failed at the most important time of his life. He huffed and headed toward the closet to gather his things. Taking a long look at the space, he tried to think of anything else he should collect before they left, but his brain refused to cooperate. The desire to flee was overwhelming. He wanted out of the building—now.

Jonah drummed his fingers on the outside of his thigh, forcing himself to stay in the moment. "All I have left to do is to find Ken's planner, then we're out of here."

Noelle turned to face him. The scrutiny behind her gaze made him shiver. It was as if she could see into the deepest, darkest places of his life. After what seemed like forever, she nodded. "Lead the way."

He hefted the duffel strap onto his shoulder and tamped down the urge to race to Ken's office.

The voices of the crime scene techs drifted in the hall. Jonah wondered what they'd discovered, but he had a mission: figure out where Ken hid his planner and get out of there.

He entered his friend's office and stopped behind his mentor's desk. "I looked in the normal places, but nada. He either had it with him or hid it. My vote is a hiding spot."

Noelle placed her hands on her hips. "Then let's think about this logically. He keeps his office tidy, so I'm guessing it'll be somewhere where it blends in or is out of sight. Like a bookshelf, closet, or cabinet."

"I'll take the bookshelf. You take the closet." Jonah strode across the room and checked out each book one at a time while Noelle headed to the single door in the office.

"Any luck?" Noelle asked as she slid Ken's lab coats aside to look behind them.

"How about you?"

"No." She stood on her tiptoes and patted the top shelf. "There's nothing...wait a second." She spun and retrieved a chair. She dragged it to the closet and stood on it. "Bingo." A black book in her hands, she jumped down and repositioned the chair at Ken's desk.

He accepted the leather-bound planner and breathed a sigh of relief. "Now that you've found it, can we please leave?"

"Gladly." Noelle accompanied him through the main lobby to the glass door at the entrance. "Wait here for a minute."

She moved outside before Jonah had a chance to respond. He took three deep breaths, but the calming technique didn't work. He pressed his fingers to his carotid artery and winced. The bruises on his neck ached. With a lighter touch, he tried again. His pulse rate bordered on tachycardia. Then again, he wasn't relaxed enough for it to be at a resting rate.

A minute later, Noelle returned. "From what I can tell, it's clear. Go straight to my car. Don't stop."

Again, she cupped his elbow and moved without his agreement.

Exposed. If he were to put a name to the trek across the small parking lot, that's what it would be.

The one positive...the warmth of the sun chased away the last bit of chill—at least physically. Make that two. He wasn't inside the death trap of the morgue anymore.

Noelle opened the passenger door, and Jonah slipped in.

Once he was safely inside, his mind spun, grappling to make sense of all the things that had happened. But Jonah knew without a doubt, Ken's final action of telling Jonah about the falsified documents had put him in danger.

He leaned his head back, rolled it to the side, and stared at Noelle. She'd stay by his side until they sorted out the whole mess, but that placed her in danger.

Could he live through Noelle placing her life on the line for him?

The thought made bile crawl up his throat. Even if they were only friends, he couldn't fail another woman that meant the world to him.

————

A slight breeze trickled through the open window of the car that Jack had parked a block away, but it wasn't enough to prevent sweat from beading on his upper lip. He stared at the entrance to the county morgue and grinned. The acid had destroyed the evidence of his art work on his latest victim. The other poor soul had been sacrificed so as to not draw attention to the girl that mattered. The doctor, on the other hand, was an uncertainty. So Jack watched—waited.

He glanced at his hands. The phone cord had left marks but hadn't cut into the skin. Given time, the reddish lines would disappear. He rolled his wrist to look at his watch and cringed. Time was something he didn't have. He had to get back to work before someone got suspicious.

Jack glanced at the office and sat up straight in the driver's seat. His target waltzed out the front door. He gritted his teeth and slammed a fist against the wheel.

If he'd had another two minutes, the doctor would have joined Dodson in the afterlife. Instead, that stupid woman— whoever she was—had to come looking for the doc, requiring Jack to leave the job unfinished. Not only had the doctor somehow survived, but Jack hadn't had time to find Dodson's planner.

Maybe once he silenced Harris, he'd show the woman his skills.

He chuckled. Yeah, that would be fun. Not one of his normal choices—a little old for that—but who's to say he couldn't deviate a little from the mission?

A plan formed. The doctor first, then he'd do a little bit of research on the chick before he snatched her.

————

Noelle gripped the steering wheel tightly enough her fingers hurt as she drove toward the EGA office. Finding Jonah in a cold storage drawer meant for corpses and seeing the markings on his neck sent fury coursing through her. An unknown attacker had come close to killing her best friend. She vowed, at that moment, to hunt the person down and make him pay for hurting Jonah.

The memories of her own time trapped by a madman wiggled into her thoughts, but she forced them aside. She couldn't afford the distraction. Jonah and the increasing threats required her full attention.

A quick glance at him squeezed her heart. He sat staring out the passenger window, the normal sparkle in his eyes no longer visible.

She wanted to cry and scream in rage at the same time. But this wasn't about her. She had to do something to get his mind off what had happened. "In all the time we've spent together, I don't think I've ever asked why you wanted to become a doctor and why the emergency department."

Jonah sat motionless long enough she thought he wouldn't answer. Then he sighed. "My sister."

"You've told me about her, but why did she make you choose medicine as your degree?" A two-word answer from the man who loved to talk told all she needed to know. Getting him out of his funk wasn't going to be easy.

His shoulders drooped. "When I was six, my parents told me to watch my little sister."

"That's a bit young to babysit, isn't it?"

He continued to gaze out the window, but at least he was talking.

"No, nothing like that. Mom and Dad asked me to keep an eye on her while they fixed dinner. She was around three at the time and had a habit of climbing on everything." He ran a hand over his face. "I was distracted with my Legos. She scaled the bookshelf next to the fireplace and called out for me to look. She'd climbed too high for me to reach. I yelled for my mom, but Wendy reached for the next shelf. Before I could tell her to stop, she fell. Her head hit the brick hearth."

"Oh, Jonah." Noelle's heart ached for the little boy who'd watched his sister get hurt. "Was she all right?"

"She had an inch-long gash, which to a child seemed like four inches. And like a typical head wound, it bled like crazy. But it was her motionless body that scared me the most."

"What happened next?"

"The ambulance came and transported her to the hospital. She had a concussion and required stitches. Mom and Dad never blamed me. But I had nightmares for weeks."

"I can understand that." Noelle turned into the EGA courtyard lot and put her car into Park. She shifted to face him. "You have to know it wasn't your fault. You were only six."

"I know that now. But then...let's just say I felt guilty for years." He leaned back and closed his eyes for a moment, then he met her gaze and gave her a sad smile. "It was then and there that I decided I'd never be helpless again. I wanted to be a doctor so that the next time something bad happened, I'd know what to do."

"I'd say you succeeded in knowing what to do. According to

the word on the street, you were the best ER doctor on the east coast—and throughout the US, if my sources are correct—until you gave it all up. And that's saying something."

"Yeah." Jonah turned away from her and stared out the window again. "I'm not all that great."

He'd never opened up to her about why he'd taken a different path in his career. The few times she'd asked, he'd said he'd needed a change and then switched topics. She'd never pressed him to divulge the reason, but the pain in his expression made her want to pry. If only to know how to wipe away the sadness from his life.

For now, she let his comment go. "I've called Alana and Juliette. Just so you know, I told them about Ken."

He jerked to face her.

She held up her hand to halt his disapproval. "They won't disclose the information until we're ready, but they're my team. I trust them with my life and yours. Bottom line, we need their help."

He studied her for a moment, then nodded. "If you say we need the others, I believe you."

Noelle released the breath she'd held, having been uncertain how Jonah would react. She laced her fingers with his. "Thank you."

"That's my line. I don't know what I'd do without you." He squeezed her hand.

In the whole time she'd known Jonah, she hadn't witnessed the vulnerability in him that she did at this moment. Noelle glanced at their entwined hands. When had her heart gotten involved? She had to tamp down those thoughts and remember a relationship beyond friendship would never happen. Not with Jonah—not with anyone.

Besides, she had a job to do and had no intention of letting her feelings cause her to lose focus. But with no idea who was behind the attacks or why, protecting him became a challenge.

She wouldn't—couldn't—let him down.

SIX

Jonah stepped from Noelle's vehicle, careful not to jostle his aching body. He stared at the walkway to her immaculate light-gray one-story bungalow in a residential area of Savannah, wondering if he had the energy to make it into the house. The attack had aggravated his previous injuries and added more to the list. Those would heal. It was the fear that had dug its teeth in and refused to let go.

For the past two hours, he'd only heard half of what the EGA ladies had discussed, but he'd gotten the gist of their decision. Whether he wanted it or not—which deep down, he did—he had a bodyguard twenty-four seven. And the most determined women on the planet digging into Ken's crime. The whole situation added a layer of helplessness to his already sour mood.

Noelle rounded the car. "I'd like to get you inside as soon as possible." She made a quick scan of the neighborhood. "I'm ninety-nine percent positive that no one followed us, but I'll feel better once you're tucked inside."

"Got it." Jonah had a strong desire to curse at Ken for

throwing away his career and reputation along with putting Jonah in danger, but what good would that do?

He trudged up the walkway edged by a well-groomed yard. It seemed like everything Noelle owned had a pristine look. Unlike himself and his chaotic life. Why would now be any different?

Noelle unlocked the door and turned off the security system. He followed her in, and she locked the door and reengaged the alarm. A typical behavior for her. He saw it every time he visited.

Jonah slipped off his shoes by the entrance and placed them neatly next to the wall. He laid Ken's planner on the kitchen table to his left, then pointed to the duffel bag hanging from his shoulder. "I'll go put this in the extra bedroom."

Without waiting on an answer, he trudged down the hall to the first bedroom on the right. He knew the house well thanks to his caregiving during her concussion. Plus, he'd spent many evenings here over the last ten months, chilling with her. Something about her house—maybe the soothing pale-green walls—relaxed him. Or it might be the company and have nothing to do with the interior design.

He placed the duffel on the white queen-sized comforter and stared out the bedroom window. A shiver ran down his spine. He grabbed the curtains and yanked them closed. His heart raced. The bruises on his neck chose that moment to throb. His fingers brushed the tender skin. He had to get a grip. Shaking off the dark path his thoughts chose to travel, he eyed the dresser and considered the bathroom at the end of the hall. No, he'd unpack his clothes and toiletries later. *Sorry, Noelle, I just don't have it in me right now.* He spun on his heels and returned to the living room.

"Hungry?" Noelle stood in the kitchen, stirring a pot on the stove.

"Maybe a little." He sounded like a sulky child. But at the moment, he didn't care.

"I had a gallon-size bag of homemade chicken noodle soup in the freezer. I dumped it into the pot and added a little more broth. It'll help it thaw faster." She tapped the spoon on the edge of the pan and placed it on the small plate next to the stove. "I figured it would be the easiest thing for you to swallow."

His throat had contusions inside and out. The soup sounded perfect. "Thanks. I'm sure you're right." Jonah collapsed on the couch and closed his eyes. How had his life gone from good to a disaster in a matter of hours?

"I'll give you until after dinner to sulk. Then you have to snap out of it."

He grabbed the throw pillow, held it to his chest, and rested his chin on it. "Fine." He heard her chuckle.

Dishes and silverware rattled in the kitchen. A few minutes later, Noelle strode in and plopped down beside him. "What's going on inside that head of yours?"

His gaze met hers. "Other than someone tried to kill me at least twice?"

"Remember, you survived. That counts for a lot. And if Alana, Juliette, and I have anything to say about it, we'll get to the bottom of whatever this is and keep you safe."

"I appreciate that." Jonah clasped her hand. The softness of her skin belied the tough bodyguard he'd witnessed in action over the past year. His gaze traveled to her eyes—a blue so bright that it reminded him of the clear waters off the coast of Jamaica. How had he not noticed before? "I trust you."

Noelle stared at their connected hands, then up at him. "I... um...thanks."

Time to confess that he'd zoned out at the office. "I have to admit, I didn't pay attention at EGA. What's the plan?"

The smile that graced her face sent a flutter loose in his belly. "When you didn't complain, I had a feeling you weren't listening."

"Oh boy, maybe I should have concentrated on what y'all discussed."

"It's not that bad." She squeezed his hand. "You're staying here since my security is top-of-the-line. Alana and Juliette will take turns monitoring the perimeter at night while I sleep. I'll take the day shift. If I need to go somewhere, one of the others will step in."

He narrowed his gaze. "So you're going to be my shadow? Everywhere?"

"I'm not going to follow you into autopsy or be always on your heels. You can go about your day as normal. If you need privacy in your office, I'll stay in the hallway. But I won't be far if you need me."

He returned the pressure on her fingers. "Thank you."

"You're welcome." She rested her head on the back of the couch and gave him a lazy smile. "Dinner will take thirty minutes or so. Would you like to rest first or take a look at Ken's planner?"

Rest sounded wonderful, but figuring out what had put him in the line of danger held a sense of urgency. "Let's dive into the planner while we wait for the soup to heat."

"Stay here. I'll go get it." She retrieved the bound calendar and returned to her seat.

Jonah scooted to an upright position and accepted the planner from her.

She shifted closer and peered over his arm.

"He didn't tell me when he started falsifying reports, but his wife died a few months ago. I'm thinking we should flip back to a few months before she died and see if anything stands out. If not, we continue to work backward."

"I agree. It gives us a jumping off point."

He turned the book to February. Jonah sucked in a breath, unprepared for his reaction to Ken's handwriting. "It's hard to believe he's gone."

Noelle stayed silent while he pulled himself together.

Meetings filled several dates during February, along with Ken's autopsy schedule. Plus, a couple of doctor's appointments were thrown in. Jonah changed the angle to read the haphazard writing. Something about the notes scribbled in the margins gave him pause.

"What is it?"

"I'm not sure." Jonah pointed to the numbers. "They aren't case numbers. Or at least, I don't think so."

She tapped one of the notations. "They're too long and not the right coding for police reports."

"There's two here." He flipped to January. "One here."

"Check the other months."

He looked through the planner, focusing on the notes in the margin. After discovering one or two each month, Jonah lifted his gaze to Noelle. "What do you think?"

"Looks like we found a possible connection. But we'll have to figure out what the numbers mean to confirm that suspicion." The timer went off in the kitchen. "Soup's done. Bring the planner, let's eat."

Noelle left him sitting on the couch.

The savory aroma reminded him of his childhood home. His mother hadn't been able to cook anything edible, but his father could have outcooked the best five-star-restaurant chef any day.

He stood and ambled to the kitchen table, mulling over the codes in his head. "So, instead of figuring out what the numbers mean, since it's giving me a headache, what about working on where to find the information we need?"

"You knew Ken best." She stirred the soup, then ladled some into two bowls.

"I thought I did." He ran a hand through his hair. "But apparently not as well as I believed."

"Don't do that. You and Ken were friends. Sometimes people don't want to burden their friends with the depressing parts of their lives." Noelle set the bowls on the table along with spoons and napkins.

"Isn't that what friendship is? Standing beside each other in good and bad?" Jonah picked up his spoon but didn't break eye contact with her.

She arched an eyebrow. "We're friends, right?"

"Good ones."

"We don't have *secrets*? Things we haven't told each other?"

He studied her for a moment. Oh, they both had hidden events in their pasts that neither wanted to share. "You have a point."

"The Ken I knew was a good guy. He probably got in over his head and didn't want to bring you into his troubles."

"In the end...he did." Stage two of grief had hit Jonah. He was angry with Ken and wanted to rail on the man for being stupid. Ugh. Only three more stages to go. Assuming he didn't get stuck in one.

For the next several minutes, they ate in companionable silence. He, lost in his thoughts; Noelle—he had no idea where her brain had gone, but by the look in her eyes, somewhere dark.

After placing her spoon next to her bowl, she clasped her hands on the table. "Where would Ken hide documents?"

"I have no idea."

"Yes, you do. Think. If he had information that he had no intention of sharing but wanted to keep for security purposes, where would he put it?"

The impossible question rolled around in his brain. He knew Noelle hadn't asked to be cruel. She was convinced that Jonah had the ability to figure it out. "His desk drawers are out. Too obvious and too neat to hide anything. I'd say maybe his file cabinet but in disguise. Like hiding in plain sight."

"That's a good possibility. Keep going."

He scratched the scruff on his jaw. "If it were me, I'd have a backup. A flash drive or something small. Maybe both documents and an electronic record."

"Now we're getting somewhere." She rubbed her hands together.

He pushed the remnants of his dinner away and slid the planner in front of him. The concept of the files tucked in with paper reports and a flash drive hidden in Ken's office took hold. "I'd like to search his belongings tomorrow, if that's okay."

"Sounds like a solid plan." Noelle cleared the table and quickly cleaned the kitchen.

"Thanks, Elle."

She shifted to face him. "That's what I'm here for—to help."

He nodded. "If it's okay with you, I'm going to shower and get comfortable for the evening."

"Go ahead. While you do that, I'll head to my office. The one next to the guest room. I'd like to work for a while before heading to bed."

He closed Ken's planner and tucked it under his arm. "I'll join you when I'm done." Once in his bedroom, Jonah placed the book on the dresser and gathered his clothes.

Had they really found the clue needed to solve the mystery behind Ken's deception?

If not, how many more attempts on his life could he live through?

———

The notes and photos of cold cases pinned to one of the office walls weighed on Noelle. She'd examined each case in detail over the past year, and if the answer lay in the information in front of her, she hadn't found it. But it was in there—somewhere. It had to be. She refused to let a serial killer go free when she had the ability to stop him.

At least she and Jonah had something to go on with Ken's

case. They might not have figured out what the numbers meant yet, but she'd bet they were closer to an answer with those than she was with the ten murders staring back at her.

She rested her hip on the corner of the small desk near the window and studied the board from a different angle.

The pictures of the cuts on her upper arms and chest caught her eye, taunting her. Her investigation into the serial killer included her own living nightmare. As the only survivor, the officers had redacted her name from the reports to prevent her identity from leaking to the public. The images in the file had no identifying features to reveal her as the victim, but Noelle knew, along with a select few detectives who'd since retired. And that's all that mattered.

She rubbed the scars on her arms through her blouse, wishing, not for the first time, for the ability to go back and make a different decision.

"Hey. Still working on those cold cases?" Jonah leaned against the doorjamb.

Tousled wet hair hung limp at his temples. He'd changed into comfortable sweats and a T-shirt. He looked more relaxed after his shower. The smell of his citrus soap drifted across the room—an aroma uniquely Jonah.

"What can I say? I'm determined."

Jonah joined her in front of her murder wall and crossed his arms. "Have you discovered anything new?"

Many nights she and Jonah had sat on the loveseat that butted up against the opposite wall, bouncing ideas off each other. She'd never explained her interest in the cold cases or this particular serial killer. Jonah knew she held a secret, but he hadn't pushed her to reveal it. Something she appreciated.

"Not much." Noelle narrowed her gaze and examined him. He'd relaxed, but the day had taken its toll. She took pity on him and motioned to the loveseat. "Let's sit down."

Without complaint, he eased himself onto the small couch.

After she joined him, he tilted his head. "Thanks. Now, run it down for me."

"Are you sure you want to do this tonight?" The man had experienced the taste of death. She had no desire to push him into a trigger.

He nodded. "I want to help. This"—he motioned to the photos—"seems important to you. We've discussed these before, but give me a rundown again."

Might as well let him a little farther into her world—at least the basics. She sighed. "As you know, I've taken an interest in these cases. You may or may not have figured it out yet, but they're all the work of a serial killer. The last case dates to eight years ago."

He pointed to the photos of her on the wall. "And the first? How long?"

Her pulse rate spiked. When they'd talked before and she'd pored over the documents, he'd been her sounding board, nothing more. "Fifteen years." She gripped her own hand hard enough to hurt.

Jonah shifted in his seat and wormed his fingers between her clutched hands. "All eleven of the other cases have names and pictures of the women. Why not the first one?"

Air refused to fill her lungs. Why had she thought Jonah wouldn't eventually ask? A stupid move on her part. She stared at the gruesome image of her cut flesh and chewed on the inside of her lips. Did she tell him?

"Elle, look at me."

Her gaze drifted to his.

"I've never asked, and you don't have to say anything. But I'd love it if you'd trust me."

His brown eyes held a depth of compassion that sent a rush of tears to the surface. "I...um..." She'd never told anyone except the detectives investigating the crime. Of course, her parents and her therapist knew, plus she'd told Lizzie the basics, but she'd always glossed over the details to everyone but the police officers. Could she reveal the ugly scars of her past—emotional as well as physical? She inhaled. "This serial killer is personal."

"You know the first victim?"

A humorless laugh escaped. "Know? Oh yeah, I know her."

"Who is it?" Jonah waited for her response, not rushing her.

Every cell in her being screamed at her to stay quiet. But this was Jonah. The man she'd shared more with in the past ten months than she'd shared with anyone else in her life. She blew out a long breath and steeled her spine. "It's me."

His eyes widened, but the silence in the room lingered.

A two-year-old required to sit still had nothing on Noelle. She forced herself to stay seated, but the lack of reaction gnawed at her. "Please, say something."

"But you're here. Not dead." He waved a hand at the wall.

That's what he'd taken away from her confession? "By a freak accident, I escaped." More like a gift from God.

He lifted his hand and cupped her cheek. "I'd like to hear about it, if you're willing to share."

She closed her eyes and leaned into his touch. Sharing with him might be the hardest thing she'd ever done. Was she willing to chance his disgust once he knew the truth? "Are you sure you want to hear this?"

"You've always fascinated me, but now..." He tucked a wayward strand of hair behind her ear. His palm brushed along her jawline before he reclaimed her hands. "Yes, I want to know. Besides, I have a feeling you haven't talked about it since it happened. I'd be honored if you told me everything."

His touch sent tingles racing over her skin. What would it be like to feel his caress as more than a friend? The black hole in her stomach grew. She'd never have a romantic relationship with him or anyone, but Jonah deserved to know the truth about her past.

Mind made up, she took three long breaths, then faced him. "It's not pretty."

"I've seen the photos and heard you talk about the reports. I don't expect it to be." His hands remained wrapped around hers.

She cleared her throat. "I was seventeen at the time. I loved hanging out with my friends. It was a Friday evening, and we'd gone to the local mall. Time got away from us. Before we knew it, it had gotten dark outside. My friends had parked on the other side of the mall. I told them goodbye and headed to my car. The minute I left the store, my internal warning bells went off."

"But you didn't listen to them," Jonah stated.

"Exactly." She slipped her left hand out from under his and rubbed the scars on her upper arm through her shirt. "I've never made that mistake again."

"I imagine not." He gave her a sad smile.

"I headed for my car. I was two steps away—almost to safety—when a hand closed over my mouth and a needle jabbed into my neck. I tried to fight, but by then it was too late." Her body shook and tears dripped from her chin.

Jonah wiped the wetness from her face with his thumb. "Easy, Elle."

The simple touch calmed her—kept her grounded in the moment. She sucked in a breath. "When I woke up, he had me strapped to a chair with a plastic tarp spread out underneath me. At first it didn't dawn on me why the floor was covered. The drugs hadn't left my system yet. Once the haze wore off, the reality of my situation hit hard. I panicked. I struggled against the restraints, but it was worthless." Her heart rate spiked to stroke level.

"You can stop if it gets to be too much." Jonah's soft tone held so much empathy she about turned into a blubbering mess.

She glanced down at their hands and took a deep breath, settling her pulse. "No. You need to know."

"I'm listening."

"Let's just say that over the next four days, the man who'd abducted me used his fists and enjoyed using a knife." She pointed to the pictures on the wall. Each victim had cuts on their upper arms and across the upper part of their chests.

Jonah's teeth clenched, and his jaw twitched.

Noelle recognized the signs of the man barely holding his temper in check. She appreciated his anger on her behalf. "Fast-forward to the day I escaped. My assailant had a thing about bodily waste. Not that he fed me, but he made sure I had enough water to keep me alive. He'd allow me to use the restroom three times a day, and if I didn't hold it, let's just say he wasn't happy about it." She waved off the stray thought. "Anyway, on that day, a noise caught his attention before he finished securing me to the chair. He rushed from the room. It gave me the opportunity to work free."

"Do you know what the sound was?"

She shook her head. "No. But I didn't care. I staggered to a door on the opposite side of the room from where he'd exited and prayed it led to the outside. It did. I was barefoot, half naked, but I didn't care. I ran as fast and far as my abused body allowed. I ended up at an old farmhouse. An elderly couple took me in, wrapped me in a blanket, and called 911."

"And since you're looking into the cases, I'm assuming the guy got away."

"Correct. I had no idea where he'd held me, and by the time the police interviewed me, my brain had shut down to protect me. I knew what had happened, but the details, like his face or his location, my mind had wiped from my memory."

"And today?"

She sighed. "It's still gone. After enough time had passed, my therapist told me that I'd probably never remember."

The crease in Jonah's forehead deepened. "Did the guy ever try to get to you again?"

"Until about eight or nine years ago, I sensed someone watching me. Needless to say, I became fanatical with my safety. But no. He never tried to abduct me again."

Jonah's gaze went to the pictures. "No one before you?"

"Not that I can find. But who knows?"

"And the one eight years ago was his last?"

"Looks that way. I checked over the next year or so and didn't find any cases that matched." And she lived in fear on the daily that he might return.

"Any idea what happened to cause him to stop?"

She paused to think over his question. The last thing she wanted was to give him a flippant answer. "The only things I can think of are, number one, he's in prison for an unrelated crime; two, he's dead; or three, he moved from the area. However, the last one is unlikely since I have contacts all over the United States and would know if a similar crime had been committed around that timeframe."

"Could he have just stopped killing?"

She shook her head. "Highly unlikely. People like him don't up and quit without a life-altering reason."

"Yeah, I assumed that, but a guy could hope, right?" He shrugged.

Even with her raw emotions and nausea swirling in her belly, she smiled at Jonah's comment.

He released her and ran his hand down her arm.

She flinched and jerked away, the memories too fresh.

"Elle?"

"Sorry. I...why don't we get some rest and start fresh in the morning searching Ken's office."

His shoulders sagged. She knew she'd hurt his feelings, but his touch—what would it be like to lean into him? Have his arms around her? Kiss him? Have a relationship with him? All the things she wanted and could never have with anyone. Not even Jonah, her best friend. Her psyche was too broken. Her body too damaged. The killer had robbed her of any possibility of a normal future.

She shook herself off the dark path of regrets her thoughts had taken her down before the emotions overwhelmed her. She stood and held out her hand to help him up. "I called Raven when you went to get your shower. She's picking up several changes of clothes for you and your mail, then plans to drop them off in the morning. She also promised to visit your house often to feed and pet Samson. Raven knows how special he is to you. She'll take good care of him."

He accepted her gesture and pushed to his feet. "Please thank her for me if I don't see her. And Elle, thank you for telling me about your past."

She swallowed the lump in her throat and nodded. "I'll see you in the morning." Without another word, she rushed from the room, leaving Jonah alone in her office. Retelling her story had opened old wounds, the events vivid and alive in her mind like they'd just happened. Her skin crawled at the recollection of her experience, making her want to take a shower and scrub away the memories.

Moments later, standing under the stream of hot water, she rested her head on the cold tile. Sobs tore through her until she had no more strength to hold herself upright. She slid to the floor and hugged her knees.

God, why?

She'd asked that question every day since the madman had left her scarred and damaged.

Taking a cleansing breath, she picked herself up off the shower floor. She'd shed enough tears over her painful past for the night. Time to let go of what she couldn't change—for now. But her memories would return with a vengeance when she least expected. It always happened, no matter how hard she tried to move on.

She glanced at her arms and sighed. She wanted a future that included a husband and maybe even children. Her closeness with Jonah had caused her desires to resurface, but knowing her arms and chest would repulse Jonah, or any man for that matter, she had to stuff her dream back where it belonged—in the not-going-to-happen column of her life.

SEVEN

Jonah stepped into Ken's old office and flicked on the light. He ran a hand through his hair. Last night had left a gaping hole in Jonah's heart. But it was Noelle's hasty retreat that had gutted him. He'd wanted to wrap her in his arms and make the pain go away. He had no idea how to handle the situation. And the one man he turned to for advice was gone.

The wedding picture sitting on Ken's desk stared back at Jonah. He'd arrived at the medical examiner's department thirty minutes ago and finally worked up the nerve to search his friend's office. Jonah ran a finger along the edge of the desk. A vise clamped on his heart as he remembered the times he'd had coffee with Ken, discussing everything from work to plans for the weekend.

The weight that had pressed down on him after the explosion returned with an intensity that took his breath away. No longer would he stop by this room on a daily basis and chat with Ken. And to make matters worse, he'd received a phone call from the county that morning, informing him they'd moved him into the chief medical examiner's position.

Jonah had achieved his goal, but not the way he'd wanted it. Ken's retirement, yes. His death—not so much. And now he'd destroy the man's reputation once he found the evidence.

Shaking off the despair, Jonah sifted through the neatly stacked papers on the desk. "Ken, what did you get yourself into?" A part of Jonah feared what he'd discover. He lifted a file and found a Post-it note. *Jonah's birthday coming in July. Don't forget.* The reminder tugged a sad smile from him. Of all the wonderful qualities Ken had, remembering dates wasn't one of them.

"All good in here?"

He jolted at Noelle's question. She stood in the doorway with one hand on the frame. She'd shared some heavy memories last night and looked no worse for wear. He, on the other hand—he ran his fingers through his hair—not so much.

"Sorry. I thought you heard me come in." She moved into the room.

"No. But that's okay. Just lost in thought."

"Anything I can do to help?"

"Not really. I'm going to examine the documents next." He pointed to the file cabinet.

"Think you'll find reports with the mysterious code on them?"

So far, he'd found nothing even close to helping uncover the answer they searched for. "It's the only thing I can think of. But if he kept them in his house…" He shrugged. "They're gone."

The file organizer on Ken's desk held nothing of interest. Jonah moved to the upright four-drawer cabinet and pulled out the one on the top left.

"I hear congratulations are in order." Noelle flashed him a sad smile.

"Not the way I wanted the job of chief medical examiner, but it is what it is, and I'll do my best." *Ken, if you were here, I'd throttle you right now*. And there it was again. When would the anger pass?

"You'll be good at it." Her gaze traveled the office. "Ken was organized and neat. You shouldn't have a hard time finding anything you need for your new position."

"I think I hear a dis in there somewhere." Jonah chuckled.

"Not me." She feigned innocent. "Seriously, though, I have no room to talk. My OCD tendencies match your chaos. We're complete opposites when it comes to our organizational habits."

"But yet, we make a friendship work." He fought the urge to pull her into a hug and never let go. When had she snuck under his radar and wormed her way into his heart? Jonah stood and moved toward her.

He watched as her throat bobbed, but she never broke eye contact with him. Without questioning his move, he cupped her cheek. "Elle?"

"I-I'm not sure..."

Last night, when she'd left him standing in her office, his thoughts about their relationship had changed. He'd stood in front of the photos that documented her injuries, and all the pieces had fallen into place. Her security system, the long-sleeved blouses, the way she rubbed her upper arms while deep in thought. All of it had burrowed into his heart.

The warmth of her skin sent a searing heat through his hand all the way to his toes. "That's okay, neither am I. But I can't deny that my heart wants more than a friendship."

She leaned into his touch and closed her eyes.

Gaze on her lips, he eased forward.

Voices drifted from the hall. Jonah froze. For the love of everything, he was in his dead friend's office looking for the documents to right a wrong. Not the right time or place to explore his new feelings for Noelle.

She took a step back, breaking the connection between them.

LYNETTE EASON & SAMI A. ABRAMS

He brushed the hair from her forehead. "I apologize for the timing, but I refuse to be sorry for my intentions."

She moved to a bookshelf and examined the contents. "We have a lot to do, so let's focus on that."

What had gotten into him? "I'll comb through the paperwork in the file cabinet. I think that's the most logical place."

"I concur. Hiding in plain sight is—was—Ken's style." Noelle glanced at him, and her gaze shifted to the window.

Her brow furrowed. She rushed toward him, wrapped her arm around his waist, and flung him toward the floor.

The window exploded, raining glass over the room.

His side hit the desk. He grunted in pain.

The two of them tumbled to the floor along with items on the desk.

When the world stopped moving, reality hit him squarely between the eyes. His attacker was back and had Jonah in his crosshairs—literally.

———

Noelle lay on the floor of Ken's office with Jonah underneath her, trying to catch her breath. If she hadn't looked up at that moment and seen the glint of the rifle scope, Jonah would be dead. She placed her hands on either side of him and pushed up. Fire shot through her arm and she cried out.

"What's wrong?" Jonah's frantic tone registered, but she had to breathe through the pain.

Eyes closed, she rolled off him. "Stay down." She clutched her right arm. Blood trickled between her fingers. The bullet had ripped a hole in her shirt and sliced her skin. Lovely. Another scar to add to her collection. What did it matter anyway? Her skin would never match up to her mother's expectations. Flawless, model-worthy smooth skin was a thing of the past.

"He can't see us down here." Jonah's hand covered hers and clamped down.

Nausea swirled in her belly from the extra pressure.

"I need to take a look."

"No. It's not serious." She had no desire for Jonah to see her damaged body.

"I beg to differ." His tone held the commanding edge of an ER doctor.

"Doc!" Bonnie's voice rose in the room.

Noelle rolled her head to the side and opened her eyes. Jonah's admin crawled to the doorway on all fours.

"I need a first-aid kit, but stay out in the hall. And call 911. Tell them someone shot at us through the window." Jonah finished giving Bonnie orders and turned his attention back to her. "Noelle, I really have to take a look."

Uh-oh, her full first name. "Fine. But let's get out of here first."

"Hold on." He grabbed a clipboard and swept the glass aside as he army-crawled across the floor and edged against the wall. He gripped the pull and closed the curtain, blocking out prying eyes.

"Smart move."

"What can I say? I'm not just another pretty face." He chuckled. A bit strained, but she'd give him an A for effort.

"Cute." She struggled to get herself upright.

"Wait. Let me help." Jonah scrambled to her side. He hadn't stood but hunched over as he hurried to her. He gripped her under her arms and lifted as she scooted against the leg of the desk for support.

A black button lay next to the phone that had broken apart when it hit the floor.

She released her bleeding arm, wiped the blood on her pant leg, and picked the item up with her thumb and finger.

"What is it?" Jonah leaned in for a better look.

LYNETTE EASON & SAMI A. ABRAMS

That's how the killer knew. She closed her eyes for a second and exhaled. Then she nudged Jonah and held her finger to her lips.

His forehead scrunched, and he tilted his head.

A listening device. He bugged the phone, she mouthed.

Jonah pinched the bridge of his nose with one hand and slammed his fist on the floor with the other.

The turmoil evident in his features made her heart ache for the man.

A year ago, she would've wanted to give him a hug and be the friend that he needed. Today...things had fundamentally changed. She had a strong desire to wrap him in her arms and make his pain disappear. To be there for him beyond friendship.

Tears clouded her vision. But that wasn't possible. Was it?

———

Jonah had taken the tiny listening device from Noelle and placed it on the desk for the police to take into evidence, then led her out of the room and into autopsy two. He pulled over two chairs and eased her onto one while he took the other. The seriousness of the situation made his nerves hum with the familiar sensation of not being able to sit in his own skin. He or Noelle could have been lying on a metal table right now instead of using the room for refuge.

"When do you think the killer planted the bug?"

Noelle continued to put pressure on the bullet wound. "I'm not sure. If I had to guess, I'd say whoever placed it there did it while Ken was alive, to spy on him."

"That makes sense." He scooted his chair forward to examine her wound. "We're going to have to tell Matt and Decia, aren't we?"

"Yes."

"Not even going to think about it?" He raised a brow.

She lifted her shoulder and grimaced. "You know as well as I do we can't wait any longer."

"I wish we had more details. I hate what this will do to Ken's reputation. And it's all based on a vague confession over the phone." He blew out a long breath. "Time to take a look." He removed her hand from her upper arm and froze. The blood-soaked sleeve sent his mind spiraling into the past.

"Jonah. You look a little green. Is it that bad?" She glanced at the tear in her shirt.

"No. Sorry." He shook his head, dislodging the horrible memory. "Blood sometimes gets to me. But I'm good." One of the main reasons he no longer worked in the ER. The other reason—his failure to save the person he loved most in the world.

"Doc!"

He leaned toward the door. "In room two, Bonnie!"

Bonnie hurried in and placed the box on the desk beside him. "Police are on the way along with an ambulance. There's the first-aid kit. Anything else?"

"No, that's all. Thanks."

The woman nodded and hurried out.

"Now that we've established I'm not the ER doctor I used to be, I'll do my best until the paramedics get here." He dug through the box and retrieved the scissors.

"No!" She jerked away.

"Elle." Jonah stared at her, then it dawned on him. The serial killer's lasting gift. The scars from multiple cuts during her captivity. "It's okay, Elle. I've seen a lot of things during my years as a doctor." He had no intention of downplaying her experience, but he wanted her to know that he wouldn't judge her. "Besides, it's not a secret anymore. At least, not with me."

She scowled at him. "Fine."

He smirked and shook his head. "Why do women always say that when things are obviously not fine?" Before he cut through the fabric, he went to the small closet in the room and retrieved a long-sleeve scrubs top. "I'll do my best to keep it between us."

"Thank you."

"You'll need antibiotics, but I can take care of that later." Even though he worked at the morgue, he still maintained his license to practice medicine. Within a few minutes, he'd cleaned and butterflied the gash closed.

"All done." Jonah cleaned up the bloody gauze and threw it away in the trash beside the desk.

"Do I get a lollipop?" Her racing pulse, which he'd noticed while treating her, belied her teasing tone.

Yes, her scars made him want to weep for the young girl who'd endured so much pain and fear. But with or without the raised white lines on her skin, he found her attractive—inside and out. He wanted her to see herself the way he saw her.

"You know..." He clasped her forearm and gently twisted it so he had a clear view of the healed slices on her skin. With a finger, he traced the lines beside her bandage. "I'm not afraid of scars."

"Please, don't." She attempted to pull away from him.

He held tight. Not enough that she couldn't break free, but enough to make his point known. "I know what happened. It's nothing to be ashamed of." He smoothed his hand down her arm and interlaced his fingers with hers. "You are beautiful, Elle." He leaned in, giving her a moment to decide what she wanted.

When she didn't move away, he closed the gap. He brushed his lips against hers, once, twice. Common sense flew from his brain, and the only thing that existed was how his heart rate spiked at the mere touch of his lips to hers. He slid his hand behind her neck and pulled her close, deepening the kiss. The moment should have scared him to death, but it was as if his out-of-control world had fallen into place with this sweet, vulnerable woman. All the dark shadows of his past scattered until only light existed.

He ended the kiss and rested his forehead against hers, both of them trying to catch their breath.

Voices carried down the hall.

He closed his eyes, not ready for the moment to end. "That's Matt. I'll go greet them while you change." He stood and handed her the clean shirt.

"I appreciate that." Her shoulders slumped.

Finger under her chin, he tilted her face. "Elle, look at me."

Her gaze met his.

"I don't want you to hide your scars, but I think you do. That's why I gave you the scrubs top. Change or not—it doesn't bother me one way or the other." He kissed the top of her head. "I'll give you time to decide."

Jonah turned and exited the autopsy room, closing the door behind him.

What had he done? He had no regrets about the beyond amazing kiss. In fact, he felt alive for the first time since Cara's death. But what if he and Noelle couldn't let go of their pasts?

Had he just ruined their friendship?

———

Noelle stared at the door. One minute, Jonah had patched up the skin where the bullet had torn through, and the next, he'd leaned in and kissed her. She hadn't kissed a man... She snorted. She hadn't even dated anyone since before her abduction. Jonah had been married, and she had no idea how to *do* a relationship. The two of them together was all kinds of wrong. Yet she couldn't muster up an ounce of regret.

Knowing she had limited time, she slipped off her bloody

shirt and replaced it with the long-sleeve scrubs top that Jonah had found for her.

Tears pricked her eyes at his thoughtfulness...and his words about her scars. No one had touched the healed cuts on her skin except for doctors. Not even her mother had stomached touching her. Jonah had cared more for her—about her—in the last few minutes than anyone in her family ever had.

A knock pulled her from her thoughts.

"Elle, can we come in?" Jonah asked from a small crack in the door.

"I'm good." She tossed the old shirt in the garbage and stood.

The door swung open, and Jonah entered with the two detectives on his heels.

Decia strode to her side. "Doc told us what happened. Are you okay?"

"He did a good job bandaging me up."

"Yeah, well, I still want you on antibiotics." Jonah pointed to the chair. "Sit while we chat. I've asked Bonnie to get us some water bottles and a few snacks. She's also picking up that prescription for you."

Noelle bit her lip to keep from laughing. She hadn't seen Jonah in mother-hen mode since her concussion. "Relax, Jonah. I'm fine."

"You will be once I make sure you have what you need."

Matt's gaze shifted between them, then to Decia, who shrugged. "Okay, then. Doc, have a seat."

Jonah moved his chair beside Noelle's and lowered himself onto it.

"First, we need your statements about the shooting. Then we want to know what you two are not telling us." Decia folded her arms, daring them to contradict her statement.

"No argument here." Jonah placed his hands between his

knees and proceeded to give the two detectives a rundown of the events.

Noelle interjected her comments when necessary.

Matt whistled through his teeth. "Someone is not happy with you, Doc."

Jonah's brows rose to his hairline. "Ya think?"

Decia finished writing her notes and tucked the pad of paper and pencil into a pocket of her cargo pants. "Now that we have that out of the way, what's really going on?"

"We planned to bring you into the loop once we had solid proof, but after the cold storage incident and the shooting, I think that idea is long gone." Noelle turned to Jonah. "Do you want to explain, or do you want me to?"

"I've got it." Jonah ran his fingers through his hair, leaving it sticking up in all directions. "I received a call from Ken Dodson on Wednesday late afternoon. He asked me to come visit him after work."

"We know that. That's why you were there when his house blew up." Matt shifted and leaned against the wall. "Tell us what we don't know."

"I'm getting there." Jonah exhaled. "When he called, he told me that he'd falsified autopsy reports and wanted me to review the cases. Set the records straight. Tell the truth. He said he'd kept the original documentation, but he died before he revealed where he kept the files."

"And you think whoever Ken falsified these reports for discovered his conversation with you," Decia stated.

Noelle rested her hand on Jonah's knee. "The hit-and-run was suspect. The attack in the morgue confirmed someone was willing to kill to hide evidence. EGA assumed full-time bodyguard status based on my assumption. I refused to take chances with his life. But it wasn't until the person used Jonah for target practice and we found the bug in Ken's phone that I realized the extent of the trouble Jonah is in."

"I sure wish you had said something earlier." Matt pushed from the wall and paced. "Any idea where Ken hid the files?"

"My guess, they might be in his file cabinet, tucked among other records. That's where I was looking when the gunshot shattered the window. However, we can't go in there and search since it's now a crime scene." Jonah rubbed his temples.

"Matt. Decia. I made a judgment call after the explosion when Jonah told me his conversation with Ken. Ken made Jonah promise not to say anything until he'd reevaluated the cases. I decided to honor that. And without Ken's testimony, or at least his statement and some type of proof, we had no clue what was going on."

"I get it. But from here on out, you communicate anything you uncover." Decia rested her hands on her hips and softened her tone. "Once we have the information, we'll investigate from our end. Ken had to have a reason not to go directly to the police. We do have to write the report, but that could take time, and I don't plan to make a big announcement, so as far as I'm concerned, Ken's secret is safe until we have solid evidence as to what's going on."

"Thanks, Decia." Noelle owed her friend big-time.

Matt squeezed Jonah's shoulder. "Be careful, man. Listen to the ladies."

Noelle stood. She had Matt's support, but she intended to make her commitment clear. "The Elite Guardians are not going to let this maniac hurt him."

Matt studied her for a moment and nodded.

"We'll let you know when the crime techs release Ken's office. Until then, send us all you've got and watch your backs." Decia gave Noelle a quick hug and strode from the room.

After Matt said his goodbyes, Jonah offered his hand to help her up.

She accepted and moved next to him. "Do you need anything from your office?"

"Nope."

"Then let's get out of here and go home."

They strode out the door toward the exit.

Noelle's mind replayed Jonah's kiss. The moment would be etched in her memory forever.

She made a mental to-do list. At the top, after protecting Jonah, she added, *Don't get your heart broken by wishing for something you can't have.*

EIGHT

Noelle sat at her kitchen table, staring at the clutter. Ken's planner lay open. Jonah's stacked mail that Raven had delivered earlier that day had fallen and scattered across the surface. She closed her eyes and fought the compulsion to clear the mess. Her OCD tendencies, a nice gift to go along with the scars from the serial killer—*her* serial killer. Control. Noelle thrived on it. And she'd never felt so out of control as she did at that moment.

The groove the bullet had cut through her arm burned, but it was Jonah's gentle touch that had seared her skin. In the past fifteen years, no one had shown as much compassion as Jonah had in that moment. Of course, few of her friends knew—but not even her best friend, Lizzie Tremaine Lee, was privy to the details.

Noelle gritted her teeth to hold the tears at bay. Jonah's tenderness was almost too much to handle. And what about that kiss? She closed her eyes and exhaled, letting the tension of the day wash away so she could focus on how to keep Jonah safe and find the person responsible for the attacks.

"I'm sorry." Jonah ran his hand across her back and sat next to her.

"About what?"

He swept his hand in an arc across the table. "The mess. I know it bothers you."

The denial sat on her tongue, but no way would she lie to him. Besides, he knew the truth whether she admitted it or not.

She shrugged. "Yes. But I can live with it for a while. Why don't you go through your mail while I examine Ken's planner again."

"Gladly, if it'll ease your stress." He sat and scooped the pile of mail together.

She grabbed the planner and opened it. "Why are you being so accommodating?"

He tore open an envelope and tossed the paper strip onto the table.

Gah! This would be harder than she'd thought. She retrieved a trash can and placed it next to him.

He grinned and threw away the scraps of paper. "I don't mean to be a hot mess. Just like you don't purposely want everything perfect. But here we are. I can try harder to pay attention to what is important to you."

She tilted her head and studied him. "Are you for real?"

He full-on belly-laughed. "I'm just me."

"Aren't guys supposed to be self-centered?"

The smile on Jonah's face disappeared. "Well, I can't speak for everyone in the male population, and even though we can be, when a guy finds a woman he wants to explore a relationship with, he treasures her. That means doing the little things so she feels cared for and loved."

She jerked to face him. "Really?"

"Now it's my turn. *Are you for real?* What kind of guys have you dated?" He tossed the current piece of mail into the trash and reached for another.

She was so out of her league it wasn't even funny. But she'd started the conversation, so she owed him an honest answer. "I don't date."

Jonah froze. "As in never?"

Noelle squirmed in her seat. How did she explain and not come off looking ridiculous? "My parents didn't allow me to date until I was sixteen. And even then, I wasn't that interested." She shrugged. "Sure, I liked boys, but I didn't have a lot of time with my sports schedule. Most of us hung out in groups after practice."

"Now, how did I guess you were a jock?"

"Because you know me."

"Apparently, not as well as I thought." He placed his hand over hers on the table. "Go on."

She inhaled. "There was this one guy, Travis, that I spent a lot of time with during track practice. I had just turned seventeen when he asked me out. Of course, I said yes. We had a great time." The memory of her first and only date warmed her heart. "He took me to dinner and then to the movies. We had a lot in common, so we had no problem coming up with things to talk about. At the end of the night, he gave me my first kiss."

"Sounds like a nice memory." He squeezed her fingers.

"It was." And then her carefree life had ended. "A couple weeks later, I was abducted." She stared at their hands, wondering how her life would have turned out if she'd listened to her gut on that fateful night.

"What about afterward? Please tell me the guys you dated treated you well."

"Didn't you hear me? I don't date."

"Yeah, but..." His eyes widened. "As in..."

She nodded. "I've had one date in my entire life."

"And the kiss?"

"One." Thirty-two years old, and she'd kissed one man—make that boy—in her life.

"So when I kissed you, you hadn't kissed anyone else but that Travis kid?"

She dropped her gaze to the table and shook her head.

"I had no idea." He cupped her chin and lifted, forcing her to look at him. "I'm honored to be your second kiss. And make no mistake, it was extremely enjoyable."

Heat traveled from her neck to her cheeks. "But you're experienced in relationships and...things. And I'm not." Great. Now she sounded like an idiot.

"All you need is a little confidence in the relationship department, but I have a feeling it's the *and things* you're most worried about." He tucked her hair behind her ear. "Am I right?"

She tugged her bottom lip between her teeth and nodded.

He leaned in and kissed her forehead. "Then I think it's time to do something about that."

"Wait. What?" Had she heard him correctly?

"I said I think—" His jaw dropped. "No. That's not what I meant." He covered his face with his hands. "I'm really botching this. What I was trying to say is that I'd like to show you what a relationship is like. And since I jumped to the kiss first, I'd like to take you on a date."

Her heart rate settled a bit, then sped up. The rollercoaster of emotions exhausted her. "I don't know, Jonah. When you realize you can't deal with my scars and walk away, you'll destroy me."

"All the more reason I want to show you what a real relationship is like. Nothing—not even scars—will scare me." He clasped her hands. "I have no idea what the future will bring between us. But I do know that I'd like you to have a positive memory—with me."

Could she take the chance? She'd opened up to him more

than anyone else in her life. Uncertain yet unwilling to let the opportunity pass, she made up her mind. "I think I'd like that."

He smiled. "Me too." He squeezed her hands one more time, then grabbed another envelope. "Unfortunately, until we solve this mystery that Ken handed us, we might have to get creative in the date department."

Glad the intensity of the conversation had ended, Noelle took a deep breath. "Explain."

Jonah slid his finger under the flap and popped it open. "I'm thinking dinner and a movie, but here at your house."

"Basically, what we've been doing for the past year?"

"Yes and no. This time my focus will be on you as a woman, not just as a friend."

And there went the flutter in her belly again. The idea of his full attention on her made her palms sweat.

She'd moved beyond being a scared young woman, and excelled in a male-dominated law enforcement career. But the concept of going on a date with Jonah terrified her.

———

What had he done? Jonah wiped a hand down his face. His comment about dating Noelle played on repeat in his head. He had no business considering a relationship with anyone—especially Noelle. He'd failed his wife Cara, but he refused to fail Noelle. And that's what would happen if he allowed himself to look beyond friendship.

But that kiss had struck something deep inside him. The completeness that had overwhelmed him...he hadn't experienced since Cara. He closed his eyes. Only the second kiss in her life. He sighed. She kissed like a dream—his dream. His heart had taken over and left his mind spinning.

He ventured a glance at her. The vulnerability in her expression would have taken him to his knees if he hadn't been sitting. He vowed right then that no matter what happened between them, he'd convince her that even with her scars, she was worthy of love.

Without pondering the consequences of his words, Jonah dumped the contents of the package onto the table. A black flash drive bounced on the surface before coming to a rest in front of them. The piece of paper that followed floated down and rested next to it.

They both stared at the items like they'd jump up and bite.

Noelle's gaze flicked to him. "Who's it from?"

"Not a clue. No return address." Jonah lifted the note and unfolded it. "It's from Ken."

"What'd he say?" Noelle leaned closer and peered over his shoulder.

"That he's sorry, and that everything I need to set the autopsy records straight is on the flash drive." Jonah picked up the small device and rolled it in his hand. "I'm not sure I want to know what's on it."

"I'd say with all the attempts on your life, you don't have a choice." Noelle covered his hand, stilling his movement. "I'll go get my laptop while you get yours. The not knowing will drive you crazy."

"You're right." He retrieved his laptop from his messenger bag and booted it up. By the time he'd inserted the flash drive, Noelle had returned from her office with her computer. "Have a seat and let's see what Ken sent me."

She scooted her chair next to him for a full view of the screen.

"Here goes nothing." He clicked on the folder named *Original Reports*. Eighteen individual file names popped onto the screen.

Noelle sucked in an audible breath. "He falsified that many reports?"

"It looks like it." Jonah opened the document labeled *Tina*

Snyder and examined the first close-up photo Ken had included and the police report. "Look at the marks on her neck."

"Strangulation?"

"That would be my guess." He squinted at the screen. "Check it out." He pointed at the handwritten note at the bottom of the page. "We don't need the fake autopsy files. At least, not initially. Ken's told me what he labeled it as. Tina's presumed strangulation was marked as a hit-and-run."

"Open another one."

Jonah clicked on the next file and studied it. "This one appears to be a drug overdose. See the marks on her arm and the dried froth around her mouth? And Ken wrote it as an accidental drowning."

"So basically, something close but where the police wouldn't continue to investigate."

"Exactly. Hold on." He scrolled down the list of names until he landed on the last file. "This looks interesting."

"All it says is extra photos." Noelle tapped the screen.

"But the question is, why make a separate file?" He clicked on the name. When the file opened, his stomach threatened to revolt.

Noelle squeaked. "Is that what I think it is?"

Image after image popped up. Each young woman's body had cuts similar to the pictures on Noelle's wall—and the scars on her arms.

"How?" Her voice quivered. "These date back three years. Long after my serial killer stopped his attacks."

"The question is, why did he stop? Was he in jail? Did he die and someone else picked up his cause?"

Noelle pushed from her chair, knocking it to the ground. "He can't be back. He just can't."

He snagged her hand. His gut twisted in knots. "Don't go there. Not yet. We have no idea what's going on."

"Jonah, these are the same!" She ran her fingers through her hair. Her breaths came in pants.

"Please, have a seat. Try to calm down before you hyperventilate." He tugged her toward him.

She nodded, then picked up the chair from the floor and sat. "Okay. I'm good."

He quirked a brow. "No, you aren't, but it's understandable." His gaze drifted to the screen and the photos staring back at him. "I was waiting for evidence, and now we have it. I think it's time to call Matt and Decia."

"I…" She swallowed hard.

He waited her out, not pushing.

"No one knows about me." The pain in her eyes raked his heart.

"Come here." He tugged her into a hug and rubbed her back. "Why is it so important that it remains a secret?"

Her cheek rested on his chest. "Because my scars are ugly, and it's a constant reminder of how stupid I was."

"Oh, Elle. The scars won't matter to your friends. Sure, they'll empathize with you, but they will not pity you. And as far as you being stupid, I don't think so. You were young. And let's be honest. Yes, you could have listened to your gut, but how many times do any of us ignore that internal warning? It rarely turns out as tragic as what you experienced. Give yourself some grace."

The front of his shirt turned damp and warm. He hadn't realized she'd started crying.

A few minutes later, she pulled away and wiped at his shirt. "Sorry that I got you all wet."

"I'll dry." He brushed the hair from her forehead. "Better?"

She stared at him through watery eyes. "Yeah, I actually am."

"Good. Are you ready to continue?"

She nodded. "You call Matt and Decia while I go get an extra flash drive from my office. We'll give them the original, but I plan to make a copy for us." Noelle strode down the hall, leaving him alone with his thoughts.

He forced himself to focus on the task at hand and not the possibility of Noelle's serial killer out there on the loose. He grabbed his cell phone and hit Matt's speed dial number.

Jonah opened another file while he waited for his friend to answer. The image knocked the wind from him. His failure slammed into him—again. A crumpled car so similar to Cara's accident it made him want to puke. The girl's injuries mimicked his deceased wife's. Injuries he'd had no power to keep from killing her.

"Detective Williams." Matt's voice drifted down a long tunnel. "Hello?"

He shook off the image of the accident. "Hey, Matt, it's Jonah."

"Hey, Doc. What can I do for you?"

He ran his finger against the flash drive. "I have something I need to show you. Can you and Decia come over to Noelle's?"

"Does this have anything to do with what y'all weren't telling us?"

"Yes." His gaze never left the photos in front of him.

"I'll grab Decia. We'll be there in twenty minutes."

Jonah hung up and stared at the accident scene on the screen.

Over the years, he'd saved so many people in the emergency room. But faced with the life-and-death situation of the person who meant the most to him, he'd failed.

How had God let him become one of the best ER doctors on the east coast and not allowed him to save his own wife?

NINE

Noelle's pulse hadn't stopped racing. Until now, she'd assumed the man who'd abducted her had disappeared, and she'd let her mind believe it. The idea her serial killer might still be out there torturing and murdering innocent young women scared the daylights out of her. What if he found her and finished what he'd started fifteen years ago? She swallowed the bile rising in her throat and took three deep breaths. She refused to fall apart.

Determination high to finish what she'd started and find the man who'd destroyed so many lives, she strode to the kitchen and stuffed her fears down tight. "Found one." She stopped in her tracks.

Jonah stared at his computer, his eyes wide.

"Jonah?"

He shook his head as if attempting to dislodge horrible memories. "Sorry, what did you say?"

"Nothing really. Just that I found another flash drive." She held it out to him. "Here."

"I'll make a copy." He transferred copies to the new drive,

then ejected it and handed it to her. "They're saved on my laptop as well, so you can keep that."

"Thanks." The man had changed since she left the room. "Is everything all right?"

"Of course." He grinned at her, but it was forced at best. "I've sat in this hard chair too long. I'm going to head to the couch, if you want to join me."

"I'll get us a couple of drinks and grab my laptop. Meet you in there in a minute."

Jonah nodded and proceeded to the living room.

She joined him and opened her computer.

The doorbell chimed.

"Must be Decia and Matt." Noelle checked the peephole, then disarmed her alarm and opened the door. "Come on in."

She ushered the duo into the living room, where Jonah sat on the couch.

Matt leaned against the wall next to the fireplace while she took a seat beside Jonah.

Decia lowered onto the easy chair that faced the coffee table. "I'm assuming you found something."

The silence in the room set Noelle's nerves on edge, but she waited Jonah out. It was his story to tell, not hers. Except for the serial killer.

Jonah blew out a long breath. "We found our proof." He wiped his hands on his thighs. Noelle clasped Jonah's hand to still his movement and add her support.

Decia's brow furrowed. "You have evidence already?"

"Yes," Jonah confirmed.

"Now we're getting somewhere. How many reports are false?" Matt asked.

Noelle's gaze met Jonah's. His silent plea tore at her heart. She could do this for him. "Eighteen over the last three years."

Decia's eyes widened. "Whoa."

"I second that." Matt strode to the kitchen, grabbed a chair, and brought it to the living room. He spun it around backward and straddled it. "So, what did you find?"

Noelle closed her eyes. How much did she tell Decia and Matt?

"Go ahead. You can do it," Jonah whispered.

Her gaze shifted from Matt to Decia. She prayed Jonah was right and no one treated her differently once they knew about her abduction. "I've been looking into multiple cold cases that date back to fifteen years ago. They all have one thing in common: a serial killer."

"How do those relate to Ken?" Matt asked.

"He's not the serial killer, if that's what you're thinking. But...the autopsies that he falsified are victims of the same killer—or a copycat."

Decia edged forward on the chair. "I know you, Noelle, and for you to make that statement you must have solid proof."

"We do." Jonah jumped in, giving her time to gather herself. "Ken left a file for each young woman with selected photos, for lack of better words, and preliminary observations. However, he made notes at the bottom to help me unravel his mess. In addition to that, he had a couple of folders on the drive. One is of the cuts on the bodies, which weren't shown in the report images. The same cuts the cold-case serial killer made on his victims."

"They match the documents I have in my office for all the cases," Noelle said.

Matt scratched his jaw. "This is definitely unusual. I'd like the flash drive Ken gave you and copies of the reports you have on the serial killer."

"Not a problem. We planned on giving the drive to you." She held the USB stick out to Matt, and he took it. "And I can email you the reports on the cold cases." She'd give them the evidence, but could she include her story?

Decia pursed her lips. "Is there anything else we should know?"

Now was the time to come clean about the past. Jonah had said it wouldn't matter, but what if it did?

"Go ahead. They're your friends." Jonah kept his voice low.

She knew Matt and Decia had heard him. How could they not in the small room? Noelle tugged on her sleeves. "There's... um...more to the story about the serial killer."

The two detectives—her friends—waited for her to continue. *God, I could really use a bit of Your courage right now.*

"Fifteen years ago, this particular serial killer abducted his first victim. At least, that's what the police concluded." She clenched her shaking hands and took a deep breath. "The killer snatched young women and tortured them until he finally decided to kill them."

Matt leaned forward. "Did the detectives figure out his motive?"

"Not exactly. But the man seemed obsessed with women who had blonde hair, blue eyes, and were around my height. He didn't like these women for whatever reason. Most likely a surrogate for whoever he was really angry with."

Matt's gaze never wavered as he digested her words. "Why work on these cases? And how do you have so much information about the killer?"

Jonah slipped his fingers into hers and held tight.

"Because..." She swallowed the bile creeping up her throat. "I was his first victim and have the scars to prove it."

When neither detective responded, Jonah jumped in. "Obviously, she escaped, but not before she paid a high price."

"How long have you known?" Matt asked Jonah.

"Noelle just told me about her connection. But ever since last summer, I've helped her toss around ideas and talk through the cases—never knowing that one of them was hers until yesterday."

Decia tilted her head and focused on Noelle. "Why didn't you say anything?"

"I felt like an idiot, and the scars aren't pretty. In fact, they're disgusting." She shrugged. "No one around here knows. Lizzie, my parents, and my therapist know the basics. Only the detectives investigating the crime know all the details. Jonah's the first person I've ever told."

Matt blinked and shook his head. "How you kept it a secret this long, I'll never know. But it explains a lot. Your apparent unease at night. The long-sleeve shirts. The intense security system."

"I became good at hiding my damaged skin. And you're right. I hate walking outside alone after dark. I might have overcome the paranoia, but the fear lingers." She looked at Decia. Her friend. Her confidant on so many things. "Dish, are we good?"

The hurt in her friend's eyes made her want to cry. "I wish you would've told me."

"I know. And I'm so sorry." Noelle lowered her chin.

"Noelle."

She lifted her gaze.

Her friend stood, stepped in front of her, and placed a hand on her shoulder. "No need to apologize. I'm just happy you confided in us."

Noelle nodded.

"You look like you could use some time to process telling us. Matt and I will leave you two alone. We'll be in touch once we've examined the files. Let us know if you discover anything else."

Jonah stood and escorted the pair to the door. "That's a promise. We haven't opened the last folder yet, but once we do, you'll be our first call with any information."

Noelle couldn't move as Jonah said goodbye to their friends. Her secret was out, and she wasn't sure how she felt about that.

Decia and Matt hadn't looked down on her or made fun of her in any way. So that gave her hope.

"Are you doing okay?" Jonah slipped beside her onto the couch and laced his fingers with hers.

"I think so. It's just weird that people know." She stared at their joined hands. "I'll admit, though, a weight has lifted."

"Good. I'm glad. What would you like to do now? Dig into that last file or take a break?"

She considered his question. The sad expression on his face from earlier nagged at her. "I want to continue with Ken's documents, but before that, I'd like to know what you saw that caused such a heart-wrenching reaction."

Jonah's face lost all color.

"Jonah? Talk to me."

He closed his eyes, and his Adam's apple bobbed. "I'm responsible for my wife's death."

———

The sun seeped through the side windows that framed the front door. Jonah's heart rate increased and his knee jiggled. After encouraging Noelle to share the past she'd hidden from her friends, he knew he'd have to fess up about the role he'd played in Cara's death. But man, he didn't want to admit his failure as a husband and a doctor, along with the guilt that continued to eat at him.

Noelle rested her other hand on top of their joined ones. "Jonah, it's okay if you don't want to tell me. Forget I asked."

"No. It's fine." Not really, but fair was fair. "One night, when I was running late at the hospital, Cara came to *drag me away*. Her words, not mine. We'd planned a date night, and I completely forgot about it. She showed up at the hospital in a dress and heels. The second I saw her, I knew what I'd done."

"Was she mad?" Noelle shifted without losing contact and settled deeper into the cushions.

"Believe it or not, no. Sad. Maybe even a little hurt. But no, she never got mad when it came to my work. Being married to a doctor is hard. An ER doctor is even worse. The hours we work and the things we see..." His mind drifted to the horrors that he'd witnessed over the years. Gunshot wounds, domestic violence, household accidents, car accidents.

"I can't imagine what it was like for either of you."

He blinked away the images. "Cara deserves all the praise. She stuck by my side through it all and never truly complained." He ran a hand through his hair. "But that night, instead of calling, she came to see me. My shift had ended a couple hours before she arrived, so as soon as I reassigned the patients, I left work."

"Did she wait for you?"

He nodded. "We talked and decided to go home and have dinner delivered. I apologized for missing our date and promised her a quiet evening together." He remembered the night like it'd happened yesterday. "I followed her home in my car. On the way, a truck crossed the yellow line and slammed into Cara."

"Oh, Jonah." Noelle's eyes widened. "You witnessed the whole thing?"

"Yes. The sickening crunch of the collision will be with me for a lifetime." He swallowed the lump in his throat. "I rushed to her vehicle and pried the door open. The front end of the car had crumpled in on her legs, and a jagged piece of metal had sliced into her upper thigh, severing her femoral artery."

Noelle whimpered. With her law enforcement experience, Jonah presumed she knew the outcome of that particular injury.

"There I was, one of the best trauma doctors in the region, and I could do little to help my own wife. I put my phone on speaker and called 911. Blood poured from Cara. My training kicked in, and I fought to pinch off the artery to stop the flow. It took me too long to get my fingers inside the puncture. Her life literally drained from her before my eyes."

"I'm so sorry, Jonah." Tears trailed down Noelle's cheeks. "But you have to know it's not your fault."

A sad smile tugged at his lips. "My head, yes. My heart, not so much. The worst thing about that night... Right before Cara died, she regained consciousness for a moment. Long enough to whisper *I love you*. Then she was gone. I failed her. More than anything, I feel guilty for not being the man she needed. Both as a husband and as the doctor she desperately needed in that moment. I wish I could go back and spend time with her. Go on dates. Take her to see the Northern Lights like she dreamed of. Love her like she deserved to be loved."

Noelle wrapped her arms around him and pulled him close. "You miss her, don't you?"

"I do. But I said my goodbye a few years ago. It's the guilt that hurts. That stays with me." He closed his eyes and let the warmth of her embrace chase away the lingering memories.

A little while later, she eased back, her own tears drying on her face. "Thank you for telling me."

He shrugged. "You're easy to talk to."

A genuine smile curved on her lips. "Back at ya."

He drew in a breath. "Would you be opposed to putting aside our investigation into Ken's wrongdoings and relaxing?" Jonah had hit his limit. The need to mentally regroup hung on him like a weighted blanket.

"Gladly. Dinner and a movie?"

"Perfect."

Her phone dinged with an incoming text. She tapped in a response. "That was Alana. She's on protection duty tonight and will be outside if we need her."

And just like that, the events of the past two days came tumbling back. Someone had painted a target on him.

Would he survive long enough to get to the bottom of the serial killer case and help Noelle break free from her past? Or would he fail another woman in his life?

TEN

Noelle placed her palms on the kitchen counter and lowered her head. The bold aroma drifting from the coffee maker did its best to clear the cobwebs from her brain. Yesterday had ripped her apart and gently started to piece her back together. After revealing her secrets to Matt and Decia, then spending the evening in Jonah's arms watching a movie, her heart had begun to heal for the first time in fifteen years.

She lifted the carafe and poured a cup of java, adding a bit of French vanilla creamer to the brew.

"Got enough for me?" Jonah stood at the entry to the kitchen, dressed in jeans and a gray T-shirt, but it was his sleep-mussed hair and bare feet that did funny things to her insides.

"Sure." One would think after spending time together over the last year, she wouldn't react to him that way. She hadn't before—well, not exactly—but now? Last night. The way he'd tugged her over and she'd snuggled against him. His tender caresses on her arms. His attentiveness. He hadn't kissed her again, except the soft kiss to her forehead when he'd said goodnight. But she'd felt loved for the first time in a long time—maybe ever.

She poured a cup and handed it to him. Their fingers brushed, sending a zing of awareness through her.

"Thanks." He glanced at the clock on the wall. "I must have been more tired than I thought. I'm usually up by six."

"Now, how did I guess you were a morning person? I mean, you did tend to be up early when you took care of me, but..." She shrugged.

"Want me to make you breakfast for old times' sake?" Mug to his lips, he grinned.

The man might be an organizational chaotic mess, but he insisted on healthy, nutritious food. He'd changed her eating habits during those short weeks that he'd hovered over her. But he had one junk food weakness.

"Sorry, but you'll have to deal with the donuts that Juliette left this morning before starting her shift." Noelle slid the pink box toward him.

He peeked inside. "Oh, I want to kiss that woman. She got my favorite. Chocolate glaze with sprinkles." He grabbed one and took a bite.

"Sprinkles?" That, she hadn't known about. "You're such a little boy." Noelle shoved down the weird jealousy at his comment about kissing Juliette and shook her head.

"What can I say? I like what I like." His gaze met hers for a long moment, then he retrieved a napkin and wiped his mouth. "Did you talk to the EG ladies after the movie last night?"

She sat at the table and chose a donut for herself. "Yes. They are now fully aware of my serial killer."

"*Your* serial killer?"

"Well, what else would you call him? I'm not a fan of what the press dubbed him. Anyway, Alana and Juliette know. Which means Alana's fiancé Cash knows, too."

"Cash is a good guy. He and I became friends when he

moved into town. He won't say anything." Jonah took another bite and groaned. The man loved his chocolate donuts. "I'm aware that you're uncomfortable with the information being out there, but to be honest, I'm surprised it hasn't leaked over the years."

"Since I was underage and the detectives refused to put me in danger by announcing it to the world, it slid under the radar of the press. They knew a girl had survived, but the story was that I didn't have any information that helped the case. Which was mostly true." She swallowed the bite of donut and took a sip of her coffee. Sugar and caffeine: a necessity to get through the day. "Soon after, I moved away for college. Then got a job in law enforcement, where I met Lizzie Tremaine Lee. I stayed away from Savannah for a long time before moving back."

Jonah snatched another donut. "That makes sense. I'd like to send those detectives a gift for keeping you out of the spotlight."

"Trust me, I've expressed my appreciation over the years. They're a couple of great men who are both enjoying retirement now."

They sat in companionable silence, finishing the sugary breakfast.

Jonah gathered the trash, placed the donut box neatly to the side, wiped the table, and refilled their coffees.

She smiled. The man was trying. When he'd taken care of her last summer, he'd kept things clean but not tidy. This time was different.

He retrieved his laptop from the living room and returned to his chair. "Ready to see what else Ken left for us?"

"Go for it. I want to get to the bottom of all this."

"You and me both." Jonah booted up his computer and accessed the files he'd saved. "I plan to reopen the cases Ken left me, but from what we've discovered so far, I want to see everything he included."

She briefly pointed to the only icon they hadn't opened yet. "Then let's take a look at that folder." Fingers wrapped around the warm mug, she scooted forward on her seat.

He clicked on the final folder. One by one, photos of a Chinese symbol on skin popped up.

The images stole her breath. Her hands around the cup shook. Proof of her serial killer glowed on the screen. She struggled to fill her lungs.

"Noelle?"

"No...that..." Words refused to form.

"Take it easy." He removed the mug from her hands, then covered her fingers with his, his entire focus on her. "Tell me."

"That's the symbol for truth. The killer repeated over and over that the truth would be revealed."

"What truth?" Jonah's tone softened.

"I have no idea." She closed her eyes. Dread pooled in her belly. When she'd mustered the courage, she looked him straight in the eyes. "My serial killer tattooed the same symbol behind my ear."

"I've never seen it."

She clutched her hair that hid the tattoo. "I wear my hair down or styled to cover it as much as possible. And when people do see it, there's nothing weird about it, so they never ask."

He motioned toward the side of her head. "May I?"

At this point, she'd do almost anything to end her nightmare. She leaned forward and flipped her hair to the side.

But the possibility that the man who'd wanted her dead was still out there hunting victims bothered her more than the tattoo that she'd never asked for.

———

The walls of the kitchen pressed in, sucking the air from the room. Jonah tamped down his anger at the faded Chinese symbol tucked behind Noelle's ear. His fingers traced the lines without touching her skin.

He glanced at the photos, then back to Noelle. "Yours is a tattoo."

The line between her eyes deepened, and she nodded.

He gestured toward the laptop. "Those are burns."

Her eyes widened. "As in this guy branded these women?"

"It appears so."

Her respirations increased to an alarming rate. Her chair scraped on the floor. She stood.

The horror in her gaze would star in his nightmares for a long time. "What is it?"

"It's a copycat." She wrapped her arms around her waist.

He studied the photo, unsure of what she'd picked up on. "How can you be sure?"

"All the original victims had the same symbol, but inked, not branded." She ran her fingers up the sides of her face, into her hair, and gripped it, like she wanted to pull it out.

"Do you have evidence that you can show me?" He'd never seen anything in the photos in her office that hinted at the tattoo.

Noelle's shoulders rose and fell. "I have the photos in my desk."

"Why not pin them to the wall with the rest of the images?"

"Because if anyone saw pictures and saw my tattoo, they'd know, or at least suspect. Even though you were the only person who knew about my work on those cold cases, I never wanted to take the chance of anyone connecting me to the serial killer if they saw my murder wall. But I guess that doesn't matter anymore." She shrugged.

He slid his chair back and stood. "Come on. Let's confirm

our suspicions." Hand out, he waited until she placed hers in his.

Once in her office, she retrieved a manila envelope.

He sat on the loveseat and patted the cushion next to himself. "Do all the victims have the same tattoo?"

She tucked her leg under herself and sat facing him. "All but one—Kathy."

The way Noelle said the girl's name sent icy fingers crawling up his spine. "Was she a friend?"

"No." She waved her hand toward the images on the wall. "After studying each case, I feel like I know them."

Unfortunately, he understood that sentiment too well. Each victim—each autopsy—became part of him.

"Kathy was a dancer. She worked at a nightclub, waiting tables in the evenings, and went to college during the day. Her major was performing arts."

"Have you figured out why she didn't have the tattoo?"

Noelle nodded. "The killer dumped her like he did the others, but the medical examiner at the time believed an animal got to her before the police discovered her body. The skin on her neck was...destroyed."

"So, let's assume she had the same ink. May I see the photos?"

She handed him the stack. He flipped through the pictures, studying them one by one.

Jonah pointed to one of the images. "These tats are well done. The guy's an artist. Why change to branding?"

"I can only think of two reasons. One, a physical ailment where he can't hold the tattoo gun anymore. Or two, my copycat theory. Someone else has picked up where he left off, so to speak, and doesn't know how to ink."

"It's time to do what Ken asked. Reopen his cases. I have a feeling your cold cases and Ken's are definitely connected. It's just a matter of how." He had the case numbers now, so he

LYNETTE EASON & SAMI A. ABRAMS

could pull the documents from Ken's file cabinet. Assuming Ken had hidden them in plain sight.

"I'd really like to see the actual police reports on all of those."

"Then let's call Matt." Jonah doubted that his friend would balk at the idea. The EGA women had law enforcement privileges, and as a medical examiner, he had access to many of the reports.

"You do that, and I'll call Alana and Juliette. I want them in on this, too."

"Sounds like a plan." He dug his phone from his pocket and hit speed dial for Matt.

An hour later, the doorbell rang.

"I'll get it." Jonah strode to the entrance, leaving Noelle, Alana, and Juliette in the living room. He opened the door. Matt stood on the front step with a file box in hand. "Come on in."

"Thanks." Matt brushed past him and joined the women. "Ladies, good to see you."

Alana lifted her gaze from where she sat cross-legged on the floor, using the coffee table as a work space. "Hey, Matt."

"Where's Cash?"

"He stayed with the kids. He trusts Rocco, but he's still not comfortable leaving Penny home without an adult."

Trauma surgeon Dr. Cash Thomas's autistic daughter had been abducted not long ago. The EGA team had swooped in and saved the day.

"Makes sense."

"What do you have there?" Juliette pointed at the box from her spot next to Alana.

"I have permission from Mayor Isaiah Lewis to read y'all in on these cases." Matt plopped onto the couch. "As if I needed it," he mumbled.

Jonah wiped his hand over his mouth to hide his smile. The

mayor had the utmost respect for EGA and called the bodyguards in frequently to help out.

"By the way, Decia sends her apologies for not coming. Her boys had baseball games this weekend. I'll fill her in on what we find."

"She works long, hard hours. Her boys deserve her undivided attention on her days off. They come first." Noelle lifted a file from the box and flipped it open.

"Want to give us the rundown so we're all on the same page?" Matt popped the tab on the Pepsi that Jonah had given him.

Noelle nodded. "Okay, boys and girls, here's the deal. We have multiple cases that Ken falsified reports on. Plus the cold cases I've reopened. You all know the details of my story now. Jonah and I discovered a possible connection."

"Why do you think they connect, beyond the obvious cuts across the victims' arms and chests?" Juliette took a sip of her iced tea.

"Because of this..." Jonah handed the tattoo photo to Matt, who passed it around the small circle. "The girls from the cold cases have the Chinese symbol for truth inked behind their ear. Noelle has the same one."

All eyes shifted to her.

She shrugged. "I try to keep it hidden."

Jonah hated that he'd brought unwanted attention to her, so he continued. He handed another image to Matt. "Thanks to Ken, we have the same photos for the newer cases. The only exception is that the killer branded the symbol instead of inking it."

Matt glared at the picture. "Copycat."

"That's what we think." Jonah crossed the room and sat beside Noelle.

"It could be the same person," Alana said.

"We considered that." Noelle's hands fisted in her lap. "If so, then where has he been for nine years?"

"Prison. Injured. Found another hunting ground for some reason." Juliette ticked off the possibilities on her fingers.

The color drained from Noelle's face.

Jonah placed a hand over her fists. "Let's focus on the investigation and not speculation."

Juliette's shoulders drooped. "I'm sorry, Noelle."

"No. You're right. It's possible. We have to consider everything."

"How about we examine the police reports? They might help us find a direction to investigate beyond the physical evidence." Matt tossed files to the two bodyguards sitting on the floor.

"On it." Alana opened the document.

For the next couple of hours, they pored over the cases. Jonah and Noelle searched online for anything and everything the others threw at them.

Matt raised his arms above his head and stretched his back. A series of cracks and pops filled the living room. "From what we've found, I agree that the cold cases and the current cases are somehow linked. I have to go with my gut on this one. I don't think it's the same killer."

"As much as I'd like to disagree, I concur." Alana straightened her legs under the coffee table. "There are definite similarities, but the differences stand out. Tattoos to brandings. The time between killings—although both of those could be explained away. It's the way the bodies are found that is the most telling."

Jonah nodded. "The cold-case victims were dumped along the side of the road for anyone to find. The newer victims are concealed, as if the killer doesn't want them discovered. Why falsify autopsy reports unless you're hiding something?"

"But why?" Matt rubbed his eyes with his thumb and index finger.

"Several possibilities." Alana rattled them off. "He's worried they can be traced back to him. The killer is protecting someone. He's a copycat and isn't confident in his abilities."

"He's someone in power." Juliette stared at the documents in her hand.

"Well, yeah, that works too," Alana said.

Juliette shook her head. "No. I mean, I found a commonality in three of the cases. Witnesses reported that three of our victims were seen with Congressman Clifton Sanford the week before they went missing."

Matt scooted to the edge of his seat. "Now *that* is interesting. Does it say where?"

Juliette squinted at the paper. "All three had dinner with him at Twilight Serenade."

Matt whistled between his teeth. "Whoa. That's upscale."

"No kidding. I'd say interviewing Congressman Sanford just went to the top of the priority list." Noelle set her laptop on the end table.

"Matt, when will the crime scene techs release Ken's office?" Jonah itched to compare the documents on the flash drive with his friend's paper documents in his file cabinet.

"I'll make sure they finish by Monday."

"Thanks, man."

"I'd like to take a peek at those reports myself. Mind if I join you?" Matt asked.

"Not at all." Jonah turned to Noelle. "That might be a great time for you and Decia to visit Congressman Sanford."

"If Alana or Juliette can cover bodyguard duties, then I'll give Decia a call."

Matt threw his hands up. "What am I? Chopped liver?"

Jonah chuckled.

"Hardly. But you'll be busy searching documents with Doc. Someone needs to have your back." Juliette rested her elbows on the coffee table and met Noelle's gaze. "I'll take the

Monday morning shift so you can go see Congressman Sanford."

"Sounds like a plan." Jonah's need to sift through Ken's files outweighed his desire to argue. "Anything else?"

"I don't think so." Alana stacked the papers she'd read into a neat pile. "We have a starting point. It's more than we had a couple hours ago."

The others tidied up the living room, leaving it spotless. Jonah hadn't noticed before how everyone took care of Noelle. They all knew she had OCD tendencies, and they catered to those needs without saying a word about it.

Documents returned to the box, Matt lifted it. "Where would you like this, Noelle?"

She glanced at the kitchen table, then twisted her mouth to the side, thinking. "I'll take it to my office."

"I've got it. Point me in the right direction." Matt pivoted, holding the box out of her reach.

Noelle pointed to the hall. "Second door on the right." She hugged her waist as she watched Matt head to her private war room.

Jonah leaned in and whispered, "He doesn't know about your murder wall, does he?"

She shook her head.

Task accomplished, Matt entered the living room. "Interesting decorations." He grabbed his Pepsi can and tossed it in the recycle bin. "I'll see you Monday morning, Doc. Let me know if you need anything before then."

"Will do." Jonah walked him to the front door. He glanced over his shoulder, then back to his friend. "Thanks for not saying much about her office."

"You knew about all that?"

"Yes. However, remember, I just found out about why not long before you did."

Matt stuffed his hands in his pockets. "I wish she'd said something before. We would have helped."

"I know, man. I do too. But I can only imagine what she's gone through over the years." Jonah scrunched his forehead.

"You have that *something doesn't add up* look on your face. What is it?"

"I can't help but wonder if there's more to her story."

"You think she's hiding evidence?"

"No, no. Nothing like that. Something personal." Jonah shrugged off the feeling and held his hand out to Matt. "Thanks for coming by."

The detective shook it. "Anytime."

Jonah turned and watched Noelle laughing with Alana and Juliette. She appeared carefree and happy. But her words about being damaged rolled around in his mind.

Sure, the scars had marred her skin, but something more lay beyond the physically healed wounds.

Would she ever trust him enough to share all her internal demons with him?

ELEVEN

The sun's glare bounced off the window of the three-story office building. Noelle held the glass door open for Decia, then strode to the elevator on the opposite side of the lobby. Once inside, she pushed the button for the second floor, which housed Congressman Clifton Sanford's office. Noelle's mind reeled from the information they'd uncovered on Saturday. How was Sanford involved? Or was it a case of coincidence?

Noelle leaned against the back of the elevator. "Thanks for coming with me."

"It's not a problem. I'm sorry I couldn't be there this weekend." Decia stood with her hands on her hips, watching the lighted floor numbers change above the metal door.

"Don't worry about it. Your kiddos deserve to have their mom home on the weekend. Speaking of, how'd the baseball games go?"

Her friend smiled. "Three wins."

"Tell the boys congrats for me."

"Will do."

The elevator came to a halt and dinged. The door slid open.

"Suite 202 is to the left." Noelle led the way. "Since you're the law around here, take the lead. I'll jump in if I have any questions."

"That works for me." Decia approached the receptionist's desk. "Hello, I'm Detective Ladecia Slaton, and this is my colleague, Noelle Burton. We'd like to speak with Mr. Sanford."

Noelle had to admit, her friend was smooth, sliding in her name without referencing EGA.

"The congressman has several meetings today. May I ask what this is about?" The middle-aged receptionist peered over the top of her glasses.

"I understand. We only have a few questions for him. I'm sure he'll want to assist local law enforcement." Decia raised a brow at the woman.

Noelle smothered a chuckle.

"I'll take it from here, Cindy." A young man in his early thirties approached. "My name's Royce Dwight. I'm the congressman's aide. How may I help you?"

Decia nodded at the aide while Noelle scanned the reception area. "Mr. Dwight, nice to meet you. We need a moment with Mr. Sanford. It shouldn't take long."

Head down, Royce tapped on his tablet. "Let me see if he can spare a few minutes."

"Thank you. We appreciate it."

Noelle shifted her gaze to him. She had a great view of the top of the man's head.

"He has five minutes before his next conference call. If you'll follow me." He spun and waved for them to follow.

She and Decia kept pace with the congressman's aide.

He gestured for them to enter Sanford's office, but remained at the doorway.

The congressman rose, his large oak desk a barrier between himself and anyone who visited. A young man with the congressman's same genetic features stood near a beverage station in the corner of the room. "Good morning, ladies. You've met my aide. I'd like to introduce you to the company's attorney and my son, Lincoln. Please, have a seat." He swept his hand out, indicating the two chairs facing his desk.

Noelle lowered herself onto the edge of the seat. "Thank you for seeing us."

"I wish I had more time, but unfortunately, I don't. So, let's get down to business. How can I help Savannah's finest?"

Decia took the lead. "As you wish. Your name came up during a homicide investigation. We'd like to know what you can tell us about a couple of young ladies that you spent time with."

"Are you implying that my father had something to do with murder?" Lincoln moved to his father's side. "Because if you are, that's the most preposterous thing I've ever heard."

"Now, son. Let them talk." Sanford rested his elbows on his desk and steepled his fingers. "Go ahead."

Decia eyed the son, then focused her attention on the congressman. "We have three young women in their twenties that were murdered. According to witnesses, their bodies were found a week after being seen in your company."

"As your legal counsel, I advise you not to say another word, Dad." Lincoln glared at Decia. "I don't trust them."

"Calm down, son. They're only doing their job. Please continue, Detective."

"Thank you." Decia pulled her phone from her pocket. "What can you tell me about Kami Zimmer?"

"The name doesn't sound familiar. Royce?" the congressman asked his aide.

"Do you have a picture?"

"Yes." Noelle had saved the photos of all the women for reference. She opened the image of Kami on her phone and shared it with the aide.

Royce stared at the floor and tapped his chin. "I think I remember her. She had dinner with the congressman at Twilight Serenade. If I remember correctly, it was a thank-you for helping with his campaign."

Noelle shifted the phone to Sanford. "Congressman, does the woman look familiar?"

The man flinched so imperceptibly that most people would miss it. But Noelle wasn't most people. And neither was Decia.

"Sorry. I don't recall her. But if Royce said we had dinner, then we must have."

"That's quite a thank-you." She flipped to the next photo. "How about Sophia Mendez? She was also seen having dinner with you."

Sanford glanced at the picture and shook his head. "I'm sorry, Detective. I don't know anything about either woman. Now, if you'll excuse me, I have a meeting to join."

She and Decia thanked the men and strode from the office. Neither said a word until they exited the building. Noelle blew out a breath. "Did you see Congressman Sanford's reaction to Kami?"

Decia nodded. "He recognized her. The question now is, why didn't he admit it?"

"An affair, maybe?" Noelle replayed the conversation over in her mind. "The aide seemed helpful, albeit a bit shy."

"Yeah, but the son was a piece of work. Like he had a chip on his shoulder or something. You saw the way he towered over his father, watching our every move."

"I did." Noelle rolled her eyes. Way to make yourself look guilty, dude. "I'll have Raven do a deep dive into Lincoln Sanford and see what she digs up."

"Good. I'll head to the station and see if Matt made it back from the morgue yet."

"I'd like to check on Jonah." Noelle retrieved her car keys from her pocket. "I'll keep you posted on anything we find."

"Sounds good. See you later." Decia waved and headed for her department-issued vehicle.

Noelle slipped into the driver's seat of her car. The visit with Sanford hadn't gone as expected, but it had been interesting nonetheless.

However, at the moment, she had an odd urge to visit Jonah. One she couldn't shake.

———

Jonah drew the curtains closed on the new window in Ken's office and moved to unlock the file cabinet. Call him paranoid, but he refused to take a chance on the shooter using him for target practice. He honestly had no idea if he'd find what he was looking for. He only hoped that Ken hadn't been too stealthy.

Between his friend's unethical actions and Noelle's story, the nerves in Jonah's skin mimicked a thousand bugs crawling on him. He hated what Ken had done. And from the little he'd discovered, money had driven the man's choices. If only Ken had taken the time to ask him for financial support instead of selling out his integrity, Jonah would have given it to him willingly. Between his career as a doctor and wise investments, he had money to spare.

Matt sat in the office chair, searching through the desk drawers. "I don't think Ken left evidence in his desk. All I'm finding are notepads and basic miscellaneous items."

"I figured as much." Jonah opened the cabinet and walked his fingers through the files. "I'm hoping he hid the information among the other autopsy reports."

"It'd be a great place to put it. Who'd look for an extra autopsy report there?" Matt shut the bottom drawer and stood. "I'll check the bookcase next." His friend strode across the room. Hands on his hips, he scratched his jaw, then started on the top shelf.

"I can't believe Ken did this." Jonah opened a file, took a long look, and slipped it back into place.

"I guess you never know what you'll do when faced with a tough decision. It couldn't have been easy for him with his wife's life at stake."

"I suppose that's true." Jonah closed the first drawer and glanced over his shoulder. "I just wish he'd said something."

"Me too." Matt removed a thick medical book and thumbed through the pages. "Speaking of saying something…Noelle dropped a huge bombshell about her abduction."

Jonah's thoughts drifted to the past year. The signs had all been there. The long-sleeve shirts in the summer. The top-of-the-line security system in the house. Her murder wall in her office. Even her OCD tendencies probably stemmed from her time in the hands of a killer. "I should have realized something wasn't right."

"We all saw the same things, and no one had a clue." Matt shifted to face him. "Except for that insanely organized murder board that you didn't tell us about."

"There is that." Jonah shrugged. "But I think back to last summer. I spent a lot of time at her house. The clues were there."

"Don't take the guilt on yourself. She hid it well from all of us."

"Maybe." The next tab caught Jonah's eye. "Well, what do you know?"

"Got something?" Matt moved to his side.

"I'd say. The little sneak labeled the file M.S. Takes"

"I don't get it."

"And you call yourself a detective. M.S. Takes as in *mistakes*."

"You have got to be kidding me. What does it say?"

Jonah opened the file. "Ken might have handed us evidence on the flash drive, but there are two Jane Does in the large cold storage here at the morgue that he never released."

Matt dropped his head back and stared at the ceiling. "Thank you, Ken."

"I'll go pull the bodies and do a visual on them." Jonah handed Matt the files. "Here, take those."

"I'll add them to the other evidence. We'll pull the documents when we have time to review them." Matt's phone rang. He held up a finger. "Williams...Okay." He checked his watch. "I'll be there in twenty minutes." Then hung up. "Sorry. I've got to go. Let me know what you find."

"You know I will." Jonah followed Matt into the hall and spotted Noelle.

"Later, kids." Matt waved.

"See ya, Matt." Noelle tilted her head and watched him hurry toward the lobby. "What's up with him?"

Jonah lifted his hands, palms up. "Who knows? How'd your visit with the congressman go?"

"Interesting. I'm not sure what's going on, but the whole conversation felt...off. Did you and Matt discover anything?"

"I think so. I'm getting ready to examine two bodies that Ken left as a gift." Jonah smiled.

"I can't wait to hear the explanation behind that statement."

"It's a good one. You're welcome to join me."

"That's an offer I can't refuse."

"I need to change first." He motioned for her to walk with him. Their footfalls echoed along the light-gray hallway. "I'll head into the men's locker room, then we can take a look."

Noelle nodded and kept pace with him. "I'd like to see if there are brandings that match my tattoo."

Jonah placed his hand on the door to the locker room. "I'll be out in a minute."

"Hold on a second. I want to clear the room." Noelle drew her gun and held it close to her leg. "Wait here." She pushed the door open and disappeared inside.

He leaned against the wall, arms crossed, and waited for her to return. When had his life become a TV criminal drama?

A few moments later, she exited and reholstered her weapon. "It's clear. Lock the door while you're in there. I'm going to use the ladies' room. I'll meet you out here when you're done."

He entered and strode to shelves that contained the county-issued scrubs. After choosing a pair his size, he changed and tossed his street clothes in his locker, then headed to the exit. He flipped the lock and pulled on the handle, but it didn't move. He tried again. The hair on the back of his neck prickled. His heart rate increased. Claustrophobia hadn't bothered him before, but since his time in the cold storage drawer, even this room seemed a bit small.

Jonah fiddled with the cell phone in his pocket, debating whether to call Noelle. Or maybe security to get the custodian to fix the door. Anything to get out of the locker room. He took a step toward the door. A splat had him glancing at the floor.

Liquid puddled at his feet. The odor of ammonia mixed with bleach. Jonah's stomach twisted, and his pulse skyrocketed. The combination could be deadly.

He pounded on the door. "Help!" He coughed at the noxious fumes. "Noelle! Help!" If no one found him, he'd be dead in a matter of minutes.

The puddle oozed farther into the space. His brain had frozen, and all intelligent thoughts had escaped. "Think." He moved to the back of the room, hoping the distance gave him more time.

The door was flung open. "Jonah!" Noelle coughed.

"Over here." He staggered toward her.

She grabbed his arm and hauled him out of the room. Once in the hall, she slammed the door shut. Arm wrapped around his waist, she led him away from the toxic air. "Stay here." She sprinted toward the main hall.

Jonah rested his head on the wall and sucked in the clean air.

LYNETTE EASON & SAMI A. ABRAMS

How many times could he evade death before the person trying to kill him succeeded?

A couple minutes later, Noelle reappeared. "I saw the janitor hurrying away when I came out of the women's locker room. He disappeared before I made visual contact. I didn't want to leave you alone and search for him."

"This is getting ridiculous. I don't know anything."

"Not yet."

"True." He inhaled three slow, deep breaths.

"Do you need medical?"

He shook his head. "No. Only a few minutes to gather my sanity and a bit of clean air."

"You got it. I'll call Decia to send a crime scene tech and someone to take our statements. And let Bonnie know and have her get someone to clean that mess once the techs finish collecting evidence."

"Tell Bonnie it's bleach and ammonia. Toxic." The adrenaline faded, and his legs could pass for jelly.

"I'm on it." She placed the calls, but her eyes never stopped scanning the area.

Noelle finished her tasks and slid to the ground next to him. "Hey, cowboy. Come here often?"

He rested his head against the wall and chuckled.

Once they gave their statements and the officers released them to leave, Noelle raised a questioning eyebrow and jutted her chin in the direction of autopsy.

"Yeah, I'm ready. If I have to." One corner of his mouth lifted.

She chuckled. "You have to. Come on. Let's examine those girls." She helped him stand.

Whoever had trapped him hadn't wanted to scare him. With that combination of chemicals, the guy had planned to kill him. Now Jonah was even more determined to find out who had murdered his friend and wanted him dead.

140

TWELVE

The bright overhead lights intensified the pasty white of the dead girl's skin. Noelle stood next to Jonah, peering at the marks on the victim as he visually examined the body. The reminder of how close she'd come to lying on the stainless-steel table with her neck in the V-shaped holder sent shivers racing up her spine. Not for the first time since her abduction and subsequent torture, she thanked God for bringing her through her living hell. There was no other way to describe it. *Nightmare* wasn't strong enough.

Her attention slid to the drain at the bottom of the table. She shivered. How did Jonah stomach the procedures day in and day out?

"Are you okay?" Jonah rested his hand on her arm.

She jerked her attention to him. "Just lost in thought. That's all."

He narrowed his gaze. "Stop going there."

"What?"

"You know what I'm talking about. Stop thinking about the

what-ifs. You survived." Jonah reached up and tilted the overhead lamp to focus on the girl's head and neck area.

"It's hard not to let it seep in." She'd struggled with it for years. Her therapist had warned her to stop trying to ignore her memories or fears but to work through them. She thought she had—until now.

"Is this too much?" He motioned to the corpse.

"I'm good." She had to be. They needed answers, and Ken had given them a way to find them. Plus, if her serial killer was still out there—she shivered.

Jonah didn't look convinced, but he didn't push. "Then let's get to it."

Noelle's respect for the man had gone up several notches. It had taken him a minute or several, but he'd collected himself after his brush with death and the toxic fumes and had gotten to work examining the only physical solid evidence they had.

He rolled the girl's head to one side. When the space behind the ear appeared tattoo free, he rolled her the other way.

"There." He used his gloved pinkie finger to point to the familiar Chinese symbol. "It's not ink. The skin's burned. He branded her."

"Just like the others." The information whirled in Noelle's mind. "What about the cuts?"

Jonah pulled the sheet down, revealing the short, crisscrossed slices across the victim's upper arms and upper chest. "If this guy isn't the same sadistic excuse for a human as the original serial killer, he knows his methods."

Noelle's breath caught in her throat. The visual of the cuts made her want to hurl. Why had she thought she could handle examining a body? Photos were one thing, but real flesh that she could reach out and touch... The material of her blouse rubbed against her arms, making her scars ache.

"Noelle?" Jonah's hand gripped hers. "What can I do?"

Her eyes drifted up to meet his.

"You look a little green."

His words barely registered. In an odd way, she recognized the way her mind had pulled back to protect itself. Almost an out-of-body experience.

"Elle?" A snap echoed in a faraway place. Jonah cupped her cheeks. The warmth of his ungloved hands penetrated deep inside her. "Talk to me."

She blinked, then blinked again. The haze lifted. "Sorry."

"Nothing to be sorry about. You worried me, that's all."

"It's different."

"Than the images?"

She nodded. "Seeing the marks on actual skin other than mine... Let's just say it messed with my head."

"I can't imagine what you're going through, but I do know you're one tough lady. Not many people could go through what you did and come out whole on the other side."

Her laugh held no humor. "Who says I'm whole?"

His thumb traced her cheekbone. "I do. You amaze me."

She had no idea how to respond. "I'll let you finish. I'm going to step out and call everyone to meet at the EGA office."

Jonah studied her for a moment, then nodded. He replaced the nitrile gloves he must have shed before he'd touched her. "Sure. It'll take me a few minutes. I want to photo document the injuries in case our attacker comes back to destroy more evidence. I'll meet you in the hall after I finish. Then we can return our Jane Doe to cold storage."

Noelle nodded and rushed from the room. Her heart thundered in her chest, making it difficult to breathe. She leaned against the hallway wall and counted her breaths. The dark spots that danced in her vision dissipated.

God, after all these years, why am I having panic attacks now?

After spending years searching for evidence to identify her serial killer, she finally had a lead. But the gnawing in her gut refused to go away. If her killer still existed, rattling the proverbial cage might put her in the guy's crosshairs. She'd never survive—emotionally or physically—if he got his hands on her again.

———

The drive to the EGA office held an eerie silence that worried Jonah. Seeing the body of the Jane Doe had shaken Noelle, and he had no idea what to do about it. He sat in the passenger seat, unsure what to say to bring Noelle out of her funk. Not to mention his own anxiety. He snorted. Weren't they a pair?

He stared out the window, mulling over the evidence in both Ken's cases and Noelle's. So many similarities, yet different. His gut told him to chalk up the current cases to a copycat. But how did the new killer know the details? And if by chance it was the same person for both, he refused to stop until they had the man behind bars. He wouldn't—couldn't—allow the serial killer to get his hands on Noelle again.

She turned the corner and aimed the car toward the three-story house that EGA called home. The lush green trees and plants in the square across from the office beckoned him, the tranquility of the small park exactly what his battered nerves required. But a more pressing matter than his own peace of mind took priority.

Noelle pulled into the courtyard parking lot and shut off the engine. The trees shaded the vehicle, allowing a reprieve from the May sun. "Sorry."

He swung his attention to her and scrunched his forehead. "For what?"

"I kind of lost it back there." The sheepish grin that flashed on her face sent warmth flooding through his chest.

How could such a simple thing affect him so much? Unable to help himself, he brushed the backs of his fingers against her cheek. "You have nothing to be sorry for. I can't imagine the memories these cases have thrown at you."

"I've worked hard to keep the damage strictly to my skin. Seeing the cuts and branding up close sent my mind into a tailspin."

Jonah narrowed his gaze, searching hers for the meaning behind her statement. "That's not the first time you've used the word *damaged* to describe yourself. Why in the world would you think that? You're a successful woman who hasn't allowed what happened to you to ruin your life. Sure, you have scars, but that doesn't mean you aren't beautiful."

Her mouth opened, then closed. "Let's get inside. It looks like everyone is already here." She exited the vehicle and stood at the back bumper, waiting on him.

They'd come a long way, sharing their pasts with each other, but she continued to hold on to something. One more layer to her pain. And he desperately wanted to be the person she trusted to confide in. Today didn't appear to be that day. He sighed and joined her.

Mild humidity hung in the air, but the slight breeze that rustled through the trees in the courtyard cooled his skin. He'd love to sit on the patio with a glass of iced tea and enjoy Noelle's company. But with a killer on the loose and a target on his back, reality dictated the necessity of meeting with the others.

He placed his hand on the small of Noelle's back and escorted her to the entrance, the jolt of awareness a pleasant but unexpected reaction to the touch.

Her constant visual sweeping of the area brought the events of the past few days to the forefront of his mind. Was his attacker out there, waiting to take a shot at him again?

Once inside, Noelle strode toward the receptionist desk. "Morning, Raven."

"Noelle. Doc. Glad to see you're both okay." Raven gestured

to the stairs. "They're upstairs in the conference room. I left water bottles for you, assuming the others didn't drink them. I mean, you know how Matt is." She rolled her eyes and muttered, "Goober."

Jonah pinched his lips together to hide his smile. Raven and Matt tended to annoy each other, yet he wondered about their behavior and the underlying reason. Wouldn't that be an interesting combo? "Thanks. We'll leave you to your work."

"Appreciate it, Doc." Raven focused on the computer that sat on the right side of her desk.

Noelle smirked. "Come on."

They climbed the stairs. She stopped by her office and tucked her purse into her desk drawer, then joined the others.

"Afternoon, everyone." Jonah greeted his friends.

A chorus of "Hey, Doc," "Good to see you, Doc," and "I'm glad you're okay, Doc" greeted him.

He moved to the two empty chairs next to each other and pulled one out for Noelle.

She arched an eyebrow but accepted the gesture.

His momma had raised a gentleman, and he refused to apologize for polite behavior. Besides, Noelle deserved to be treated like a treasure.

"Thank you all for coming." Noelle clasped her hands on the table.

He noticed the slight tremor but kept the fact to himself.

Noelle continued, "I'm assuming you've all reviewed the current cases and the cold cases."

"Plus, we have our additional research ready." Juliette lifted a small stack of papers.

Jonah leaned back in his chair and crossed his ankle over his knee, preparing to listen to the group do their thing. He excelled at autopsies and medical jargon, but criminal investigations were beyond his expertise.

"Perfect." Noelle grabbed a pad of paper and a pen from the

center of the table. "I propose for simplicity's sake that we refer to the different sets of cases as current and cold."

"That works for me." Matt flipped open a file and clicked the top of a pen. "As a quick review, we have multiple autopsies that Ken falsified the records on. From his notes and photos, it appears the torture methods match or are similar to the injuries in Noelle's cold cases. The cuts and the brandings and tattoos are the same."

"Do we have cause of death on the cold cases?" Alana asked.

"I can answer that." Jonah spoke up. "From what I can conclude from the police reports and ME documents without doing an actual autopsy, all the victims we have information on died from sharp force injury to the abdomen."

"They bled out from a stab wound after he mutilated them." Decia scowled.

Noelle sucked in a breath.

Decia cringed. "Oh, girl. I'm so sorry. I didn't mean—"

"No. You're right." Noelle fisted her hands. "That's exactly what he did."

"Why? What was his motive for doing that?" Juliette tilted her head. "Noelle, did he ask you questions? Did he say anything during your captivity?"

Jonah held his breath. The inquiries had become personal to Noelle. His attention never left her. If she even flinched, he wanted to hustle her away from everyone. But she needed to face the past head-on so she could put it behind her, no matter how painful.

Instead of falling apart, Noelle straightened in her chair and placed her hands in her lap. What he'd come to recognize as her law enforcement mask dropped into place. "Funny you should ask that. There are a lot of things I don't remember and a few that are fuzzy. I hadn't remembered his words until now. He kept asking if it was worth it."

"What was worth it?" Alana's nose scrunched.

Noelle's right shoulder rose and dropped. "I have no idea. It was almost like a mantra. He never waited for an answer. He'd ask, then slide the knife over my skin."

"I wonder if our current cases experienced the same thing." Matt went from clicking his pen to tapping it on the table.

"The cuts are similar. And let's not forget the Chinese symbol *truth*." Jonah slipped his hand under the table and clasped Noelle's.

"I'm assuming you confirmed the brandings on the two Jane Does." Decia's gaze met his.

"Yes. Both Jane Does have the exact marking that Noelle has, but it was burned—branded—into the skin instead of inked."

Matt rubbed his forehead. "Tattoos can be painful, but branding is a whole new level of cruelty."

"You're still thinking two different killers, aren't you?" Alana asked.

Matt stopped the tapping. "The ritual sounds similar, but I find it hard to believe the cold-case killer up and switched his methods."

"What if he couldn't tattoo his victims anymore? Would he change his technique?" Jonah had his opinion but wanted the professionals to weigh in.

Noelle shook her head. "I don't think he'd change."

"Run with that thought." Matt flipped his pen end to end through his fingers. If the man didn't stop with the pen, Jonah might throw the writing instrument across the room.

"The way he used the ink gun..." Noelle's forehead crinkled. "It had a professional feel to it."

Decia's finger tapped her lower lip. "I agree. If he was an artist, there's no way he'd switch to branding. It's too much a part of who he was. I suppose the change is possible, but I'm with Noelle on this. Let's not forget, the causes of death are different. According to the documentation, the causes of death were strangulation, overdose, among other things. Not exsanguination like the cold cases."

"So we're in agreement. Two sets of cases. Two different killers." Juliette's gaze swept the conference table.

"If that's true, then how does the current guy know so much about my serial killer?" Noelle's jaw twitched.

Matt threw his hands in the air and pushed a puff of air through his lips. "Great. Why can't it be simple? Two bad guys. And as for the cold cases, we're chasing a ghost."

"Exaggerate much?" Jonah shook his head. "Where do we go from here?"

"We break it into two different investigations." Decia leaned forward, her elbows on the table. "Then we find the thread that links them together."

The room grew silent.

Decia had voiced his internal question. The killers had a connection, but what? And where did his and Noelle's safety fall within the new madman's plan?

————

Noelle wiped her sweaty palms on her pant legs. The eyes of the others around the conference room table zeroed in on her, waiting for her reaction. Well, they'd have to wait, because she wasn't sure what to think. The memories hadn't overwhelmed her while digging into the cold cases. She'd kept a certain detachment. Photos and words on paper from the past were one thing. New victims in the present...something else. The terror she'd experienced as a teen hovered above, waiting for the perfect moment to envelop her and drown her.

Jonah's hand squeezed hers. The warmth of his touch grounded her in the moment. She willed her racing pulse to slow. "What do you need from me?"

"If you're okay with it, let's start with your abduction and move to our current cases." The sympathy in Decia's eyes gripped Noelle's heart and twisted.

She knew her marred skin would never hold the same smooth, unblemished perfection her mother had preached to her, but pity from her friends only enhanced her parents' reaction to her now-healed wounds.

The tightness of Jonah's grasp shoved the hurt into the background. "Ask your questions."

Jonah spoke first. "Tell us where you hung out as a teen and what you did for fun."

Matt's eyebrows rose. "Are you sure you aren't a detective?"

"Stuff it." Jonah gave his friend a playful scowl.

The mood in the room lightened. Her best friend had thrown her a soft ball, allowing her to ease into the past. She took a moment to consider his request before responding. "I tended to hang out with friends on Friday and Saturday nights. With practice for whichever sport I participated in at the time on the weekdays, I had no time to just relax. So, on the weekends, a group of us would go to the mall. We'd get ice cream at the food court and talk. Other times we'd walk around and window shop. None of us had the money to do more than that."

"Did anyone not like your group?" Juliette asked. "You know, the whole teenage drama thing."

"Not that I can remember." She searched her memory for even the slightest clue. "There was one kid. I always felt uneasy around him. He was a year younger than me. His father owned the convenience store where he worked. Our group would go there to grab snacks and drinks after school or after practice, depending on the day."

"What was it about him?" Alana leaned forward, her gaze pinned on Noelle as if she held a national secret.

"It was the way his gaze traveled up and down my body, like I was a prime rib dinner. But the weird thing—he'd scowl at me the whole time. I think his father noticed, because he'd yell at the kid to get to work." She'd forgotten all about the guy—and the creepy feelings.

"Name?" Matt's firm tone startled her.

She tilted her head back and stared at the ceiling. What was his name? "The store was called Henderson's Market." She snapped her head forward. "Yancy Henderson."

Matt jotted down the name. "I'll build a dossier on the guy."

Noelle shook her head. "Yancy's too young. The man who tortured me was probably in his forties."

"Like the dad?" Jonah asked.

"Maybe." Her brain struggled to keep up with the group's line of thought.

"Noelle."

Her gaze met Decia's.

"It's worth considering." Decia continued. "Anyone else stand out? Even if it seems impossible. Go with your gut."

How many times in the past had that internal voice saved her life? Too many to count. "My high-school art teacher, Mr. Larsen, paid a little too much attention to me. Or at least, it felt that way. He'd ask me to stay after class to discuss my work. Then he'd touch my shoulders and arms." She shivered as though Larsen's hands ran down her skin. "I'd insist I had to get to my next period and leave, but I sensed his eyes on me until I walked out of sight."

Jonah's fingers flexed in hers. "I don't like that guy."

She shifted to face him. "You don't even know him."

"I know enough." He practically growled the words.

"Age?" Matt's tone mimicked Jonah's.

"What's with the one-word questions?" She rolled her eyes. "I'd say mid-forties."

Matt grunted and continued to write on the notepad.

"And before you ask, that's it. I led a pretty boring life. I mean, sure, a couple of my father's clients hit on me when they came into town for a quick business trip. But none of them had the opportunity to pull off multiple murders."

"I want a list of every one of your father's clients that you can think of." Juliette's demure tone turned harsh.

"I agree." Decia flipped to a clean page on her notepad. "That's a start. Let's move on to what you remember about the abduction."

And here it came. The ultimate question. What did she remember? Too much for her peace of mind. Gaze on the wall across from her, she avoided any and all eye contact with the others.

She pulled in a steadying breath and detached herself from the events. "I had parked on the opposite side of the mall from my friends that day. When we said goodbye, I exited out the food court doors. Night had fallen and the parking lot lights had turned on. I remember an odd sensation. You know, that sixth sense that something isn't quite right. But I ignored it."

"You're doing good, Elle." Jonah's nickname for her eased the knot forming in her belly.

"I did what any single female does when walking alone. I had my car key between my fingers. A lot of good that did me." She huffed. "I hit the car fob to unlock my car. When I reached for the door handle, a hand closed over my mouth, and a needle stabbed me in the neck. I struggled to get away, but whatever the guy used didn't take long to knock me out. The next thing I knew, I woke up in a room inside a bare cabin or some kind of outbuilding—I'm not sure which—strapped to a chair." She could taste the musty room. Smell the sweat—hers and her killer's. The leather straps tight against her.

"Elle?" Jonah squeezed her knee.

She blinked away the consuming memory.

The rustle of papers registered in her brain. She glanced at Decia. "What is it?"

"From what we've uncovered, it seems you weren't the only

one that happened to." Decia jotted a note in the margins. "Sorry. Please continue."

Noelle fought the nausea roiling in her stomach. "The guy came in and out of the room. Each time, he'd uncuff my hands and take me to the bathroom by gunpoint, then ask if I was ready to tell the truth yet while he...well, you know." Tears burned behind her eyes. Her skin flamed with pain as if it were happening right here—right now. "I had no idea what he meant. The night he tattooed me, he drugged me and laid me on a couch instead of sitting me in the chair—I'm assuming to get a better angle to get behind my ear. When he'd finished, he returned me to the chair and started to recuff my hands, but a noise caught his attention. I pretended to be out of it. Although, that wasn't hard to do. The drugs made it difficult to think straight, but I knew it might be my only chance to get away. He left before securing me. I wiggled out of the restraints and staggered to another door I'd seen him use. And the rest, as they say, is history."

Jonah lifted his hand and wiped his thumb under her eyes, drying the tears that streamed down her cheeks.

She brought her gaze to his, unwilling to face the others. But Jonah—he made her feel secure, almost whole again.

He cupped her cheek. "It's over. You did great."

His praise filled the cracks in her heart. With him by her side, she just might be able to face the past and not crumble.

———

Jonah resisted the urge to demand the team stop after Noelle had given the account of her abduction and torture. His jaw ached from clenching his teeth. The tremble of Noelle's hands in his unleashed a protectiveness within that he hadn't experienced in a long time—if ever. He wanted to take her away to a private island so she never had to worry about her serial killer again.

"Now that we have information and possible suspects to investigate on the cold cases, what do we have on the current ones?" Jonah steered the conversation away from Noelle. The team had asked a lot from her, and he'd risk everything to give her time to regroup.

"I'd like to reinterview the congressman and everyone in his office." Decia tapped her pen to her lips. "Something about the conversation with that man bothers me."

"Me too, but I'm not sure what." Noelle's tight grip relaxed.

"I'll take that assignment." Juliette spoke up. "Decia, if you'll shoot me the notes, I'll dig a little deeper and see what I can find."

"As soon as we finish, I'll email them to you." Decia jotted down the reminder.

"Has anyone interviewed the waitstaff at the restaurant about the two young woman who dined with the congressman?" Alana's gaze touched on everyone around the table. "Since that's a no, I'll do that."

Matt leaned back in his chair and swiveled side to side. "Since those girls were last seen there, that's a good call. And who knows, maybe there's a connection besides to the congressman. Another patron, maybe?"

"If the original killer was a tattoo artist, someone might know him from his work." Jonah shifted to face Noelle. "Let's get Raven's input on the tattoo shops in Savannah, then make a plan."

She nodded. "That's a great idea. Raven should be able to narrow down our search radius so we don't waste time."

Decia's phone buzzed. She glanced at it, then gathered her things and stood. "We have to go, but I think we have a good way forward. Stay in touch. We'll compare notes after we finish our assignments. Matt, you ready?"

The detective's chair popped forward. "Sure. See y'all later. Happy hunting." Matt strode from the room. "Yo, Decia, wait up?"

"Let's go pick Raven's brain." Noelle pushed from her seat.

Jonah closed his eyes and groaned. "Are we going to hear a history lesson about each tattoo shop?"

Alana laughed. "Probably."

"Fine. Come on, Elle. Raven awaits." He placed his hand on the small of Noelle's back and escorted her from the room.

After retrieving her purse, they maneuvered down the stairs in silence.

"Noelle. Doc. The detectives just left. I assume the meeting is over." Raven tucked a strand of long black hair behind her ear, highlighting her dangling skull earrings.

"We're finished." Jonah rested his elbows on the counter of her desk. "We need your help."

Raven mimicked him. "Shoot."

"What are the top five tattoo shops in Savannah?"

Her perfectly manicured brow rose. "Looking to get some ink, Doc?"

He chuckled. If only Raven knew his secret. After his white-coat ceremony as a doctor, he and his classmates had piled into a tattoo parlor. He'd chosen the tat *Primum non nocere*, the Latin phrase for *First, do no harm*, for the celebration—a mantra his mentor had drummed into him. Jonah shook his head at the memory. "Nope. Part of an investigation."

Raven grabbed a pen and notepad. "Anything special about the artwork?"

"Chinese symbols," Noelle added.

"Do you have a picture? A lot of artists sign their work."

Noelle froze. "Excuse me?"

The goth receptionist rolled her eyes. "Not like that. They leave a special flare to designate their art."

"Oh. In that case, hold on." Noelle retrieved her phone and

scrolled through the photos. She stopped on one from the victims. "Here."

Raven held Noelle's wrist and studied the picture. "There's not much to go on, but I think I can give you the best places to start." She wrote down several names and handed the paper to Noelle. "Try those. But watch out for Mack at the Red Rose. He's a bit cranky."

Jonah smiled. "Thanks, Raven."

"Anytime, Doc."

He strode with Noelle toward the door. "What do you say we head to your place and grab something to eat while we take a look online and see what we can find out about these shops?"

"I want to do a little research on tattoos as well. I don't like going into a situation uneducated." When they approached the door, Noelle signaled him to stop. "Stay here for a second." She slipped on her sunglasses and exited the building.

For a moment, he'd forgotten about his attacker. He hated relinquishing his safety to Noelle. Not that he didn't trust her with his life—he did. But he had a protective streak for her, and the situation had stomped all over it.

She opened the door and motioned him to join her. "It's clear."

He stepped outside and scanned the area.

The reality of his situation sent a shiver running up his spine.

One simple mistake or misstep and he'd be singing with the angels, or so his grandmother used to say. They had to discover who'd killed Ken and had Jonah in their sights, because he couldn't live like this much longer.

THIRTEEN

WEDNESDAY, 6:30 P.M.

The hot shower had relaxed Jonah's muscles from the stress of the day and cleared the fog from his brain. His own brush with death had had him reeling, but Noelle's heart-wrenching description of her abduction had gutted him.

He used the hand towel on the counter to wipe the condensation from the mirror and ran his fingers through his wet hair. Noelle deserved a carefree evening.

Who was he kidding? She deserved a carefree life after what she'd endured. Mind made up, he nodded at his reflection. He'd put his worries and fears aside for the evening and focus on her. Once they finished researching the tattoo shops, he'd treat her to a date.

Jeans and a Henley T-shirt on and bathroom tidy to appease Noelle's OCD tendencies, he tapped the doorframe on the way out. Tonight mattered. Failure wasn't an option. The second date of her life had to be...not perfect, but had to make a statement.

"There you are. Feel better?" Noelle finished pouring two glasses of iced tea.

"I hope one of those is for me."

"Yup."

He placed a hand on the middle of her back and accepted the beverage.

She tilted her head and studied him.

He winked at her and smiled. The baffled expression made him want to laugh. Operation Second Date for Noelle had begun.

"I...um...shall we get to work?"

Her inability to string together a coherent sentence after a simple touch stroked Jonah's ego. The woman hadn't been kidding when she'd said she had little to no experience with romantic relationships. His expectations for the results of the evening had shot through the roof. Forget Operation Second Date. Operation Treat Her Like a Princess had commenced.

"Sounds like a plan." Jonah placed his glass on the table, then pulled out her chair and motioned for her to sit. "Let's get busy."

She blinked. Her confusion was the cutest thing ever.

"Problem?" He did his best to remain serious.

"No." Noelle sat and he helped her scoot into the table.

He took his seat and popped open his laptop, ignoring her stare. "We have five shops to research. You start at the top of the list, and I'll take the bottom. We'll meet in the middle."

"Okay." Noelle slid her laptop in front of her and opened it. "Why did you do that?"

"Do what?"

She tapped her chair. "This."

He folded his hands on the table and gave her his full attention. "Because you're special and should be treated as such." The air conditioner kicked on and filled the otherwise quiet room with a soft hum. He reached over and smoothed the crease between her eyes. "You're thinking too hard."

She opened her mouth, closed it, then opened it again. "I don't get it."

"You will." Jonah smiled and returned his focus to work.

He heard her huff, then the click of keys.

Thirty minutes later, research complete, Jonah stored his computer. "Ready for dinner?"

"Beyond ready." Noelle leaned back in her chair. "I'll make spaghetti."

"No. I want to take care of you tonight." He moved to the cabinets and pulled out the ingredients for the quick-fix meal.

"You don't have to do that."

"I want to. Consider this our first date."

She spun on her seat. "Date?"

He chuckled. "I can't exactly take you out to a nice restaurant or to the movies, but I can make do here at the house."

"I guess." She folded her arms. "What can I do to help?"

"Absolutely nothing."

She shook her head.

He crouched next to her. "Tonight is about you and only you. I want you to relax and enjoy. That's your job for the evening." He'd never seen her pout before, and he found it adorable. He tapped her nose. "Go find a movie for later. I'll let you know when dinner's ready."

The bewildered look on her face kicked his plan up a notch. Noelle had no idea how to navigate a simple date. A combination of sadness on her behalf and delight that he had the opportunity to introduce her to dating played tug-of-war within him.

He could not mess this up. Jonah laughed. No pressure there.

Noelle had chosen a comedy for herself and Jonah to watch, and her stomach ached from laughing so hard. She snuggled deeper into Jonah's embrace, enjoying the tenderness and affection. So different from their typical evenings together where they sat on opposite sides of the couch and talked. The man had exceeded her expectations of date night. Of course, those expectations had limits due to her lack of relationship experience. She could get used to more evenings like this one.

Jonah's hand caressed her arm. "What are you thinking so hard about?"

"Hmm. Wouldn't you like to know?" She bit her lips to keep from laughing at his expression.

He rolled his eyes. "Come on, spill."

"I'm happy. Tonight is exactly what I needed. A wonderful dinner. A funny movie. And a great guy who makes me feel special."

Jonah's chest rose and fell. A smile spread on his gorgeous face. He leaned in. "You are special."

And cue awkward. He'd kissed her once. Did he plan to kiss her again? Did she want him to? Yes...no...maybe.

"Elle, relax. I'm not going to kiss you."

Her entire body sagged. Their first official date, and he didn't want her. What had she done wrong?

"Please, don't do that."

She glanced at him. "What?"

"It's not that I don't want to. I do, very much so. But I want you to enjoy the night without the worry or stress." He swiped a finger down her nose. "That doesn't mean it won't happen in the future, though."

She rested her head on his chest. "I think I'd like that."

He chuckled. "Good."

"Jonah?"

"Yeah, babe?" His lips brushed her hair.

"Do you have a tattoo?"

He stiffened. "Why do you ask?"

"Raven asked if you planned to get one. I don't know." She shrugged. "You seemed to get lost in thought."

He tucked her in closer. "Yes, I do."

"What is it?"

"The Latin words for *First, do no harm.*" His fingers trailed along her arm. "A memory of my mentor."

"Can I see it?"

He choked. "That would be a no."

She twisted to look at him. "Why not?" Her eyes widened. "Never mind. Forget I asked." Heat flamed her face.

He threw his head back and laughed. "Oh, honey. That pink flowing up your neck and onto your cheeks is adorable."

"It's not funny. It's embarrassing."

"Elle, look at me." He placed his finger under her chin and lifted. "It's not that private. My tattoo is on my upper thigh. I chose a place where no one can see it."

"Oh." She burrowed back into his arms. "Do you regret it?"

He exhaled. "Regret? No. Would I choose to do it now that I'm older? Probably not. I am glad that I decided to have something meaningful, though."

"I can understand that." She closed her eyes. "I didn't get a choice with mine."

"Would you like to have yours removed?" His tone held no judgment, only kindness.

"I've thought about it. But ultimately, no. I can't see it unless I look in a mirror at the right angle, so that helps." She played with the buttons on his Henley shirt. "It serves as a reminder that I survived."

"That's a nice way to look at it." He laid his cheek on her head. "Thank you."

"For what?"

He squeezed her tighter against him. "Tonight. Us. This."

"I should thank you. No one has ever treated me like this before."

"You deserve it."

Tears dripped from her chin and onto his shirt. Never in her life had anyone cherished her like Jonah had tonight.

God, it feels too good to be true. Am I setting myself up for heartbreak? Or is this my future?

Jack clenched his jaw and pounded on the arm of his easy chair in his living room. How had the doctor survived? Jack had skills. His daddy had taught him to hunt, and the internet was a treasure trove of information. Not to mention his mentor. The only answer to the failed attempts was that the doctor was the luckiest fool alive.

He'd followed the man home to discover the lady security guard watching the house. Sure, he could sneak past the woman, but he decided to wait for another opportunity to take the man out.

Ken had royally messed up his plans. Why did the man have to grow a conscience?

Jack took a sip of his Coke. Normally, he'd add a little extra kick to the drink, but until he eliminated the one person who could expose his secret, he had to keep a clear mind.

The TV droned in the background, and a couple of dogs barked outside. Jack stared at the wall, formulating his plan for tomorrow, and the end of Dr. Harris. With the doctor gone, he'd be free to focus on his next victim. He couldn't ignore his responsibility. The women who seduced men had to die. Only one failure marred the mission, and that one was his father's. The one that got away. Someday he'd find her and finish what dear ol' Dad had started. But he'd save that for later. The doctor took priority.

Tomorrow, he'd follow the doctor and end his life once and for all, eliminating the potential for evidence against him.

Stupid Ken had killed his friend. He just hadn't realized it. It was all Ken's fault Dr. Harris's life had to end.

FOURTEEN

Armed with facts about tattoos and the shops that Raven had suggested, Noelle parked her car in front of the Ink Shop and turned off the engine. The time she'd spent with Jonah last night had soothed her battered nerves from yesterday's truth session and his near-fatal encounter. No one had ever treated her the way he had. Working side by side, fixing dinner for her, and snuggling on the couch while watching a movie had her off balance—unsure how to process the evening.

"Before we go in there, thanks for last night."

Jonah flicked off his seatbelt and shifted to face her. "You don't have to thank me. I enjoy your company."

"It's..." How did she say it without sounding stupid? "I don't know how to do this relationship thing."

"You're *doing it* just fine." He brushed his knuckles along her cheek. "There's no right or wrong. There's only what works for us."

Thirty-two years old and she'd only had one date and one

164

kiss in her life—until this week. She'd missed out on so much because of the creep who'd planned to kill her.

"We'll go slow. I refuse to rush you into more than you can handle. If hanging out and holding hands is your limit, then that's what we'll do. I'm too old to care about what's normal. We do us." Jonah cupped the sides of her face and kissed her forehead. "Come on, before you overthink things."

Her mind scrambled to process his words. She shook off the disorientation. "Wait there. Let me make sure it's safe." She exited the car and scanned the area for threats. Once satisfied, she skirted the vehicle and opened his door. "We're good."

Jonah stepped onto the sidewalk and slipped off his sunglasses. "You take the lead. If you want to switch, give me a nod."

"Thanks." It couldn't be easy to be a take-charge man and let a woman protect you. Not that Jonah was sexist, but he was a protector, and she could see the struggle written on his face. "Let's go."

They entered the shop and moved to the counter. Designs lined the walls—everything from skulls to crosses, including a wicked-looking devil that gave Noelle the creeps.

"May I help you?" A man with a full-sleeve tat of angry clouds that started at his shoulder and merged with lightning bolts streaking down his arm, ending at his wrist, interrupted her perusal of the artwork.

"I hope so." She retrieved her phone from her back pocket and swiped to the photo of the Chinese symbol. "Do you have or have you had anyone that might have done this ink?"

The man studied the image. "Not much to go on." He scratched the stubble on his jaw. "Can't say it's any of my artists." He straightened. "Sorry I can't help."

"Thank you for trying."

The man pointed to her phone. "If you're interested, I can do that for you."

LYNETTE EASON & SAMI A. ABRAMS

His offer sucked the air from the room. Noelle's heart rate spiked. The idea of the needle and another tattoo on her body sent bile churning in her belly.

Jonah's hand rested on her lower back. The warmth grounded her in the moment.

"I'm good. Have a nice day." She strode to the door. The urge to run—overwhelming. But she held back. She had a job to do. "Stay here for a second while I take a quick look around."

The pressure on her back, a silent acknowledgment.

She stepped from the building and swept the area with an experienced eye. Less than a minute later, she motioned for Jonah to join her. "All clear from what I can tell." She escorted him to the car and stayed by his door, scanning the area. Once he was safe inside, she moved to the driver's side and slid behind the wheel. She closed her door and started the engine.

"Are you okay?" Jonah placed his hand on her forearm.

She nodded. "The guy's question caught me off guard. Yesterday affected me more than I care to admit." She inhaled and released a long, slow breath. "What's next on the list?"

Jonah had taken Raven's suggestions and mapped out a plan for the day. "Forever Inked." He rattled off the address.

"I guess it was too much to ask for our first stop to be the right one."

He chuckled. "That would be a bit optimistic."

"Here's praying it's the second one." She smiled at him.

His brow furrowed, and he looked away.

"Jonah, what just happened?" She pulled into traffic and followed the GPS on her dash to their next location.

He sighed. "How do you do it?"

"Do what?"

"Pray."

She opened her mouth, then closed it. They'd talked faith and beliefs in the past. How had she missed his uncertainty? "I thought you believed in God. I'm gathering you don't?"

He shifted and angled himself to face her. "Oh, I do. I believe He is very real."

"Then why the question about prayer?" She glanced at him and then returned her focus to the road.

"Let's just say He and I aren't on speaking terms."

"That's too bad." God had been and still was her lifeline.

"So I ask again. How do you pray after all that's happened to you?"

She clamped her mouth shut and thought about her reply. She had no intention of brushing off his question. Her answer mattered.

"Noelle, I didn't mean to upset you."

"That's not it. I don't want to give you a flippant response." She tightened her grip on the steering wheel. Where should she start? "I grew up in church. In fact, I found my faith and friendship with Jesus when I was twelve. I can't say that everything I experienced in church was positive. Sometimes I wonder how people claim to know God and act the way they do."

He laughed, but it had no humor in it. "I hear you on that one."

She glanced at him and smiled. "But you know what I decided?"

"What?"

"That we are all human and respond with human actions." She shrugged.

Jonah rubbed the back of his neck. "I guess I've never looked at it that way. Human nature tends to make us view the world through our own lens and not always God's."

"Exactly. But to answer your original question, it was all I had to keep me sane."

He straightened in his seat. "While you were being tortured." His whispered response was more of a statement than a question.

Sweat beaded on her forehead. She adjusted the air vents, even though her body's response had nothing to do with the temperature. "You see, as I sat there in pain, with blood dripping from the cuts on my body, I knew the only person who could hear me was the same person who had any idea how I felt at that moment."

"Jesus."

"Yes." She swallowed the boulder-sized lump in her throat. She'd never admitted that to anyone. "So I prayed. It started out with begging to get me out of there. Then over time, it turned into a conversation. I didn't feel alone. And my panic faded. Oh, I was still scared, but I knew no matter what—alive or dead—I'd be okay."

"Are you?"

"You mean okay?"

He nodded.

"Most of the time. But I do have my moments when I'm not." She relaxed her grip. The hard part was over. "I'm alive. I have friends. I enjoy my life. Do I have insecurities? I think you know that answer. But I'm not that frightened teenager anymore." She pulled into the parking lot of Forever Inked. "I'm taking it you don't pray."

He shook his head. "Not for a while now."

She had a choice to make. Continue their conversation, or do what she referred to as a drop-and-run: give him time to digest what she'd said, and come back to the conversation later.

"Let's see if anyone inside can help us." She exited the car and came around to open his door.

"I hate this," Jonah grumbled.

She attempted to hide her grin but failed. "Come on, cowboy."

"Ha, ha. Very funny."

They strode to the entrance.

The hairs on the back of her neck prickled. She froze.

"Something wrong?" Jonah's gaze swept from left to right and back.

Her hand slipped behind her back and under her shirt. Her fingers slid around the grip of her Glock. She searched the street. Nothing appeared out of place. Maybe her mind was playing tricks on her. She shook her head. No, she refused to dismiss her instinct.

"Come on. I'll feel better once we get inside." Whoever had Jonah in his sights had her rattled.

———

The hanging bell on the door jingled when Jonah entered the second tattoo shop of the day. Noelle's reaction had his nerves sparking like live wire. He shook off the foreboding sensation and focused on the mission to find the guy who'd hurt Noelle.

He examined the interior of the shop. Similar to the first one but had a classier impression. The same types of images lined the walls, except Forever Inked sported happier artwork. An abundance of flowers and hearts dotted the wall alongside the traditional skulls and crossbones.

"Am I imagining it, or does this place seem a little more reputable?" Noelle whispered in his ear.

Before he responded, a woman who appeared to like butterflies, if the four he saw on her arms and neck were any indication, approached them. "Welcome to Forever Inked. What can I do for you?" Her cheery tone—a huge contrast to Mr. Serious at the last place.

Noelle stepped forward. "I'd like to know if you have any idea as to the artist who did this." She presented the image on her phone.

The woman tapped her lips with her finger. "The swoop at the bottom looks a bit familiar, but I can't say for sure."

"Do you have a name?" Jonah asked.

"No. It's only a sense." She took one last look then lifted her gaze. "Sorry I'm not more help."

"That's okay. It's a long shot anyway."

"None of my guys have that signature, but we've only been around for a few years. I don't know all the artists in the area. Maybe try Body Murals. That shop has been in Savannah for twenty years or more. The owner is an old guy in his mid-fifties."

Jonah bit back a laugh. He supposed to someone in their early twenties, fifty did seem old.

Noelle elbowed him. "Thank you. We appreciate your help."

"No problem. Come on back if you ever want a tat." The girl tilted her head and studied Noelle, then smiled. "I think a cross with a spiral of butterflies fits you."

Noelle stiffened. "Why do you think that?"

"You have a strength, yet you have a newness about you. Like you're flying for the first time." The young woman shrugged and walked away.

"That was…weird."

He clutched her shoulders and spun her to face him. "No. She's right."

"Are you trying to tell me she's psychic?"

"Not at all." He tapped her ear. "You're wearing your cross earrings."

"Oh. Yeah, I kinda forgot about that." Her sheepish grin was adorable.

He chuckled. "Plus, you do have a certain happy glow to you." He leaned in next to her ear. "I'm hoping I have something to do with that."

She smacked his chest and gave him a gentle shove. "You're a dork."

"But I'm your dork."

Her eyes widened.

Great. Had he messed up?

A smile spread across her lips. "Yes, you are."

His pulse raced at her admission. He wanted to throw his arms around her and kiss the living daylights out of her. But he refrained. Not only were they in public, but she reminded him of a deer. Ready to bolt at the slightest movement.

"What do you say we get out of here and check out Body Murals." He guided her to the exit and allowed her to do her job before he joined her outside.

Once in the car, she programmed her GPS. "Ready?"

He buckled his seatbelt. "Yup."

Halfway to their destination, Noelle reached over and squeezed his hand. "Tell me why you quit praying."

He jerked his gaze to her. "What?"

"I want to know why you quit praying."

His mind traveled to the past—to his ugly failure. Noelle had opened up to him; he owed her an explanation. "I've told you about the accident that killed my wife. I tried with everything in me to save her, but I knew deep down it would take a miracle. So I prayed for one. I prayed hard. Begged, even." Emotion thickened in his throat. "But God didn't listen."

Noelle's mouth opened, but he stopped her.

"I know. It's not that He didn't hear me. It's that he chose to let a different outcome happen. But I'm not going to lie. It hurt. I felt abandoned. Like He didn't care about me." Jonah pinched the bridge of his nose. "It became easier to not pray than to accept that His way wasn't mine. If that makes sense."

"Sure it does. Chalk it up to human nature. We want what we want. It doesn't matter about a bigger picture."

"True. I guess at first, I wanted to hang on to my anger. Then it became easier to blame God for not listening." Her words settled in his heart. He hadn't talked with God in a long time due to his stubbornness. And he hated to admit it, but he'd lost out on the comfort and peace that went with the relationship. "I'm beginning to rethink my stance."

"Good. Life's a whole lot easier when you can talk with your best friend."

"That's how you see Him, isn't it? Not as God, but as a friend you can chat with."

"I believe that's what He really wants. He wants us to reach out to Him. Wants a friendship with us."

He spotted the shop up ahead and tucked her bit of wisdom away to ponder later. "There it is, on the right."

"Got it." She turned into the parking lot and found a spot in front of the entrance. "Fingers crossed we get a lead."

"Thought you did prayer." He smirked.

She rolled her eyes. "Ever hear of something called an expression? Now, come on."

A minute later they stood inside Body Murals. Unlike the last two places, chairs and tables filled the interior. The buzz of the tattoo guns hummed in the air, several clients in the middle of a tattoo.

A burly guy that reminded Jonah of Popeye stalked toward them. Jonah leaned close to Noelle. "This could be fun."

Noelle backhanded him in the stomach. "Knock it off."

"Morning, y'all. How can I help?" The man's easygoing tone shocked Jonah. He'd expected the guy to be grumpy, or at least brusque.

"We'd like to see if you recognize the artist who did this Chinese symbol." Noelle held out her phone.

The man gripped her wrist and lifted for a better look. The gesture had Jonah ready to defend if the guy moved wrong. "Hmm. Looks a bit like Vincent's work."

Now they were getting somewhere. Jonah leaned his hip against the counter. "Does Vincent have a last name?"

"Nah. That's his artist name. As in Van Gogh."

"Oh." The defeat in Noelle's tone was noticeable.

"His given name was Richard Nelson."

"That helps. But you said *was*."

"Yeah, the guy walked out of here about eight years ago and never returned. Left all his gear here, too. Oddest thing."

"Why wouldn't he take his things?" Jonah flipped the information around in his mind.

"Not sure. The equipment is expensive."

"Where is it now?" Noelle slid her phone into her pocket.

"I stored it in the back for six months, then sold it. Kept the cash for another three months, but when he didn't call or come by…" The guy shrugged.

"I get it." Jonah straightened. "Thanks for the information."

"Anytime."

Energized for the first time all day, Jonah and Noelle headed to her car and got inside.

"We finally have a name." The smile that graced her face made his insides turn to mush.

"It all fits. The timing. The artwork. We might just solve your cold cases yet." He couldn't help but share her enthusiasm. Her delight was contagious.

The atmosphere in the car as they drove through the backroads heading to the main part of town had changed. Happiness replaced the intensity that had overwhelmed them both.

"Call the team and let them know." Noelle slipped her phone from her pocket—not an easy feat considering she was driving—and handed it to him.

He tapped on the screen to open her favorites on the phone. "I'm hoping they've made progress too."

Her eyes darted from the rearview mirror to the side mirror and back.

"What is it?" Jonah glanced over his shoulder.

"A truck, coming up on us fast."

Jonah huffed. "I knew the peaceful day was too good to be true." A long horn blast jerked his attention to the road ahead.

He grabbed the armrest on the door. "Noelle. There's a train crossing on the tracks ahead of us."

"I see it."

"What are you going to do?"

"I can't flip a U-turn. There's not room. The road's too narrow. And even if there was, he'd T-bone us before I could get the car turned." She slowed the car a bit.

"What are you doing?" His voice rose an octave.

"Giving us space. He's going to ram us, I can't stop that. But by slowing down—" The truck slammed into the rear of their car.

Jonah whipped forward and jolted back. The seatbelt caught across his chest and knocked the air from his lungs. The momentum pushed them straight toward the train.

Jonah grabbed the handle above the door and pointed at the tracks. "There's the end. Can you keep us from colliding?"

"Hold on." Her knuckles had turned white gripping the steering wheel, and her eyes flitted from one mirror to the other, then to the train.

He braced a hand on the dash at her command, searching for any outlet on the road that she could take. None existed.

She hit the brakes hard. The tires squealed and black smoke rose around them. A second later, she jammed the gear into reverse and hit the gas.

His head hit the passenger window. He blinked away the black dots exploding behind his eyes. Their forward progress slowed, but the truck pushing them toward the train had the advantage.

Noelle's gaze was pinned to the rearview mirror. "How much longer?"

He did a quick estimate in his head. "Twenty seconds."

"That's about five seconds too long." She practically growled. "Don't let up!"

"As if!"

"Fifteen," he called out as the last railcar approached the crossing but remained too far away for his liking. The distance between the front bumper of the car and the fast-moving train diminished at a rapid rate.

Her eyes moved from the mirror to the horror in front of them. "Any ideas?"

She couldn't be serious. "None. You're the professional. Ten seconds." He stole a glance at her and witnessed the moment a plan had formed. "Five."

"Hang on!" She slammed the older model sedan into drive and ripped the steering wheel to the left.

The idea was a good one, but it didn't give enough room for a clean getaway. The metal cattle guard of the rear-facing engine scraped the back quarter of the car, sending it spinning through the crossing-gate arms on the other side of the tracks.

A scream split the air. His? Hers? He had no clue.

He flung his hand to the center console and braced for impact.

The car crashed into an electrical box and flipped nose first. Glass exploded. It skidded along the pavement on its front hood and came to a stop.

He hung upside down, his seatbelt holding him in place. The ringing in his ears, along with the headache blooming, had him wanting to let go of consciousness. But what if the assailant hadn't driven away and decided to confirm he'd finished the job? Noelle. He forced his eyes open and rolled his head to the side.

Noelle's blonde hair floated down, covering her face from view. Her arms hung limply from her upside-down position.

His heart pounded at the lifeless sight.

God, I know we haven't been on speaking terms lately, but please don't let her die.

His first prayer in years and he had to choose another life-or-death situation with a woman he deeply cared for. He'd laugh at the irony if God's answer didn't terrify him.

LYNETTE EASON & SAMI A. ABRAMS

He braced himself and released the seatbelt mechanism, hitting the floor—ceiling—ground—whatever—with a thud. He sucked in a breath and held it as he placed his fingers to the side of her throat.

A pulse. But was it his or hers that thumped against his skin?

FIFTEEN

The whoosh of blood pulsed in Noelle's ears, but it was the hand on her throat that made her heart race. She snatched the person's wrist and clamped down. No way would she allow anyone to strangle her again.

"Easy. It's only me."

"Jonah?" She opened her eyes. Why was the roof of the car below her? She searched her memories, struggling through the fog in her brain. The train. The accident. "Are you hurt?"

Noelle released his hand. What if the guy who'd tried to kill them stopped and lay in wait to finish what he'd started? She had to get outside now and protect Jonah.

Jonah removed his finger from her throat. "Nothing a few ibuprofens and a couple of ice packs won't fix."

Her fingers fumbled with the seatbelt release. Coordination wasn't her friend right now.

"Here. Let me. Brace yourself on my shoulders so you don't fall." Jonah placed her hands on himself and clicked the button.

Her knees hit the steering column on the way down, and she

bit back a cry. Once crouched on the ground, she took inventory of her surroundings. The front windshield had cracked and popped out, the side windows had shattered, and the hood had sustained the majority of the damage. It was a miracle they could walk away from the accident with only minor injuries.

Thank You, God, for the protection.

Who had targeted them? Her mind wandered. Why? Her thoughts kept floating away. She must have hit her head harder than she thought. She blinked to clear the haze. The world snapped into place.

"My gun." She tapped the small of her back. Her holster and weapon in place, she exhaled. "Stay tucked in here. I'm going to make sure the area is clear. I don't want this guy succeeding in killing you."

Jonah cupped her cheek. "Be careful."

She nodded, drew her Glock, and crawled from the crumpled vehicle. Sirens whined in the distance. Her muscles relaxed a smidge, but until the cavalry arrived, she had to maintain her vigilance. After a sweep of the area, she sagged against the car.

"Is he out there?" Jonah poked his head out the broken window.

"He doesn't appear to be. But stay there until the police show up." She had no desire for him to come out in the open until she had backup.

Twenty minutes later, sitting on the bench seat in the back of the ambulance, the ache where the seatbelt had caught her across the shoulder intensified.

Noelle would feel the full damage from the car accident tomorrow. She'd survived—and make no mistake about the gratitude she felt—but the slices on her forearms from the debris caused her stomach to roil. More scars to add to her collection. Wouldn't her mother be proud.

A humorous laugh fell from her lips.

"What was that for?"

She lifted her gaze to Jonah, who sat beside her in the ambulance. The man hadn't left her side. "Just thinking about my parents."

His eyebrow arched.

"A story for another time." She lifted her hand to her temple and probed the bandage that covered a gash from the wreck. "How did he find us?"

"Well, we were asking a lot of questions. Maybe one of the employees at the tattoo shops tipped him off."

Noelle waved a hand, dismissing his suggestion. "If the owner of Body Murals is correct, my serial killer isn't around anymore. So who is after us?"

Jonah commandeered the supplies from the paramedic and took over cleaning her cuts.

The young guy shook his head and hopped from the medic unit. "I'll be right out here if you need anything, Doc."

"You just kicked him out of his own ambulance."

"I figured you'd prefer taking care of your upper arms in private." He pointed to the tears in her sleeves and shrugged. "And don't you mean who's after me—not us?"

"Maybe. But what if the two sets of cases are linked?"

"We considered that. Remember the markings?" Jonah examined the cuts.

The commands and comments of EMS workers and the hum of heavy equipment droned outside. She sat in her own little world and stared at Jonah with morbid fascination while he worked. "I know that. I'm thinking a deeper connection, not just a copycat."

"Talk me through it."

"Honestly, I'm probably grasping." Jonah tweezed out a piece of glass, and she sucked in air through her teeth. "It's more of a gut feeling than solid proof."

"I trust your gut." After dousing her right arm with saline solution for a final clean and smearing ointment on the wounds, he wrapped her forearms like the professional he was. "I vote we go to your place and call the others instead of holding a meeting at the EGA office."

Her head did hurt, and her body ached. She'd be shocked if Jonah's torso didn't have bruises that he was hiding. "I like that plan."

"I'll take care of the rest of the cuts once we get there." He cleaned up the mess and set the supplies aside. "I'll talk with one of the officers on scene and get us a ride while you fill out the refusal of transport paperwork."

Unable to summon the energy for more than a nonverbal agreement, she nodded. She appreciated the fact that Jonah hadn't pushed her to go to the emergency room.

A few moments later, the paramedic handed her a clipboard. "I'm not even going to ask. Go ahead and sign it." He hooked a thumb over his shoulder. "You're in good hands with Doc."

She scribbled her name on the line. "You know him?"

"Who doesn't? He was—still is—one of the best ER doctors around. We lost a good doctor at the hospital when he left."

A vise tightened around her heart. He'd thrown away a career he loved because he couldn't let go of the perceived failure. "If you get a chance, let him know that."

The paramedic studied her, then grinned. "Will do." He glanced at the forms. "You're good to go."

She accepted his hand and stepped from the ambulance into the bright sun. She squinted, wishing she knew where her sunglasses had landed in the wreck.

Jonah strode toward her. "Officer Adams is going to take us home. Plus, he has your things."

"All of them?" She quirked a brow. When the officers had arrived on scene, she'd mentioned her backup gun in the center console of the car.

"Yes. He said since you hadn't fired it, there was no need to log it into evidence. And of course, your law enforcement privileges helped as well."

Reality came crashing down on her. The near-death experience had scrambled her thoughts. Even with officers on the scene, Jonah's safety took priority. She had to get her act together. "I want you out of here and behind closed doors."

"My, my, Miss Noelle. Whatever do you mean?" He fanned his face. His fake Southern-belle accent and high-pitched tone made her laugh.

She playfully smacked his arm. "Not like that, you dufus."

He chuckled. "Let's get out of here."

They slid into the backseat of Officer Adams's cruiser, and she rattled off her address. "I appreciate the lift."

The officer glanced in the rearview mirror and smiled. "My pleasure." He pulled away from the chaos and aimed the vehicle toward her home.

Noelle retrieved her phone from her pocket and called Raven. The admin promised to fill in the others and set up a conference call for later. Noelle glanced at Jonah. He'd leaned his head back, but his gaze darted along the sides of the street through the tiny slits of his lowered eyelids. If only they both could rest. But the day's events had her mind spinning.

Her attention shifted from the side mirrors to the surrounding neighborhood, not letting her guard down, as the officer made his way to her house.

"Ms. Burton. Dr. Harris. Is there anything else I can do for you?" Officer Adams pulled his squad car next to the curb.

Noelle breathed a sigh of relief. A few more minutes and she'd have Jonah safely inside with the security system on. "No, I think we're good. Thank you."

Jonah straightened.

"Ready to go?"

He grunted and swiped his face with his hand. "I can move if I have to."

She chuckled. "You have to."

The officer hurried around the car and opened the backseat passenger door for them. "Sorry for your troubles. I'll send you a copy of the report from your accident."

"I appreciate that." Noelle slid from the car.

"Would you like assistance clearing the house?" Adams shut the car door.

"No, thank you. I think we're good." Noelle shook the man's hand and stepped onto the sidewalk.

With a final goodbye, she and Jonah strode up the walkway and entered the house. She punched in the security code, then rearmed the system.

Jonah stared at the red light on the panel. "I'd like to say that's not necessary, but instead, I'll say I'm grateful." He shook his head as if dislodging the thought. "I'll grab the first-aid kit and clean the rest of your cuts."

"Thanks for that, by the way." Noelle appreciated his thoughtfulness at the scene. The last thing she wanted was someone else seeing her scars. "I'll go change and meet you in the kitchen. It seems to be our triage center." She flashed him a grin and laid her weapons on the end table next to the couch.

He rolled his eyes. "Go."

Once in her room, she pulled her shirt off, careful not to rub her sleeves against her wounds, and tossed it in the garbage. The slices in the material didn't leave much hope of salvaging it. She eyed her normal three-quarter-sleeve tops and decided to ignore her mother's voice that crept into her mind. She donned a tank top and changed her jeans. Jonah had seen the white lines that marred her skin, so why worry? The man didn't seem bothered by them. But, unable to bring herself to go without a cover, she gathered a white button-down blouse before closing her closet, just in case she had unexpected company.

When she entered the kitchen, Jonah had the supplies lined

up on the table like a surgeon with his instruments. She struggled to hold back a laugh and failed.

His gaze lifted and landed on her bare arms. He froze for a moment—so brief she thought she'd imagined it. "What? I may be a hot mess with everything else, but I'm dialed in when it comes to my skills as a doctor." His sheepish look reminded her of an embarrassed little boy.

"Riiiight." She drew out the word, hoping for a smile. And he didn't disappoint.

"Have a seat. Let me tend to those cuts."

Cuts. Which ones? The recent or the past? He hadn't judged her when he'd seen her scars. In fact, he'd even touched them. But over time, would they disgust him?

"Come on. I want to make sure you don't have glass embedded in your skin." He patted the chair.

She hung her cover-up blouse on the back of another chair, then sat. "I think you enjoy your job a bit too much."

"I'll never tell." He chuckled and got to work tending to her injuries.

The antiseptic solution he used on the open wounds stung. Tears pooled, but she blinked them away. She'd experienced worse. Much worse.

A few minutes later, Jonah cleaned up his mess and washed his hands. "Good as new."

"Sure," she muttered, hoping he hadn't heard her. "Thanks for taking care of me so that I didn't have to go to the hospital."

He brushed the backs of his fingers along her cheek. "Anything to make you feel more comfortable." His brown eyes connected with her blue ones.

His touch made her belly flutter. She swallowed past the lump in her throat. Could she really have it all?

The front door handle jiggled.

Jonah's eyes widened. "Are you expecting anyone?"

"No." Noelle slipped on her blouse, then snatched her Glock

from where she'd placed it when she entered. "Stay in the kitchen," she whispered. Taking time to cover her arms was stupid, but ingrained actions died hard.

She moved without sound to the door. Taking a deep breath, she widened her stance and took aim.

Whoever stood on the outside would have to get through her to kill Jonah.

Jonah tucked himself behind the partial wall of the kitchen and resisted the urge to step beside Noelle. It went against every protective fiber in his being to let her stand between him and danger. But he wouldn't interfere. The woman he'd admired for the past year and who he'd come to care about more than he'd like to admit was an Elite Guardian. He trusted Noelle with his life.

Not having a line of sight made his pulse race. He closed his eyes and listened.

The door opened and footfalls hit the entry tiles.

"Freeze. Hands up!"

A scream filled the air.

"Raven?" Noelle's question had him joining her by the door. "What are you doing here?"

One hand covered Raven's heart, the other shaking as she held a travel carrier of coffees. Her breaths came in pants, and her bag and envelopes lay scattered on the floor. "You scared me."

Noelle holstered her weapon, then hurried to close the door. She turned and tapped in the security code before the alarm blared.

"I brought some yummy goodness from Bitty and Beau's along with Jonah's mail and extra clothes." Raven offered the cardboard carrier to Jonah. He took it.

If not for the stoppers in the cups, small puddles of coffee would have lined the interior of the tray. "Thanks for the drinks." He placed them on the table and returned to where the women stood.

Raven gathered the items from the floor. "I thought you'd still be at the scene. I wanted to surprise you."

"Oh, you surprised us all right." Noelle smirked.

"When I heard about the accident, I had just left Jonah's house." Raven gave him his mail. "By the way, your cat is fine. A little needy, but Samson's a sweetheart." She put the duffel bag next to the couch and collapsed onto the cushions.

"I appreciate you taking care of him." He wished, not for the first time, that his little angel with claws was with him. He'd adopted Samson soon after losing Cara. He was man enough to admit the furball had helped with the gut-wrenching pain. And now Samson eased the stress from a hard day at work. Better than blood pressure meds.

"Are you two okay?" Raven asked.

Jonah handed Noelle her coffee and spun his to see what Emma or whoever made the brew had written on the cup. *Believe in yourself.* He loved Bitty and Beau's. Anytime he needed a lift in his day, they never failed to deliver.

"Thanks." Coffee in hand, Noelle lowered herself next to Raven. "There was a moment I didn't think we'd make it, but as you can see, we're good."

"Phew. I'd hate to break in a new office manager." Raven grinned.

Jonah eased onto the recliner and took a sip. He groaned at the rich chocolate-infused brew.

"Yo, Doc, would you like a moment alone with your coffee?"

He lowered the cup and glared at Raven. "Haha. Very funny." The woman had a wicked sense of humor, that comment only a peek into what lay beneath the surface. "Are the others ready for the conference call?"

"It's all set. I have everything scheduled for an hour from now. Will that give you enough of a break before diving in again?" Raven clutched a throw pillow against her abdomen.

"This and a little food will do the job." Noelle lifted her cup before taking a sip.

"Is there anything you need me to do? Oh, wait." Raven rummaged through her purse, which looked more like a beach bag, and pulled out a large manila envelope. "Alana got the video footage from the restaurant. I pulled stills and printed them for you."

"Perfect." Noelle took the packet. "We'll look at these in a bit."

Raven tucked the pillow behind her and stood. "I've got things to do, unless you need something else."

"I think we're good. Thanks again for taking care of Samson and getting my stuff." Jonah walked her to the door.

"Sorry about holding you at gunpoint." Noelle cringed.

Raven waved a hand like shooing a fly. "I don't blame you after all the chaos. I'll announce myself next time. Let me know if I can help with anything." With that, she left.

Noelle closed the door and reset the alarm.

"You scored when you found Raven. If I could, I'd steal her from the Elite Guardians." He nudged Noelle. "But I think she'd protest."

She gave him a playful glare. "Don't you dare. That woman keeps the office running smoothly. I couldn't do it without her."

"What do you say about fixing lunch, or should I say a midafternoon snack, before our call?"

"Sounds great."

For the next hour, they avoided conversation about the cases. The downtime gave them the break they needed.

With the kitchen clean, Jonah joined Noelle on the loveseat in her office.

He scanned the images on the wall. Since she'd announced

that the set of faceless pictures were of her, his stomach churned whenever he looked at them. The woman had survived a brutal few days. Her ability to still stand with confidence about life amazed him. Her words about God wanting people to reach out —wanting a friendship—had struck something deep inside. Maybe he should try harder to talk with God again. Because she definitely hadn't made it through those dark moments alone.

The laptop balanced on Noelle's thighs came to life.

"Ready for this?" she asked.

"More than. I want this over. I think I'll pray for resolution in both sets of cases."

Without lifting her gaze to him, she smiled at his comment. "That would be nice."

He knew she wasn't only referring to closing the cases but to his willingness to pray.

Squares of their friends' faces filled the screen.

"Hey, everyone." Noelle waved.

"How are you? I'm glad you're okay. What were you thinking? Are you feeling okay?" Questions and comments came at them rapid-fire.

Jonah held up a hand. "We're fine. Minor cuts and bruises."

"I guess we can trust Doc. He is the professional," Matt grumbled. "But I talked with Officer Adams..." He let the statement hang.

Might as well stop the conversation before it crumpled around them. Jonah inhaled. "You all know the basics. But what I can tell you is that Noelle's quick thinking and skills saved our lives."

She shook her head, but he stopped her.

"Seriously. It was a close call, but her instincts made the difference between us sitting here now and us taking up tables in the morgue."

"Can we move this meeting along?" Pink filled Noelle's cheeks.

He clutched her hand and squeezed.

She gave him a shy smile.

"Juliette, what happened at the congressman's office?" Apparently, they had convinced Decia that he and Noelle were in one piece, and she was ready to move on.

Juliette brought her tablet in front of her. "I did a little digging before chatting with Congressman Sanford. Did you know he has a thing for younger females?"

"Oh, ick." Matt grimaced. "How young?"

"Not like that." Juliette shook her head "Think the male version of a cougar. His tastes are women in their early twenties."

"And he's what? Sixty?" Decia asked.

"Not quite, but getting close," Juliette said. "I'm not dissing all couples with a large age difference, but when an older man targets women half or less than half his age...nothing good can come from it."

"What else?" Noelle asked.

"It's fairly well known within his circle that he cheated on his wife before her death."

Juliette scrunched her nose. "What a peach. How did she die?"

Matt raised a finger. "I can answer that. Car accident. Hit-and-run. The officers never discovered who killed her."

"So it could have been on purpose." Alana's words stopped the conversation.

"I'm not sure SPD ever considered that angle. The report states the person responsible ran a red light and smashed into the driver's side, killing her instantly, then drove off."

Wet crimson covered Jonah's hands. How many lives had he saved, and the one that meant the most had slipped through his fingers. Bile crept up his throat. He shoved his failure to the back of his mind and fought to keep his late lunch in place. He blinked away the blood. "Then it's possible Mrs. Sanford's death wasn't an accident."

"After everything we've heard, I think it's a real possibility. Or at least one we shouldn't ignore." Decia twirled her pen. "We have a cheating husband and a wife who died under unknown circumstances. What about the son and others in the congressman's office?"

"The son is protective of his father and is against him 'talking with the cops.'" Juliette used air quotes. "I guess he considers me law enforcement. Anyway, he's secretive. I'm not sure if it's his personality, the attorney in him, or he's actually hiding something."

"What about the aide and the administrative assistant?" Decia asked.

"The admin is knowledgeable of everything that goes on in that office. I'd be surprised if anyone makes a move without her knowing." Juliette sighed. "But beyond that, nothing had me questioning her involvement in illegal behaviors."

"She might be a source of information once we have specifics to ask," Matt said.

"And the aide. What was his name?" Noelle snapped her fingers. "Royce Dwight."

"Now, he's an interesting one." Juliette scrunched her nose as if smelling a rotten egg. "From the outside, he looks squeaky clean."

The air conditioner kicked on, and the cold air tickled the back of Jonah's neck. "There's dirt on him?"

"Not really. He's too clean, if you catch my drift." Juliette shrugged. "Sanford was a friend of his father's during high school. The congressman offered him an internship because of it, and Royce has become an invaluable part of Sanford's political team. If I had to guess, I'd say the aide is willing to do *anything* for the congressman."

Matt rubbed the back of his neck. "So, we have a whole lot of nothing. We can't point at anyone, and yet we can't rule them out either."

"Do you think the congressman is our killer?" Alana asked.

Decia squinted at the screen. "I get the feeling you have a reason you asked."

Alana's brow furrowed. "Maybe."

"You visited the restaurant where the congressman was seen with the current victims. What did the waitstaff at Twilight Serenade say?" Noelle continued to hold Jonah's hand.

"They recognized several of the victims." Alana eased back in her chair and swung her seat side to side. "They remembered Sanford wining and dining the women, but each employee insisted that the congressman treated the ladies well."

"That does not prevent him from being a killer," Decia stated.

"True. But why? His platform is tough on crime. Is he hiding behind his words?" Jonah ran the fingers of his free hand through his hair. "What else, Alana?"

"The bartender, Austin James, who I discovered, when I asked about security footage, is also the owner, gave me consent. He emailed me the videos for the weeks in question. I think Raven gave everyone copies of the stills." Alana raised a brow.

"I got ours." Matt answered Alana's unspoken question for himself and Decia.

"Us too." Jonah lifted the envelope. "However, we haven't looked at the photos yet."

"No worries. Y'all had a lot going on," Juliette said.

"You can say that again," he mumbled.

Noelle tilted her head. A smile graced her beautiful face. She grabbed the packet and slid out the contents.

Jonah leaned in and got his first look at the photos.

"I circled the victims and wrote the dates and times on the pictures." Alana gave everyone time to examine the images.

Decia spoke first. "On photo number four, is that the congressman's son?"

"Yes. In fact, his son Lincoln and aide Royce made multiple appearances in the videos," Alana confirmed.

"Who's the guy in the background? I can't see his face." Noelle lifted one of the images to the camera and pointed to the person in question.

Alana squinted at the screen, then flipped through her copy of the pictures. "That's the owner/bartender."

The crease in Noelle's forehead deepened as she studied the photo.

Jonah shifted to get a better angle of her face. "Is there a reason you're interested in him?"

"No, just curious. I'm trying to place all the players."

"So, back to the original question. Could Congressman Clifton Sanford be our killer?" Alana asked.

"I haven't met the man, but I watched one of his news interviews on TV. He favors his right side." Jonah hated speculation when it came to medical conditions, but he decided now might be the time to throw out his thoughts for the others to consider. "If I had to guess, the man had a stroke at some point in the past."

"Meaning?" Matt leaned forward, his face close to the screen.

"I don't think he's physically capable of overpowering these women." There. He'd said it. Jonah examined one of the pictures of Sanford. "Not unless he had help."

"I'm not a fan of who he seeks out for his dates. Noelle." Decia waited for Noelle to look at her. "Is it possible that Clifton Sanford is your cold-case serial killer?"

Noelle's breath hitched.

Jonah placed his hand on her knee, hoping the connection calmed her.

She swallowed hard. "I don't think so."

"Are you sure?" This time it was Matt who asked.

"No. I'm not positive. But when I met him face-to-face, I had no reaction to him." She scowled. "I think my subconscious would know."

"Maybe. Maybe not. I'll do a deeper dive into him." Decia jotted down a note. "Okay, Jonah, Noelle, what did you find out on your tattoo shop hunt?"

Jonah took the question, giving Noelle time to reset her mind. "After visiting several different shops, the owner of Body Murals gave us a possible name."

"Shoot me the name," Matt said.

"Richard Nelson. The owner told us that the guy's artist name was Vincent." Noelle offered the ID of the possible suspect.

"Was?" Decia asked.

Jonah nodded. "Apparently, Richard disappeared eight years ago, leaving behind all his equipment."

"I'll take a look into his history and see if I come up with anything." Matt wrote on a pad of paper.

Decia rubbed her eyes. "Anything else?" No one spoke. "That's what I was afraid of."

"Look, I know we have a twenty-four-seven plan for Doc, but I think we need to up that, especially after the attempt with the train." Alana crossed her arms as if daring them to go against her.

"I agree," Juliette added.

"It's not a bad idea. I, for one, would feel better knowing Doc is covered by two of you. Unfortunately, we can't pull SPD manpower to help, but sign Matt and me up for a shift on our off time." Decia's mom tone made Jonah smile.

"I appreciate it." Jonah hated that he'd put Noelle in the crosshairs of another killer, so if Decia's offer meant an extra set of eyes on Noelle as well, he was all in.

SIXTEEN

Southern Café, not far from Colonial Park Cemetery, bustled with people. The inside tables and booths had filled in the short time since they'd arrived, including the six tables enclosed by a black iron fence in front of the establishment. Not exactly what Jonah had had in mind for an intimate brunch, but then neither was Juliette sitting out on the patio for extra protection. With the exception of last night's quiet moment snuggling on the couch with Noelle, yesterday had scared the daylights out of him.

"Hey." Noelle waved a hand in front of his face. "Where'd you go?"

"Sorry. I'm a bit preoccupied." And not for the reasons one would think.

"Understandable. A lot has happened in a short time." She sipped her orange juice, then folded her hands on the table. "I've been thinking about all our suspects. It's confusing. I keep feeling like there's something we're missing. Or someone."

LYNETTE EASON & SAMI A. ABRAMS

"Like who?" His gaze landed on Juliette, grounding him in the danger that continued to lurk.

"Someone close to my killer? Or maybe he went to prison and bragged to another inmate?" She tucked a strand of hair behind her ear. "I'm grasping."

"No. It's worth considering." Jonah let the ideas simmer and took a sip of his dark brew. "Do you really think Congressman Sanford had anything to do with your abduction?"

She shook her head. "I don't think so. But the age seems right. If it's him, then how could I not know?" She sighed and tugged on her three-quarter-sleeve blouse that covered a bright blue tank top.

He hated that his question had her retreating to her insecurity. He reached across the table, stilling her hand, and jutted his chin toward her arms. "I noticed you left your extra shirt on last night after our video chat."

She cringed.

"Don't."

She tilted her head. "Don't what?"

"Don't hide. Don't be ashamed. Take your pick." He hadn't meant to make her uncomfortable. He only wanted her to see herself as he saw her. A beautiful woman inside and out.

"It's kind of hard with the evidence on my arms."

"You trusted me with your secret. You let me into your nightmare. Please, let me show you that your beauty isn't dictated by the white lines on your skin."

Tears pooled in her eyes. Her chin quivered. "Isn't it, though?"

Her quiet words had him straightening in his seat. Who had led this woman to believe her worth was linked to her looks? "Why are you so preoccupied with your appearance?"

The waitress chose that moment to serve their food.

He wanted to groan at the timing but refused to continue with the topic until their server left.

"Is there anything else I can get for you?" The woman smiled.

"No. I think that's all." He thanked the waitress and returned his attention to Noelle. "So, why are you so fixated on your scars?"

She picked up her fork and played with the Denver omelet she'd ordered. "It's ingrained in me."

To lessen the focus on her, he took a bite of the strawberry banana pancakes he'd ordered. Once he'd swallowed, he met her gaze. "How come?"

Inhaling, she set her fork aside and tucked her hands in her lap. "My mother was—is—obsessed with flawless skin. My grandmother was a model, so looks were always a thing in my house. But when she died of skin cancer a month before I turned five, my mother changed. As a child, she'd remind me at every opportunity that I had to take care of my skin. I look back now, and at first it made sense. Use sunscreen to prevent cancer. Wash your face so you don't get acne when you get older. All the normal things. But at some point, it became more."

"How?"

She shrugged. "The typical superficial stuff. Any scar I got, she'd use whatever the hype product was at the time to make it fade. My skin became tied to my value as a person—as a potential partner in life."

The bites of pancake he'd consumed sat like a rock in his stomach. "That's not typical superficial stuff. Noelle, you have to know that isn't true."

She tapped her hand over her heart. "Here, yes." Then she touched her temple. "Here? Not so much."

Jonah closed his eyes and pondered what to say to the woman who had slowly claimed his heart. When he opened them, he glanced around the café, realizing he'd pulled his attention away from their surroundings.

As if Noelle had come to the same conclusion, she scanned the room.

Juliette still sat outside, pretending to focus on her phone. He knew she had their backs, but he hadn't paid attention to the people around them. Even though Noelle and Juliette were his bodyguards, he refused to put his safety entirely on them.

Convinced danger didn't lurk in the background—at least at the moment—he cleared his throat. "I don't want to drop this conversation. I think it's important to you—to us—but..."

"Let's stay focused on the cases for now." She sent him a pleading look.

"That works for me." He wiped his mouth with a napkin. "Do we have any other leads in either the current cases or the cold ones?"

"Not that I've heard. Decia texted me this morning saying that she has an officer taking a deeper look into Lincoln Sanford and Royce Dwight. Plus asking about the congressman's friend."

Plates and glasses crashed to the floor.

Jonah whipped his attention toward the noise. A man with a knife stumbled toward him and shoved the blade in his direction.

Noelle leaped from her seat and swung her hand at the guy's arm. The knife's trajectory changed, but not enough to miss.

A searing pain like a hot poker spread through Jonah's side.

The man pushed Noelle out of the way and ran out the front of the café.

"Jonah!"

He grasped his side, then lifted his hand. Blood covered his palm. The maniac had stabbed him.

"Call 911! Juliette, stay with him!" Noelle's commands brought him out of his daze.

He glanced up in time to see her sprinting from the café after the person who'd targeted him in a public place.

"Noelle, don't," he gasped.

Someone shoved a towel at him. He grabbed it and pressed it to the wound. "Juliette, go help her."

Juliette positioned herself as a barrier between him and the rest of the patrons. "She has the assailant. My duty is protecting you."

The idea of Noelle chasing down the suspect and getting hurt—or worse—scared the life out of him.

His heart cried out, *God, please, I can't lose her too.*

———

Stupid. Stupid. Stupid. Noelle sprinted down the tree-lined street toward the cemetery, wanting to kick herself for getting distracted. She'd allowed Jonah to draw her into the discussion about her mother and had forgotten, for a moment, the danger that prowled around them.

If the guy half a block in front of her hadn't bumped into the waitress, Jonah might be dead. A man around six feet, give or take an inch, a baseball cap pulled over his eyes, and dark sunglasses. That's all she had. Some former LEO she was. *Yeah, Officer, he's your average Joe. Nothing discernable to make him stand out.* Great, just great.

People jumped out of the way as the man pushed through the crowds.

"Coming through!" She pumped her arms, trying to catch up with the attacker. Her Glock sat comfortably against the small of her back. Her fingers itched to reach for it, but withdrawing it in the middle of the crowd would create more panic than already existed.

Sweat dripped down her temples and between her shoulder blades. Thank heavens for the shade trees and the slight breeze. Even in May, the humidity hung heavy in the air.

She spotted Jonah's assailant entering the cemetery.

Only two ways in or out. An advantage and a concern.

Pushing her speed, she gained ground. She grabbed the fence post and launched into the graveyard.

The perp ran toward the back exit.

Noelle changed her direction, her new course intended to cut the man off. She leaped over grave markers, hating the disrespect of her action. She hoped those who'd gone before understood.

Thanks to Raven's fascination with weird historical facts, Noelle had toured the cemetery multiple times and had the layout committed to memory.

She ducked under the low-hanging Spanish moss, keeping her target in sight. Her breaths came in pants, but she continued to press on. She refused to let the man get away.

After exiting out the back of the cemetery, the guy dashed across the street.

She hurdled the last of the tombstones and followed him out the gate.

The man jumped on a tour trolley before the driver pulled away from the curb.

Noelle yanked her Glock from the small of her back and followed him on. "Stop!"

The passengers clapped at the confrontation, unaware that the showdown wasn't part of the scripted tour.

The attacker stood at the back of the trolley, the bloody knife used on Jonah held out in front of him.

The driver slammed on the brakes.

Noelle maintained her hold on her weapon and grabbed a seatback, steadying herself. The forced halt caught the suspect off guard. He dropped the knife and tumbled against the bench seat. His sunglasses flew to the floor.

Screams filled the air, the passengers now aware of the danger.

No matter how hard she tried, Noelle couldn't move her gaze from the man's eyes. She knew those cold, heartless, ice-blue eyes. She'd stared at them each time the serial killer had come in to torture her.

The guy scooped up the knife, jumped out the back window, and dashed away.

Unable to respond, she stood stunned.

"Noelle!" Jonah's frantic tone jerked her from the black hole her mind threatened to fall into.

She secured her Glock, flashed her credentials, and apologized to the driver. After directing the man to call Savannah PD and give a statement about the incident, she stepped off the trolley and met Jonah and Juliette on the sidewalk.

Jonah's hand covered the blood-soaked cloth on his side.

"You should be at the hospital getting that taken care of. And you, Juliette, should have kept him away from the danger."

"I'm not going to bleed out. I couldn't let you go after that guy alone. Don't get mad at Juliette. I didn't give her a choice."

The adrenaline crash edged its way in, and she had to sit down before it struck. She pointed to a bench not far away. "Let's go over there." Not allowing herself to get complacent, she continued to scan the area in case the attacker circled back around.

Jonah clutched his side and ambled over to the bench. He lowered onto the seat and patted the metal next to him.

Noelle joined him and tipped her head back. She sucked in several deep breaths. The attacker had gotten away, and now Jonah sat beside her with a knife wound that he refused to have tended.

Juliette stood to the side, arms crossed. "I can connect the dots as to what happened. But why do you look like you've seen a ghost?"

Noelle exhaled. "Because I think I did."

Jonah shifted to face her. "Come again?"

"I got a good look at your attacker's eyes." Noelle clasped her shaking hands together.

"And?" Juliette raised a brow while her gaze assessed their surroundings.

"They were those of my serial killer." The words came out as a whisper.

Jonah's breath hitched. "But how is that possible? That guy was, what? Late twenties? He would've been in his teens when he abducted you."

"It's not possible." Noelle let her gaze dart from Jonah to Juliette and back. "But yet, somehow it is."

SEVENTEEN

One would think that the antiseptic odors of the hospital wouldn't bother Jonah. But they would be wrong. Somewhere in the plastic bag near the exam table were his possessions, including his ruined shirt. They should have just thrown the thing away. He dropped his arm over his eyes. The fluorescent lights of the emergency room bay the paramedics had landed him in buzzed like a hive of bees. The white curtain that provided privacy—closed. At least everyone couldn't see him brood. Small favors and all that.

He hated being on the other side of the stethoscope. His old coworker and smart-aleck friend Dr. Walden had cleaned the knife wound and stitched him up. The man had lectured him to be more careful, told him to lie still for a bit, and left him waiting for the discharge papers.

Yeah, right. Lie here and do nothing. No way. Jonah rolled to his side and pushed up to a seated position. The paper on the bed crinkled beneath him. He reached for the scrubs shirt the nurse had left on the small table and winced. The world spun. He gripped the edge of the bed.

"Whoa there, cowboy." Noelle strode in. "Let me help."

He wanted to assure her that he was perfectly capable of dressing himself, but in truth, he needed her. "Thanks."

Her eyebrow arched. "No complaining?"

"Not today." The crease in her forehead had him hurrying to explain. "I'm fine, and if you don't believe me, you can ask Dr. Walden. But my side hurts anytime I move, so I'd appreciate it if you'd hand me that shirt." He pointed to the light-green top.

She studied him a moment, then nodded. "I can do one better." Noelle slipped the shirt over his head and held it out for him to slide his arms in, then pulled it down over his torso.

"I feel like a two-year-old," he grumbled.

"Well, sometimes you act like one." She flashed him a cheesy smile.

"Everyone decent?" Decia popped her head around the white curtain.

"And what if I had said no?" Jonah shook his head and sighed. So much for privacy. "I'm good." He shifted to stand and Noelle held out her hand. He considered ignoring her, but common sense took over. He'd been horizontal for a while, and between that and the blood loss, he had to be careful with dizziness.

Noelle waited for him to find his balance. "Good?"

"Yup." He turned toward Decia. "What's going on?"

"Think you can snag us a conference room? Matt's working on your Richard Nelson lead from the tattoo shop, but Alana and Juliette are here. We'd like to hear directly from you what happened today."

"I'll go work my magic." He took a couple of tentative steps, confirming he wouldn't fall flat on his face.

"More like throw your weight around," Noelle teased.

"Har har, very funny." He moved past Decia and headed out to find an old coworker.

Five minutes and a promise to visit the hospital staff more often later, he ushered the women into a conference room on the next floor up and flipped on the light.

"Have a seat." He chose a seat near the door and lowered himself onto a cushy office chair.

Alana and Juliette sat across from him, Decia at the head of the table, and Noelle beside him.

"This is perfect. Thanks, Doc." Decia set her notebook in front of her. "I've read the report, but give us a quick rundown of the events."

Noelle spoke before he'd collected his thoughts. "As you know, we had brunch at the Southern Café near the Colonial Park Cemetery." She explained the attack and her subsequent pursuit of the assailant.

He sat stunned as she told them about chasing the attacker through the graves.

"Then he jumped on the trolley. The passengers thought it was part of the act. The driver slammed on the brakes, which made the attacker stumble and lose his sunglasses." Noelle's breath hitched. "His eyes. I'd seen those eyes before."

"Where?" Even though Decia had already heard Noelle's account of what'd happened, she asked anyway.

"My serial killer." Noelle shoved her trembling hands under the table.

Jonah reached over and clasped her fingers, hoping his touch encouraged her to continue.

Noelle shook her head. "But it's not possible."

"How so?" Decia leaned in.

Jonah glanced at Alana and Juliette, who remained silent, worry etched on their faces.

"The age is all wrong. This guy is in his late twenties, early thirties. The man who abducted me would be in his late fifties if not early sixties by now. There's no way it's the same person."

"A son, maybe?" Alana offered.

Decia rubbed her temples. "I'm not saying it is, but what if it *is* a father-son connection like we considered?"

"Congressman Clifton Sanford and his son Lincoln?" Juliette asked.

"Maybe." Noelle rubbed her eyes. "But I don't think so. Sanford's eyes are blue, but not the same. And Lincoln's were brown."

"Contacts?" Alana rested her elbows on the table.

"Anything is possible." Noelle sighed.

Decia narrowed her gaze at an invisible spot on the table. "The aide, Royce Dwight, has blue eyes. They had this strange, almost icy look to them."

"What?" Noelle jerked her attention to her detective friend.

The description wasn't lost on Jonah. She'd described the eyes that haunted her to him. He squeezed her hand.

"They weren't your normal blue. That's why it made an impression," Decia said.

"He didn't make eye contact with me. Always seemed to have his head down." Noelle's voice quivered. "I never saw them."

Jonah's gut twisted at the implication. "Alana, call Raven and get her looking into Royce Dwight. And while she's at it, into his father too."

"On it, Doc. I'll catch up with y'all later when I have answers." Alana had her phone to her ear as she strode from the room.

"Decia, I know you have an officer researching Royce and his dad, but we need to move on this." Jonah's heart threatened to beat out of his chest.

"I agree. I'll gladly accept Raven's help." Decia's cell rang. "What's up, Matt?" A pause. "Are you serious?" Another pause.

"I'm on my way." She hung up. "Matt has the address for Richard Nelson along with a search warrant."

"How'd he secure that?" Jonah hadn't thought they had enough evidence to convince a judge.

"EGA has friends in high places." The detective smiled. "Since the man is missing and a possible link to a serial killer, they agreed."

Noelle stood. "I'm coming."

"I'm not sure that's a good idea." Decia's calm tone belied the worry stamped across her features.

Jonah glanced at Noelle, and it hit him. She'd opened the dam on her past, and if she ever wanted to recover from her personal nightmare, she had to see this through for her own sanity. After all she'd endured, she deserved to be there. "I'll go with her." He stared down Detective Slaton, determine to give Noelle what she needed.

"Fine. But, Doc, you stay right by my friend's side."

"There's no place I'd rather be." That was a lie. He'd rather be at Noelle's house waiting on the news instead of taking her to the possible home of the man who'd tortured her. But he'd be what she needed him to be: the person that stood beside her as she faced her biggest fear.

———

The birds chirping in the trees surrounding the old house that sat away from the county road set Noelle's nerves on edge. Hip resting on the hood of her car, she wrapped her arms around her waist and waited on Matt and two other officers to search Richard Nelson's modest single-story house. Sweat beaded on her forehead, but not from the heat. What if Nelson was her serial killer?

She should have stayed home.

No. She had to come.

LYNETTE EASON & SAMI A. ABRAMS

"Are you doing okay?" Jonah's concerned tone snapped her from her thoughts.

"I'm not sure if I want it to be Nelson or not."

"What do you mean?"

"If it's him and they find him, I'll come face-to-face with the man who took my life. Not in the literal sense, but in many ways just the same."

Jonah settled next to her. "You'll handle it."

She flicked her gaze at him. "How do you know that?"

"Because you're one of the strongest women I know. And I refuse to let you do this by yourself." He shrugged.

"Thanks," she whispered, unable to make her voice work. The man had kept her grounded since they'd arrived.

Matt had given her an update that the house appeared abandoned, and so far, they hadn't found Nelson.

Jonah scooted closer and slid his arm around her.

She laid her head on his shoulder and sighed. "What's taking so long?"

"Matt's doing a thorough search of the house, then moving out from there to the small shed and building beyond. Give him time."

Matt strode their way with a sour expression on his face. "Doc. Noelle."

She straightened and shoved her hands into her jeans pockets. "What'd you find?"

"The house is clear. I'd say with the dust an inch thick and the petrified food in the kitchen, no one has lived in that house for quite a while. Years, in fact." Matt rubbed the back of his neck.

"Then why the grim look?" Jonah moved to Noelle's side as if to protect her from the bad news.

"It's what we found in the outbuilding." Matt's gaze landed on Noelle. "I want Noelle to come see it."

Jonah stepped forward, fists on his hips, staring at Matt. "Not without a heads-up first."

She placed her hand on his shoulder. "It's okay, Jonah."

"Calm down, Doc. You know I wouldn't do that." Matt glared at him.

Jonah grumbled but shifted to the side.

"What is it that you want me to look at?" Her stomach twisted in knots at all the horrible possibilities her mind conjured up.

"We believe the outbuilding is Nelson's 'workshop.'" Matt used air quotes around the word.

"Richard Nelson is the serial killer?" She swallowed the bile crawling up her throat.

Matt nodded. "It's my opinion that he is."

Her eyes darted along the tree line, and her breaths came in pants. Was he watching? Would he finish what he'd started fifteen years ago?

Jonah laced his fingers with hers. "Calm down before you hyperventilate. Matt and I won't let anything happen to you."

She mentally kicked herself for her reaction. "Where is he?"

Matt's gaze dropped to the ground, then up to her. "We haven't found him yet." He held up a hand to stop Jonah from speaking. "He's not in prison. We've questioned his friends. At least, the few we know about. It's like he vanished."

"Detective Williams." An officer called from the front porch. "I have something you need to see."

Matt motioned for them to follow. "Come on. Let's see what Officer Taylor found, then I'll take you out back."

Noelle gripped Jonah's hand tighter as they trailed Matt. Jonah had broken down her walls and become her confidant. She hadn't told anyone the personal things she'd confessed to him. But with each step toward the house, she felt herself emotionally pulling away.

"What is it, Taylor?" Matt asked.

Officer Taylor waved them inside. "I found a photo tucked behind those books." With gloved hands, the man held the image for all three of them to see.

Jonah's head jerked up. "He has two sons."

"That's what it looks like." Matt yanked his phone from his pocket. "I'm on it. I'll ask Decia to investigate."

Noelle fell down the black hole of memories. The killer's muffled voice swam in her mind. Ice-blue eyes stared at her. His hot breath made her cringe. The sharp blade slid against her skin, sending fire ripping through her. She struggled to allow herself to stay in the moment and recall details.

A memory popped into her brain. "There was a kid. I saw him. Or rather, he saw me." She squeezed her eyes shut. The musty odor in the house swirled in her nose and mouth. "But this isn't where I was held."

"From the documents I read, they found the shed attached to an abandoned cabin where he kept you, but never the person responsible."

"What else do you have to show me?" A shiver ran down Noelle's spine. She wanted out of the house but was unsure what came next.

"There's an outbuilding set approximately twenty-five yards away from the main residence." Matt pinched his lips together and scratched his jaw. "It appears similar to the place where he held you."

"You can't be serious!" Jonah narrowed his gaze. "Matt. You're asking too much."

Tears blurred her vision. No one had ever really stood up for her like Jonah. The man treated her better than anyone had in her life. Including her family. "Jonah, it's okay. If it solves multiple cold cases, then I have to do this."

He spun and cupped her cheek. "I don't care what Matt says. If it gets to be too much, say so, and I'll take you away from here."

Words refused to form. His protective streak had stolen her ability to speak, so she nodded.

"The outbuilding is over here." Matt motioned for them to follow.

A shed the size of a one-car garage sat near the tree line. The roof required repairs, and several sections of siding hung by one end. The building had seen better days. More evidence that Nelson hadn't lived here in a very long time.

Matt opened the door and stopped. "Noelle, I know it's a lot."

"You think?" Jonah muttered under his breath.

She placed a hand on Jonah's forearm to reassure him she'd be okay. "No. I get it. I'll be fine." She hoped. Studying documents and pictures was a far cry from visiting in person.

"Before you go in, I need to warn you about what we discovered in there." Matt struggled to meet her gaze. "There's a chair and a bed. But it's the spots on the floor that are the most disturbing."

She stiffened. Could she stay detached and not relive every moment of horror?

God, I need You. I can't do it without You.

Noelle swallowed. "Let me see it."

The door opened, and she and Jonah stepped inside. Dust covered every surface, the only light the duty flashlights supplied by the officers. She rubbed her nose, attempting to prevent a sneeze. A chair sat in the middle of the room, and a bed not far away. Ropes littered the floor around the minimal furniture.

Noelle accepted a flashlight and shone it around the room. The beam landed on dark brown spots of various sizes, staining the floor.

Her heart pounded, and a whimper escaped.

"Noelle?" Jonah's hand warmed her lower back.

She shrugged off his touch. The hurt in his eyes gutted her, but the contact was more than she could handle and maintain her sanity.

With one last visual pass around the room, she darted out the door. Hand over her mouth, she hurried toward the bushes near the house.

The memories flew around in her mind like a swarm of gnats. Hands on her knees, she gasped for air.

Jonah crouched next to her but didn't make physical contact. "What can I do?"

After several minutes, she drew in a long breath. "Nothing. It caught me off guard. I'm okay now."

"I kinda doubt that, but I'll trust you."

Leave it to Jonah to speak the truth. She straightened. "Where's Matt?"

"Standing about ten feet away, looking guilty."

The corner of her mouth hitched. "Poor guy."

Jonah snorted.

"Seriously. Even I didn't think I'd have that kind of reaction." Noelle shoved her hands in her pockets. "Let's go talk with him."

Jonah joined her as they strode toward the detective.

Matt grimaced. "I'm sorry. I shouldn't have asked."

"No, Matt. You did the right thing." She chewed on the inside of her cheek. "I can say without a doubt that the room setup and methods are identical."

"That's what we thought, but we wanted to make sure." Matt blew out a long breath. "Now for the million-dollar question. Where's Richard Nelson? And who is his son?"

"As for the *where* part, you've checked all the possibilities you thought of. But what if he's dead?" Jonah swept his hand in an arc. "There's a lot of property."

"You think someone killed him and buried him out here?" Matt's eyes widened.

"Anything's possible. No one has seen him in nine years." Jonah shrugged. "Got a better idea?"

"Not really." Matt pulled his phone from his tactical pants. "I'll get the dogs."

Noelle refused to get her hopes up. Not that she wished death upon anyone, but the thought of never worrying about her serial killer again brought tears to her eyes. She ambled to her car and sat on the hood, forcing the memories to fade.

Jonah boosted himself next to her. "Do you want to stay or go home?"

"Stay. I need this. I have to know." She stared off at the wooded area behind the house. "Jonah, I'm sorry."

"You have nothing to be sorry for."

She shook her head. "I meant I don't think there can be an us. At least, not more than a friendship. After what happened out there, I've realized I'm more messed up than I thought. You deserve so much more than I can give."

"I disagree." He held up a hand to stop her. "A discussion for a later time."

An argument sat on the tip of her tongue, but she'd keep it to herself—for now.

Four hours later, the cadaver dog found a body buried on the property near the woods.

Was it her serial killer? And if so, who had tried to kill her and Jonah?

EIGHTEEN

THURSDAY, 9:00 A.M.

Arms wrapped around her waist, Noelle stood several feet away from the metal autopsy table that held the remains of the man unearthed in Richard Nelson's backyard. Her pulse raced. The body, the torture room similar to the one he'd used for her, and Matt finding her serial killer had sent her into an internal black hole that she hadn't climbed out of. From the moment she'd flashed back to her abduction, she'd pushed Jonah away, unsure how to deal with the kaleidoscope of emotions whirling through her. Nelson had taken her security—her self-confidence.

Jonah tied his apron and snapped on nitrile gloves. "All right, ladies and gentlemen. I plan to record the findings, but are there any questions before I start?"

Matt stood across the table from Jonah and cleared his throat. "I'd like it on record that the remains are confirmed through dental and medical records as those of Richard Nelson. He had a unique crack in his jaw noted by old dental X-rays and identical evidence of previous broken bones. We still need DNA verification, but I believe that is a formality at this point. The crime scene techs are continuing to collect evidence, but the initial assessment, along with the cold-case files, shows that starting fifteen years ago, Nelson kidnapped, tortured, and killed for over six years until he disappeared."

"Noted." Jonah adjusted the overhead lamp.

"Any information about the young boys in the photo?" Juliette had insisted on backing Noelle up, knowing last night had taken a toll on her.

Matt nodded. "We discovered that Nelson had at least one child. Beyond that, we can't find any information."

The conversation swirled around Noelle. She swallowed against the smell of dirt and decay, but it was being in the presence of her killer that made her stomach roil. She hated to admit weakness, but the scene had thrown her off-balance. "Juliette, you have protection duty. I'm stepping outside."

Jonah paused his work. His gaze met hers.

She couldn't respond to his silent question. The whole situation had numbed her from the inside out. She hurried from the room.

The door swung closed behind her, and she rushed out the exit into the parking lot.

She drew in fresh air and tilted her face to the sun. Tears spilled over her temples.

God, I should be thanking You for finding the man who hurt me. And I am grateful. But how am I supposed to deal with this? Then there's Jonah... She closed her eyes. Why had she thought a relationship with Jonah was possible? Life experiences had damaged her more than the physical scars on her arms and chest. Jonah deserved a whole woman, not someone who retreated when memories came crashing down.

Footfalls clomped to her right. She lowered her head, not wanting to bring unwanted attention to her meltdown. She turned to greet the person walking down the sidewalk.

Icy blue eyes met her gaze.

213

The air was sucked from her lungs. The man who'd attacked Jonah stood a few feet away. She reached for the Glock that pressed against her back.

"No, no." The man closed the distance and held a gun to her side. "Get your keys. We're going for a little ride."

"Who are you?" Noelle slid her fingers into her pocket.

"Easy there with the hand." He nodded toward her jeans. "You can call me Jack."

The man's eyes had her heart pounding. The same unique color and sinister look as Richard Nelson. She fought against the flashbacks, retrieved her keys, and held them up.

He snatched them from her hand and jabbed the barrel of the gun into her side. "Slowly walk to your car."

Noelle scanned the empty parking lot. So much for covertly signaling someone to alert security. And the cameras on the outside of the building were useless. The assailant had positioned himself in such a fashion that the video feed would show the two of them strolling to her car like friends. Besides, with the Glock in her back, it would be a death sentence to do anything bold.

"Go to the passenger side and get in."

"I know why you're trying to kill Dr. Harris, but why take me, Jack?" She followed his instructions and slipped into the car, all the while searching for a way to take the guy down.

"The ME knows too much. He'll die soon. But you..." He brushed a strand of hair from her cheek.

She jerked away. Her skin crawled from his touch.

"You are a loose end. The elusive whale, if you will." He flashed a grin at her.

"And you're *Moby Dick's* Ishmael?"

He shook his head and chuckled. "Ishmael? No." Jack flipped down the car's visor and winked. "Gotta block the view."

Bile rose in her throat. A list of horrible things he could do to her swirled in her brain. Even with God by her side, she'd never survive another abduction like the first one.

Jack held out the loop of flex cuffs. "Hands."

She stared at the plastic. Sweat beaded on her forehead. Her heart rate skyrocketed from the memories.

"Now!"

The rage in the man's gaze had her following his instructions. First order of business—survive. If she stayed alive, she could escape or be rescued. She slid her hands into the cuffs, and he tightened them, cutting into her flesh.

At least he'd cuffed her hands in front of her. She had options.

Jack withdrew a folded handkerchief from his pocket. "Time to have some fun." He placed it over her nose and mouth.

The sweaty odor of chloroform registered in her brain. She bucked against Jack's hold, but he pinned her to the seat.

The world dimmed.

His hot breath fanned her ear. "My father loved Moby Dick. I prefer Jack the Ripper."

A muffled cry fell from her lips, and she lost the battle to stay conscious.

———

Jonah lifted his gaze from Richard Nelson's decomposed corpse and glanced at the clock in the autopsy room. An hour had passed since Noelle had made her hasty escape. He hadn't said a word about her departure, knowing her struggle with the turn of events. She'd retreated into herself last night and hadn't shaken off the shock as of that morning. He wasn't surprised she hadn't returned to the room, but for some reason—call it his gut screaming at him—worry wrapped him and squeezed, sending a shiver snaking up his spine.

He examined the hole in Nelson's skull one more time. The

man's death...definitely not natural causes. He'd request that the crime techs search the grave for the bullet. But if it hadn't lodged in Nelson's head, the dirt wouldn't contain the evidence. And who knew where his final breath had taken place?

With the condition of the remains, the autopsy hadn't taken as long as he'd expected. He snapped a few final pictures. "Anyone heard from Noelle?"

Matt checked his phone. "Not me. Juliette?"

"Sorry. No text message or call. She tasked me with your protection, so as you know, I haven't left the room. And as harsh as it sounds, you are my priority. But something's not right. She'd never leave you for this long without checking in." A scowl formed on Juliette's face. "Matt, I'm turning Doc's safety over to you while I go find Noelle."

The detective nodded, and the petite bodyguard hustled from the room.

Matt folded his arms over his chest. "Noelle looked a bit green when she left."

"It had nothing to do with witnessing an autopsy, and you know it." Jonah covered the body with a sheet and dealt with his instruments.

"I do. I've known her a while now, and her reaction yesterday surprised me."

"Have you read her entire case file?" Jonah wondered how much his friend knew about Noelle's past.

Matt rubbed the back of his neck. "Enough. That, along with what she told us—I can only imagine what she went through."

Juliette rushed through the door. "Her car is gone, and she's not answering her phone."

Jonah shed his gloves and paper apron, tossed them into the biohazard can, and scrubbed his hands in the sink. "I have a bad feeling about this. I'll have security run through the video feed." He placed a call to the security office in the building and then one to Bonnie to have an assistant take care of Nelson's body.

Matt's phone rang. He put it on speaker. "What's up, Decia?"

"I heard from Alana. The restaurant, Twilight Serenade, is owned by a company linked to Congressman Sanford."

"I thought the bartender, Austin James, or something like that, owned the place." Jonah's worry for Noelle had slowed his reasoning abilities.

"Hi, Doc. He very well might. But even so, the congressman has a hand in it."

The room phone rang. Jonah picked it up. "Dr. Harris."

"Doc, this is Mitch with security. I found your lady. She left in her car with a man. I've never seen him before."

"Thanks, Mitch." The situation was all kinds of wrong.

"Doc, wait. There was something odd about it."

Jonah's spine stiffened. "Go on."

"I don't have specifics, just a gut feeling. But the way they walked together...it didn't look natural."

"Good enough for me. I'll be in touch." Jonah hung up and relayed the message to his friends.

Matt widened his stance and placed his hands on his hips. "I think it's time to have another chat with Sanford."

"I'm coming with you. Give me a minute to change clothes." Jonah hurried to his office with Juliette and Matt on his heels.

Juliette held up her hand. "Let me clear the room first."

He leaned against the wall and waited. After Juliette had cleared the small room, he changed into his jeans and polo. "Ready."

Matt turned to Juliette. "See what you can find out from the security cameras. We'll go meet with Sanford. Then we can exchange info."

"Sounds like a plan. But since Noelle left me in charge of Doc's safety, I'm counting on you to play bodyguard."

"Done. I'll call you and Alana when we finish." Matt motioned toward the exit. "Let's go, Doc."

Twenty-five minutes later, they entered Sanford's office building and marched to the receptionist's desk.

Matt flashed his badge. "We need to talk with Congressman Sanford immediately."

"Yes, sir." The woman notified Sanford and stood. "Follow me." She opened the door to the congressman's office for them.

Jonah stepped next to Matt and folded his arms.

"What can I do for you, gentlemen?" Sanford stood behind his large ornate oak desk.

"What is your relationship with Richard Nelson?" Matt's tone held a lethal edge that Jonah hadn't heard before.

Sanford rubbed his chin. "We were friends growing up."

Matt arched a brow. "Keep going."

"He disappeared nine years ago. What more do you want me to say?"

"We found his body."

Jonah flinched at Matt's abrupt words.

Sanford blindly reached for the arm of his chair and collapsed onto it. "You found Richard?"

Jonah nodded. "Yes, sir."

"You found my dad?"

He and Matt spun to the doorway.

Royce Dwight, the congressman's aide, pressed a hand against the wall. Jonah studied the man's pallor.

"We discovered his remains yesterday on the property of his old address."

Royce's gaze met the congressman's. "I don't understand. What's going on?"

Jonah decided to follow Matt's lead and go with blunt and gauge both men's reactions. "We have reason to believe Richard Nelson killed multiple women starting fifteen years ago."

"What? No way. Not my father." Royce straightened and strode farther into the room.

Sanford shook his head. "I don't believe it. The man was

devastated when his wife left him. We spent quite a bit of time together. I would have known."

"Maybe. Maybe not. And now there's another serial killer mimicking Nelson. It has to be someone who knew what he had done. There are too many similarities." Matt's eyes darted back and forth between Royce and Sanford. "Royce, why doesn't your last name match your father's?"

The man's shoulders drooped. "I took my mother's last name when I turned twenty-one."

"Why?" Jonah asked.

Royce pinched the bridge of his nose.

"That's okay, son. I've got this." Congressman Sanford rose and placed a hand on the younger man's shoulder. "Royce and his brother Austin didn't get along. He wanted separation from the family name, so I supported him."

"What happened between you and your brother?" Matt asked.

"When we were younger, he changed. One day we were best friends, the next... But years later, after my father disappeared, it was like a switch flipped in him," Royce said.

"I remember that." The congressman continued. "After Richard left without word, I took his boys in and helped them get started in the world. I gave Royce a job here in my office, and I invested in Austin's restaurant. Both boys work hard. Royce is invaluable, and Austin bartends at his own business."

"The one you frequent with, shall we say, young women?" Matt tilted his head as if challenging the older man to disagree.

Sanford dropped onto his chair. "Fine. Yes, I take my dates there. But there's nothing illegal about that. They are all of age."

"I'm not going there about the age difference. But the fact several have turned up tortured and killed makes me wonder, Congressman."

Sanford jerked back in his seat. "Tortured?" The shock on

the man's face—evident. No way was the man that good an actor.

Jonah pondered the new information while Matt continued to pepper the men with questions.

Noelle's reaction clicked in his brain. "Royce."

"Yes, sir."

"Does your brother have your father's eye color?"

The man nodded. "Yes. I have a cross between Mom's and Dad's blue eyes, and he got Dad's unique icy blue."

Jonah spun toward Matt. "It's the bartender—Austin."

Matt's entire body went rigid. "I thought his last name was James."

Royce shook his head. "No. For some reason, eight or nine years ago he started introducing himself using his middle name, going by Austin James, but unlike mine, his last name never changed. It's still Nelson."

Matt gave Jonah a knowing look, then shifted his gaze to the congressman. "If Austin wanted a private place, where would he go?"

"I'm not sure." The creases in Sanford's forehead deepened.

"Hold on." Royce strode to a cabinet next to the desk. "I saw him here this morning. I thought he came to talk with Mr. Sanford, but..." The aide opened the door, revealing a row of keys. One of the hooks was empty. "Your cabin."

"Where?" Matt demanded.

Sanford wrote down the address and handed it over.

"Don't leave town." Matt hurried toward the door. "Come on, Doc."

Jonah rushed to keep up.

Matt hurried down the stairs. "The one that got away."

"Excuse me?"

"I don't know, man, but what if Austin saw his dad hurting Noelle when he was young and that's what changed him?"

"It's possible. And it makes sense."

"She was the only girl to escape." Matt pushed through the glass doors at the entrance of the building and jogged to his car. "Hear me out. What if Austin had planned all along to finish what his dad started?"

"How did he know who Noelle was?"

"Officer Taylor found pictures of the girls Nelson killed. It's possible Austin saw them, but with the age difference and lack of information, he couldn't find her. That is, until he came face-to-face with her."

"Then why target me?" Jonah slid into the passenger seat while Matt tapped the address into his GPS.

"To keep you from exposing his kills. He hadn't anticipated Ken revealing the truth to you. He's mitigating the fallout." Matt pulled from the parking space and raced down the street. "But when Noelle saw his eyes on the trolley, he must have realized who she was, and the opportunity to finish her became his priority." Matt called Decia and gave her the rundown. "Decia will meet us at the cabin. She's informing the boss man and asking for backup."

Jonah lay back against the headrest and mulled over Matt's theory. "I think you're right."

"My theory? It's nonsense." Matt adjusted the air vents.

"It's not. In fact, it makes perfect sense." Jonah shifted and peered out the passenger window. *God, please let her be there and keep her safe. I'm trusting You with her life.* He stiffened. Had he really taken the leap to trust God again?

"You okay, Doc?"

"How can I be? Some maniac has the woman I love. So no, I'm not all right." Jonah froze.

"You didn't mean to say that, did you?" Matt's soft tone surprised him.

He shook his head. "No. But that doesn't mean it's not true."

"I'm happy for you, Doc. You've carried the guilt over your

wife's death for a lot of years. It's time to let go and live again. And I can't think of a better woman for you."

"What happens if we can't find her? Or worse yet, we're too late." Tears pooled on his lashes.

"We will find her. We will bring her home—alive." Matt's hands tightened on the steering wheel, turning his fingers white. "No other option is acceptable."

But what if?

Jonah swallowed past the lump in his throat. Noelle needed him, and he'd do anything to save her.

He'd allowed anger to control him for too long. He wanted the peace of giving God his fears and allowing Him to take control, like he'd done so many times in the past during an emergency surgery when he thought he'd lose the patient no matter what he did.

Jonah tossed aside years of resenting God and prayed like he hadn't since the day his wife died.

NINETEEN

The woman who'd caused Jack's father's obsession sat on a chair in the middle of the cabin's detached garage with a clear plastic tarp spread under her. Jack paced the length of the room. He'd used the old picture his father had had of the girl to search for the one that'd gotten away. For years he'd scoped out the mall and other known hangouts without any luck, until he'd finally picked up where his old man had left off. What choice had he had? He had to protect Sanford from those women.

He checked his watch. Three hours. The dumb broad was still out cold. He ran a hand through his hair and continued pacing. He'd planned to take care of business, clean up his mess, and get out so Sanford wasn't the wiser. With the cops and Dr. Harris in the mix, he'd avoided his normal workroom in case they found out his name.

After two more laps, he stomped to the chair. He slapped her face. "Wakey wakey."

Nothing. He did it again, a little harder this time.

She stirred, but her head drooped.

He squeezed her chin and lifted. "Wake up!"

Her lids fluttered and popped open. She whimpered and tried to pull away.

"That's right. It's me."

She squirmed under his hold. "What do you want?" Her words slurred from the effects of the chloroform that remained in her system.

"For you to die." Her wide eyes made him smile. "Dad never got over losing you. The one blemish on his mission."

"What mission?" she mumbled.

"Mom cheated on him. When he confronted her, she lied. The next day, she was gone. Dad always did have a mean streak in him, but Mom deserved what she got."

"But why me? Why any of us?"

Jack laughed. "You? Right place, right time. Plus, you look like her. The rest?" He shrugged. "Who knows where he found them? He took that secret to his grave. It doesn't matter. He rid the world of liars." He threw her chin to the side, whipping her head. His tools sat on a small table a few feet away. "I didn't have time to grab everything, but I have enough. Besides, dear ol' Dad already marked you."

He felt her eyes on him, watching every move he made. Good. He wanted her to know what he had in store for her.

"I don't understand."

Jack picked up the knife and studied the blade. "All my father ever wanted was the truth from my mother."

"That's why he tattooed the Chinese symbol for truth?" Her glazed eyes stared at him.

"Yes. Unfortunately, I don't have those skills, so I use a hot iron. It's fascinating how the skin sizzles and puckers against the heat. Too bad I can't show you. But my skills with the knife will do." He flicked the blade with his thumbnail.

She scrambled to push away from him, but he had her zip-tied to the chair with no way to escape. He chuckled. They always tried to get away.

His watch beeped. Someone had breached the perimeter. He tapped the tiny screen and checked the video from the cameras he'd strategically placed at the entrance of the driveway.

How had the cops found him?

Jack tossed the knife down, grabbed the gun from the small table, and threaded the suppressor onto the barrel of his weapon. They might be in the middle of nowhere, but he refused to take the chance of someone hearing a gunshot. "So much for all the fun I had intended for you." He shrugged. "But plans change." He lifted the weapon.

The woman bolted toward him, chair and all, tackling him to the ground.

He hit the ground, wheezing out a breath, and squeezed the trigger. He shook off the ringing in his ears and shoved her off him. Pushing up on all fours, he glanced at her still form.

Blood pooled on the floor next to her body. Good riddance.

It's done, Dad. I got the one that got away for you.

He took off out the back door, into the woods behind the cabin.

———

Jonah stared at the cabin with a detached garage. He itched to get inside. Who knew what horrible things Noelle could be experiencing while he and Matt waited on Decia? He leaned against the car at the entrance to the property, then pushed off and paced, unable to contain the jolt of energy shooting through him.

"You're making me edgy." Matt checked his weapon and holstered it.

In the distance, birds screeched and scattered.

Jonah's gut screamed at him that something was wrong. "We have to get in there."

"We will. Once we have backup." Matt flipped his wrist and glanced at his watch. "Decia will be here in a couple of minutes."

He ran his fingers through his hair. What if Noelle didn't have that much time?

"There she is."

Detective Slaton pulled her vehicle up next to Matt's and stepped from the car. "Ready?"

"Yes." Jonah answered for Matt. No way he'd let his friend delay finding Noelle any longer.

"You heard the man." Matt shook his head. "One thing before we go. Doc, you have to stay behind us. No rushing in before we get a read on the situation."

"Fine. Just move." His attitude toward his friends had turned snippy, but his patience had worn thin.

Matt and Decia took off toward the cabin.

Jonah sprinted after them. His thoughts ran wild at what he'd find when they made it inside.

Movement came from behind the garage. The trio veered away from the cabin, toward the other building.

The detectives stood to the side of the door and counted down. They breeched the side door in a synchronized fashion and ducked into the garage.

He plastered his back against the exterior. *Come on. Hurry up.*

"Doc, get in here!"

Jonah bolted through the door and came to a dead stop.

Noelle, still tied to a chair, lay on a plastic tarp that covered the ground, a growing puddle of blood underneath her.

Not again. He swallowed hard. Sweat popped out on his upper lip. The coppery smell coated his tongue.

"Doc!"

He blinked, shaking off the past. He wouldn't let his insecurities stand in the way of helping Noelle. "I'm on it."

"I'm going after Austin!" Decia hurried through the open door on the back side of the garage.

"Take care of her." Matt pointed to Noelle. "I'll cover Decia. An ambulance is on the way."

When had they called for medics? "Go." Jonah spotted the knife on the floor. He retrieved it and sliced the rope around Noelle's torso, then cut the zip ties on her wrists. He chucked the chair aside and rolled her onto her back.

"Hang on, honey. Don't leave me." He lifted the hem of her shirt and gasped. A bullet had entered her abdomen. He slipped his hand under her, felt for an exit wound, and found one. Two holes. And blood everywhere. At that moment, Jonah knew his own abilities would fall short. He'd watched Noelle fight through her past trauma with God by her side. He wanted that in his life again. That overwhelming soul-deep peace.

God, I never wanted to be in this position again. I need Your help.

He trusted God with Noelle. But unlike last time, he'd do his best work and accept the outcome. Oh, he might not like it and would give God an earful, but he wouldn't turn away from Him, no matter what happened.

The realization settled deep inside him, giving him the calmness he needed to do his job. Jonah jerked his undershirt and shirt over his head. He bunched the undershirt, lined it up with the exit hole, and rolled her onto the cloth. With his shirt against the entrance wound, he pressed down, stemming the blood flow.

She arched and cried out.

"Sorry, honey. But I refuse to let you die on my watch." He hoped—and prayed—his determination helped.

Her eyes fluttered open, then closed.

"Come on, sweetheart. Let me see those beautiful blue eyes." Jonah's hands cramped at the constant pressure, but he ignored the discomfort. It was nothing compared to the pain Noelle was experiencing at the moment.

Where was that ambulance?

Matt strode in, his breathing labored. "Decia got him. Tackled and cuffed him. It was a thing of beauty."

"Is everyone okay?" Jonah asked without taking his eyes off Noelle.

"We are now that Austin Nelson is in custody." Matt crouched next to him. "The ambulance is three minutes out. How's she doing?"

Jonah shook his head. The chances of Noelle making it to the hospital were slim.

TWENTY

The clunk of the vending machine near the hospital waiting room grated on Jonah's nerves. He paced along the wall of windows on the far side of the room. Three hours. Jonah smacked the glass with an open hand. They'd taken Noelle into surgery three hours ago and still no word. It had been touch and go in the ambulance, but the paramedic had worked with him to keep her alive.

"Easy, Doc." Decia rested her hand on his shoulder.

"What if..." He couldn't say it.

"Don't go there. You did everything you could, and now, we pray. That's all we can do."

He placed both palms on the glass and lowered his head. *God...* His mind spun in so many different directions his thoughts refused to gel. Wasn't there a verse that talked about the Holy Spirit stepping in during times of weakness? And Jonah had weakness in spades.

"Dr. Harris?"

He lifted his head. A nurse in scrubs with an untied mask

hanging from her neck stood at the entrance of the waiting room. "Yes."

"Dr. Kincaid asked me to update you."

Jonah strode across the room. Decia, Matt, Alana, Juliette, and Raven joined him. "And?"

The woman smiled. "Ms. Burton made it through surgery. She's in the recovery room as we speak. Knowing that she's special to you, Dr. Kincaid is staying by her side to monitor her for the next hour."

Jonah's knees buckled.

Matt's hand shot out and gripped his elbow, steadying him before he face-planted on the floor.

He blinked away the black dots that danced on the edge of his vision and took three deep breaths. "Please tell Dr. Kincaid thank you."

"I will." The nurse turned to leave but stopped. "And Dr. Harris, from what I witnessed in the OR, you saved that woman's life. If you hadn't acted when you found her and helped the paramedic during transport, we'd be having a very different conversation right now."

"I did my best." And he had, just like with Cara. That's all anyone could do. He saw that now. "I'd like to see her as soon as possible."

The woman nodded. "I'll let the nurses know to come get you when they transfer her to ICU."

"Thank you." He knew the drill. Had lived it for many years. But that didn't remove his impatience to see Noelle for himself.

Once the surgical nurse had left, he and the others took a collective breath. Noelle had survived. He knew she had a few more hurdles to clear before she was out of danger, but so far, so good.

"Now that we know she's okay, I'll go get food from the cafeteria. We need to eat, or none of us will be fit to care for her." Alana grabbed Juliette's arm. "Come on. I need an extra pair of hands."

Without argument, Juliette joined Alana and disappeared down the hall.

Jonah dropped onto a waiting room chair. He rested his elbows on his knees and held his face in his hands.

"You okay, Doc?" Decia rubbed circles on his back.

"Things could still go wrong."

"I know. But don't borrow trouble. She's alive. We can work with that." Her hand had stilled, but the warmth of her touch soothed his battered nerves.

"Why do I feel like one of your boys?"

Decia laughed. "Caring. That's what moms—and friends—do."

He smiled. "Thanks."

"Anytime."

Two hours later, Jonah sat next to Noelle in the ICU. Cords and medical equipment crowded the head of her bed. Her hospital gown exposed the scars on her upper arms, and her pale complexion against the crisp white sheets tugged at his heart.

Her lids fluttered but didn't open. The nurses said she'd woken once since they'd moved her, but he'd yet to see it happen. Those quiet moments had given him time to reflect, and he'd come to a conclusion today. Now that he and God were back on speaking terms, the past no longer held him prisoner. Could he return to his previous job as an ER doctor? Yes. Did he want to? Probably not. However, he'd consider filling in for his hospital friends if the need arose. He returned his focus to the woman he loved.

"Elle, it's Jonah." He laced his fingers with hers. "Please, wake up, honey. I want to see those beautiful eyes of yours."

The beeping sped up. He glanced at the monitor and watched the line spike.

A nurse rushed over. He held his hand up, stalling her forward progress.

"Easy, honey. Calm down. You're safe." He brushed the hair from her forehead and kissed her temple. "I'm right here. I'm not going anywhere."

Her head rolled into his touch, and her heart rate slowed.

The nurse studied the monitor, then nodded and returned to her station.

"Come on, Elle. Wake up for me."

Noelle's dry lips parted, then closed.

"Here." He dribbled a few drops of cool liquid onto her lips.

She swallowed the small amount of water.

"There you go. Now that your mouth isn't glued together, let's try an ice chip."

She gave a slight nod.

"You're sore from the endotracheal tube they placed down your throat during surgery. It'll go away soon." He added another ice chip onto her tongue. "That's enough for now."

"Thank you," she whispered.

"You are more than welcome." He resumed his position in the chair next to her bed. "Can you open your eyes?"

She struggled, then her lids lifted.

"Hi there, beautiful." He smiled. "It's good to see you."

She shifted and grimaced. "Stomach hurts. What happened?"

"Let's not worry about that for a bit." He straightened the sheet on the bed.

She quieted, and he thought she'd fallen asleep, but her forehead scrunched. "Got shot."

"Yes." Jonah tucked a strand of hair behind her ear. "Rest. We'll talk more later."

"M-kay." Within a minute, she'd drifted back to sleep.

Jonah sat and stared at the precious woman lying in front of him. She'd stolen his heart before he'd realized what had happened. And to be honest, he didn't want it any other way.

He laid his head on the edge of the bed and closed his eyes. *Thank You, God, for giving her back to me. I promise to take good care of her.*

Once Noelle was coherent enough to remember their conversation, he planned to lay out his wants and dreams.

———

Sunday, 3:00 p.m.

The recliner had never felt so good. Noelle sank deeper into the cushion and closed her eyes, letting herself drift. She'd arrived home several hours ago, and Jonah hadn't stopped fussing over her. He'd stayed by her side at the hospital, refusing to leave except for when their friends forced him to eat or go home to shower.

When her parents had visited her hospital room, her mother had tsked at her bare skin. Jonah had about come unglued and faced off with the prim and proper woman. He'd stated in no uncertain terms that her mother wasn't allowed anywhere near Noelle until she changed her attitude. Her mother had stomped out of the room without so much as a goodbye.

The rejection hurt, but Jonah had stood up for her, and that was all that mattered. She'd never felt so loved in her life.

Since all of her friends had seen her marred skin, she'd decided to let go of the shame that had imprisoned her for so long—the insecurities forced upon her by her mother. Today, she wore a loose-fitting sleeveless top that did nothing to hide her scars.

"Can I get you anything?" Jonah ran his hand over her arms, then bent down and kissed her scars.

She jolted.

He arched an eyebrow.

"Sorry."

"Nothing to be sorry for." He smiled. "You'll get used to it."

The idea of her ugly skin as a thing of beauty—his words, not hers—continued to baffle her. But the way he treated her... Wow! She resisted the urge to fan her face.

"Feel up for a conversation?" He sat on the arm of the couch next to her.

"Sounds serious."

"It is."

Concern churned in her belly. Had she misjudged his interest in her? Nope. She refused to go there until she had a reason. "Go ahead."

He leaned in and clasped her hand. His gaze met hers. "Cara's death gutted me for years. Then I came to terms with her being gone. The suffocating darkness lifted. The memories no longer had a hold on me. But there was one thing I couldn't shake: the guilt from not saving her—failing her—that continued to consume me."

Noelle sat and listened. She knew about his guilt. Her heart ached for the man she'd come to love. First as a friend, and then as more.

"When I saw you lying in that pool of blood, a part of me died. I thought I had lost you, too." His Adam's apple bobbed. "My heart shattered. But one thing filled me with regret."

"What was that?" She squeezed his hand.

"That I never told you that I love you."

Her breath caught in her throat. Had she heard him right? "You love me?"

"More than anything in this world." He slid from the arm of the couch and crouched next to her. "I love you, beautiful."

Tears streamed down her cheeks. She had no doubt in her mind that the man loved her, scars and all. "While Austin held me in that garage, I realized that I had trusted God with everything except my insecurities—the very thing that kept me from living my dream of a husband and family." She shook her head. "How could I have peace in the middle of Richard Nelson torturing me but not trust God with someone to love me?"

Jonah kissed the back of her hand but remained silent.

"At that moment, I decided that if I got out of there alive, I'd fix that problem." She licked the salty tears from her lips. "I love you, Jonah Harris. But more than that, I trust *you* to love me."

"Your trust means the world to me. I understand your fears, and I will do my best to make you feel special every day that God gives us together." Jonah stood and held her face in his hands. "I love you."

He closed the distance. His lips brushed hers, their touch soft and gentle.

Her inexperience worried her for a moment, then she melted into his touch.

As if he'd waited for her uncertainties to fade, he palmed the back of her head. He drew closer, careful not to jostle her, and deepened the kiss.

When he pulled away, he rested his forehead on hers. "That could get addictive."

She struggled to slow her breathing. "And dangerous. You take my breath away."

"Then it's a good thing I'm a doctor." His smile warmed the remaining cold places in her heart.

Today marked a new beginning for Noelle. Her serial killer's body had officially been identified and the cold cases and current cases solved. She had a man who treasured her, scars and all. The road ahead would have potholes and speed bumps. But with Jonah by her side, for the first time in her life she was ready for whatever came her way.

EPILOGUE

SEPTEMBER 30

The setting sun flickered on the gravestones in Colonial Park Cemetery. The Spanish moss on the trees dangled like fingers from the branches. During the day, Noelle loved the look, but at night, not so much. She hated all things nighttime. A byproduct of the serial killer who'd kidnapped and tortured her.

Her fear of the dark had intensified since her recent abduction, but Raven had decided Noelle deserved a celebration of freedom. And how did her friend want to celebrate? Another Savannah Historical Tour, of course. What had possessed Noelle to agree to the evening tour? Her fondness for Raven and the opportunity to spend time with her friends, that's what. Right now, she hoped they finished the tour before it got dark.

Four months had passed since Jack, aka Austin Nelson, had abducted and shot her. A few days ago, she'd received word that Austin had died while awaiting trial. He'd mouthed off to the wrong person while in prison and had paid the ultimate price.

Relief from surviving her ordeal mixed with sadness for all those who'd died and their grieving families.

She refused to lie and say that she wasn't happy that she wouldn't have to look over her shoulder anymore. But in reality, it hadn't made the anxiety disappear. Dead or alive, Richard and his son Austin had done irreversible damage to her body and mind.

Jonah's arm tightened around her waist. "Doing okay?"

Shadows danced along the buildings, giving way to the diminishing light. She snorted.

"That's what I thought." He leaned in and whispered in her ear: "We can bail before it gets dark if you want."

"And spoil Raven's fun?" She shook her head. "The tour's almost over. I'll be fine." She hoped.

They exited the cemetery and continued along the path, listening to the tour guide drone on about the history of Savannah. Noelle had joined Raven so many times on these tours that she could probably recite the entire speech.

"Thank you for joining us tonight." The tour guide finished her spiel and bade them goodbye.

"Wasn't that fun?" Raven flipped her black hair over her shoulder. She'd chosen an orange highlight for the month of September.

"You have a strange sense of fun." Alana chuckled.

Raven glared at her.

Alana extracted herself from Cash and threw her arm around Raven. "I admit, I had a good time."

"See. I told you. The history of this town is so amazing. I'm hungry. Let's find a place to sit and eat." Raven motioned for them to join her.

Noelle started to follow, but Jonah stopped her. "What?"

"We'll catch up with them in a bit. Come here." He tucked her in close and kissed her.

"Hmm. You always know what I need."

"I hope so." He drew in a shaky breath and stepped back.

"Jonah?"

LYNETTE EASON & SAMI A. ABRAMS

"Elle..." He chuckled. "Wow, I can't believe how hard this is."

Her pulse raced. "You're scaring me."

He clasped her hands in his and dropped to one knee. "Elle, I think I fell in love with you when you smiled at me after I hit you with the line drive. You stole my heart in that moment. I was just too stupid to realize it. I never want to live without you." He pulled a black box from his jeans pocket and opened it. "Will you marry me?"

The diamond ring glittered under the streetlamp.

She'd decided in that garage months ago that she wouldn't stand in God's way. And He was offering her the future of her dreams, if she'd reach out and take hold.

Tears pooled on her lashes and spilled down her cheeks. "Yes. I'd be honored to be your wife."

He slipped the gorgeous princess-cut diamond onto her finger and rose to his feet.

Both hands cupping her face, he brushed a kiss on her lips. "I love you."

She smiled. "Show me."

"Gladly."

All her fears faded away when his lips met hers and he deepened the kiss, showing her his heart and dreams.

———

Thank you for reading *Hunting Justice*! Return to Savannah again with the next Elite Guardians: Savannah romantic suspense, *Guarding Truth*. Read on for a sneak peek!

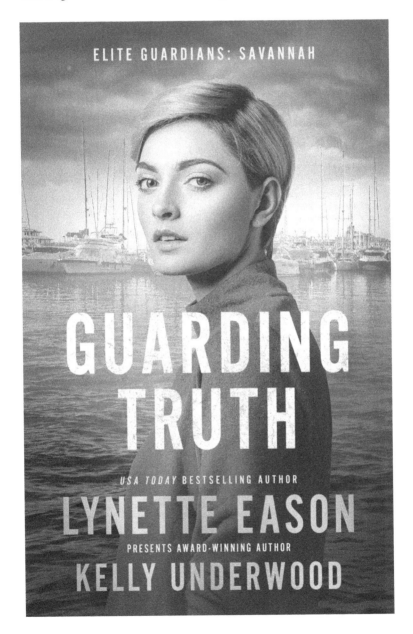

ELITE GUARDIANS: SAVANNAH

GUARDING TRUTH

USA TODAY BESTSELLING AUTHOR

LYNETTE EASON

PRESENTS AWARD-WINNING AUTHOR

KELLY UNDERWOOD

GUARDING TRUTH

ELITE GUARDIANS: SAVANNAH | BOOK 3

CHAPTER 1

REMOTE VILLAGE IN THE HINDU KUSH MOUNTAINS OF AFGHANISTAN, NEAR THE TAJIKISTAN BORDER

THURSDAY, 4:00 A.M.

"Time's up. Hostile vehicles spotted. Approaching in less than five minutes."

Caleb Styles nodded to his fellow Army cyber intelligence analyst, Lazlo Thomas, without taking his eyes from the screen in front of him. "And...done. I just uploaded the last software patch. Time to get out of here." He powered off his laptop, shoved it in his backpack, and followed Laz out of the makeshift tent that served as a command center for the Army outpost.

Not that he could miss the man's dark curly hair with a length that tested the boundaries of Army standards. Caleb preferred his dark-brown hair trimmed with military precision, never knowing when he'd be called into the field on trips such as this.

"Slow down a bit, would you?" Caleb caught up and matched Laz's warp-speed pace. Dirt swirled around his feet, the moonlight illuminating the path through the camp. He matched two steps to every one of Laz's long strides. Despite Caleb's six-foot fit and toned frame, Laz had a good four inches on him.

They walked past four other identical brown temporary structures used to house a contingent of soldiers and supplies. Men hustled, preparing to help defend the nearby villages from the impending Taliban forces.

"Sorry, I'm not slowing down until there's plenty of space between us and the Taliban."

"Yeah, I'd like to get out of here before the fighting erupts." Even though they'd both made it out of basic training alive, Caleb spent most of his days behind a computer screen, keeping cyberterrorists from taking down the Army's system. It meant being in the field on special assignments on occasion to make sure communications hadn't been compromised.

Laz slowed to a normal pace. "I can only imagine the kinds of torture devices the enemy would use on intelligence analysts if we got caught here."

Caleb glanced at his friend through glasses fogged from the sweat dripping from his brow. Despite being shielded by mountain ranges on both sides, in the valley, sweltering temperatures ruled the day and night. Even in October.

"Don't worry," Caleb said. "I'll do everything in my power to get you back to base so you can ship out. I know you've got a girlfriend back home. Ready to propose yet?"

Laz's pearly whites lit up under the moonlight at the mention of his girlfriend. What would it be like to have someone waiting for him back home? The trajectory of Caleb's life didn't include a wife and kids. However, one glance at Laz's face, and for a second Caleb reconsidered.

But he'd never been able to risk his heart for a chance at happiness.

"You know," Laz said in a singsongy cadence, "I heard the Rangers have made a special trip to pick us up. And do you know who made it out of Ranger School in one piece?"

Oh, he knew all too well.

Juliette Montgomery.

Caleb would have elbowed Laz in the ribs if the man hadn't been moving at the speed of a cheetah. "You just had to go there. Juliette and I will always be friends. There are lots of Rangers in the area. I'm sure she's—"

"Caleb?"

His heartbeat ticked up at the sound of his name from the voice he knew instantly. He slowed and turned.

"Jules." His basic training days came flooding back to him. They'd partnered up on many assignments, partly because most men didn't want to be on duty with a woman. But the other part of him had volunteered because he'd enjoyed spending time with her.

Juliette stood with three other men, dressed in fatigues. Despite her petite five-foot-three stature and shoulder-length dark-blonde hair, she looked every bit the part of a warrior.

Her golden-brown eyes twinkled in the moonlight for a fraction of a second before going into soldier mode. "No time to catch up. We've got to move." She motioned to one of the three vehicles, and just like that, they were a team again, as if no time had passed since they'd last been together.

Caleb and Laz helped hoist supplies, duffel bags, and weapons into the trunks of the vehicles, as four aid workers were also being evacuated because of the expected danger.

Once loaded, Laz, Caleb, and Juliette took the middle of the three-car caravan. Laz took the front passenger seat, leaving Juliette and Caleb in the back seat.

"Buckle up," Juliette said. "Our driver is Sergeant Hank

Williams, better known as Hank the Tank. He's got a lead foot. That's why we're in the second car. To slow him down." The bucket car seat looked like a child's dollhouse chair when Tank's muscular frame slid under the steering wheel.

"Better watch it, *Hazard Pay*," the driver said, adjusting his mirror to smirk at Juliette.

"They still call you that?" Caleb tried to stifle a laugh but it came out as a snort. Laz joined in. "At least some things never change."

Juliette folded her arms. "One crazy stunt in basic training and I'm branded for life."

"That one stunt solidified your career as a soldier," Caleb said. "Four armed men had you trapped. It was game over. That would have sent most men packing."

Caleb had cleared the path for her but couldn't get to her in time. He hadn't expected Juliette to rush into enemy lines like a bullet shot from a gun.

Laz laughed. "I watched you take down those guys headfirst. The look on their faces was priceless. No one saw that maneuver coming."

Caleb remembered the day with perfect recall, thanks to his eidetic memory. "To this day, soldiers still refer to that as the Kobayashi Maru. You know, where Juliette changed all the rules to get herself out of a jam."

Juliette groaned. "You and your *Star Wars* references."

"*Star Trek*. When are you going to get that right? Captain Kirk changed the rules of the test—"

Juliette and Laz burst into laughter. "Some things don't change," Juliette said. "You still drone on and on about sciencey techy stuff that most of us can't comprehend."

"We all learned our lesson after that stunt." Laz turned his neck to look in the back seat. "Never underestimate Juliette Montgomery."

Caleb glanced at her. They always fell back into that

comfortable rhythm as if no time had passed. "Jules can hold her own, that's for sure."

Tank chuckled and turned to look at Caleb. "Well, that and no one calls her *Jules*."

Heat crept up Caleb's neck. Had he overstepped? She'd worked and fought her way through Ranger School, a feat very few women accomplished. Maybe she had changed.

"I'll allow it, Tank," Juliette said. "We go way back. And Caleb has pulled me out of trouble too many times to count. He's earned the right to call me *Jules*." She caught Tank's eyes in the rearview mirror. "But you two better not try it."

"Never." Laz saluted her and watched out the windshield. Tank put the car in gear and hit the gas to follow the lead car.

Caleb longed to take a deep breath that didn't consist of dirt and diesel, but this was just the start of their journey to the Tajikistan border. While not far, their destination meant crossing through the mountain pass on roads that barely qualified as safe for a bicycle, let alone a three-vehicle caravan filled with people and supplies.

"So, what brings you all the way out here?" Caleb shifted in the cramped back seat so he could talk to Juliette over the grinding of tires against the earth and rocks below. "Since when are Rangers doing extractions?"

She nodded. "We happened to be in the area on another assignment when we got word that the fighting had shifted and were called in to help with the evacuation. But I could ask the same of you. Even though I'm sure you can't tell me about it, given your super secret clearance level."

"Looks like both of us are doing what we love. Congrats on making it through Ranger School."

She smiled. "I had plenty of practice with all those overnight duties we pulled in basic. I mean, we had some good times on patrol. Hanging out and dreaming of our futures while patrolling the camp—it wasn't all work."

His dreams had always included her. Maybe one day he'd have the courage to tell her.

A bump threatened to send him airborne except the seat belt locked him in place. He grabbed the steel handlebar on the side of the Humvee to steady himself. They climbed higher up the mountain.

"How is your niece?" Juliette asked. "Ivy, right?"

"Ivy's a handful—super smart. I went home last month to see my sister. Tessa will need to stay on top of things with that girl. Already skipping grades."

The sunrise backlit the mountains, changing their dark shadows to splashes of light and color. A bright spot in an otherwise dreary brown, never-changing setting.

Kind of like being in the presence of Juliette. She added a hint of adventure and mischief to his usually quiet and introverted life. Most of his time was spent in front of a screen, not jumping out of planes on dangerous missions like Juliette.

"Whoa, hang on folks." Tank's booming voice rose above the rush of wind outside the Humvee. The car in front slammed on the brakes, and Tank skidded their vehicle close to the edge of the road.

Caleb looked out Juliette's window and stared at the murky blackness below them. The space between them and the edge of a cliff shrank to a few feet. Juliette morphed into warrior mode, her hand reaching for the M16 perched in a rack behind them. "Why did we stop, Tank?" Her eyes flickered between the side window and the front seat.

"Looks like something in the road. I don't have a good feeling about this." Tank also reached for his gun, and Caleb rested his hand on the butt of his sidearm.

The whistle of the rocket-propelled grenade hit Caleb's ears before the blinding light of the explosion lit the darkness. The car in front of them burst into a fireball, sending shrapnel flying into their car.

A chunk of Humvee door hit the front of their vehicle with enough force to knock them closer to the ledge. Tank stomped on the brakes, but the car spun. The front of their vehicle teetered on the edge of the cliff and then took a nosedive.

Metal creaked and Juliette screamed. The vehicle skidded down the side of the mountain. The seat belt dug into Caleb's shoulder, but it was the only thing keeping him from hitting his head on the roof.

Boom.

The car collided with...something. What was it? Dust poured into the cabin, so thick Caleb couldn't see inside or out. Someone coughed. He reached out his hand to feel around the back seat and connected with Juliette's hand. She squeezed back.

"Nobody move," Caleb said. "We must have hit a tree or rock that broke our fall." At least they were upright, but his side of the car had taken the brunt of the crash. He tried the door but it wouldn't budge.

He needed to make sure everyone survived. "Everyone okay? Call out."

"I'm alive," Juliette replied.

A grunt sounded from the front seat. "I—I'm alive but hurt." The voice was Laz. "I'm pinned under the dashboard and can't move my leg."

Tank didn't reply. The smell of diesel burned Caleb's nostrils, and the vehicle let out a slow groan. They needed to move. Now.

A seat belt unbuckled. "I'm going to go out the door and get Tank and Laz out. You get ready to jump out when I have them."

"Jules, no. If you move, we might fall. It's not safe." If a rock was blocking their fall, it might not hold them for long. "We're not done falling."

Caleb's gut clenched at the sound of the opening door.

"I have to get them out. I'm the lightest in the car. We have to try."

From Caleb's vantage point, he saw nothing but the sun rising outside the front windshield. Out the window, he saw the outline of the boulder that had slowed their descent down the mountain. The boulder was the fulcrum and their car the seesaw. "Be careful, Jules. We're still in danger of dropping some more."

Once the dust settled, he could see the front seat. Tank wasn't moving, and a streak of blood trickled from his forehead down his cheek. The door scraped.

"I'm out," Juliette called back. "We crashed into a rock, but it kept us from going over the side of the mountain. It's steep."

More daylight lit the sky, and Caleb watched Juliette hold on to the vehicle for support while she made her way to the front.

She reached through the glassless window of the driver's side door. "I can't find a pulse. I'm heading around to Laz. We've got to get them both out of here—"

Rocks and pebbles tumbled down the side of the mountain, causing the Humvee to shift. Juliette lost her footing and slipped out of his sight with a yelp.

Smoke filled the cabin. Caleb crawled through the back seat and went out Juliette's open door.

"Please, Lord, let this rock hold us," he whispered.

He maneuvered his way to the edge of the rock.

"Jules!"

"I—I'm stuck." He followed the sound of her voice and saw her clinging to a tree branch. Her speech slurred and a gash on her forehead seeped blood.

A pop sounded from behind him, and he turned to see black smoke pouring from the engine. Not a good sign. The car might explode.

He had to save both Laz and Juliette.

"Laz, you have to get out."

"Can't move, bro. Save Juliette. Get her out of here. I'll be all right. I'm sure help is on the way."

His lie cut to Caleb's core.

One of his two friends could die here tonight.

Caleb sent up a prayer and committed to his choice.

He lowered himself off the rock and down toward Juliette's position. The tree branch was her lifeline, and that head wound was still bleeding. He grabbed her arm just as she let go, and strained to lift her. When he got her into his arms, he said, "Wake up, Jules. I'm never going to leave you behind."

We hope you loved the action, adventure, and romance in this riveting story. Discover more exciting romantic suspense from Sunrise Publishing!

GET READY . . . THINGS ARE ABOUT TO GET HOT!

With heart-pounding excitement, gripping suspense, and sizzling (but clean!) romance, the CHASING FIRE: MONTANA series, brought to you by the incredible authors of Sunrise Publishing, including the dynamic duo of bestselling authors Susan May Warren and Lisa Phillips, is your epic summer binge read.

Follow the Montana Hotshots and Smokejumpers as they

chase a wildfire through northwest Montana. The pages ignite with clean romance and high-stakes danger—these heroes (and heroines!) will capture your heart. The biggest question is...who will be your summer book boyfriend?

A BREED APART: LEGACY UNLEASHED!

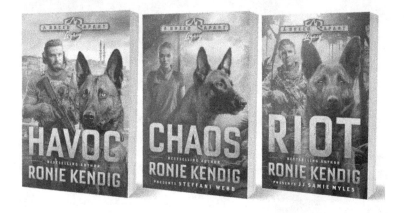

Experience the high-octane thrills, danger, and romance in Ronie Kendig's A Breed Apart: Legacy series.

FIND THEM ALL AT SUNRISE PUBLISHING!

CONNECT WITH SUNRISE

Thank you again for reading *Hunting Justice*. We hope you enjoyed the story. If you did, would you be willing to do us a favor and leave a review? It doesn't have to be long—just a few words to help other readers know what they're getting. (But no spoilers! We don't want to wreck the fun!) Thank you again for reading!

We'd love to hear from you—not only about this story, but about any characters or stories you'd like to read in the future. Contact us at www.sunrisepublishing.com/contact.

We also have a monthly update that contains sneak peeks, reviews, upcoming releases, and fun stuff for our reader friends. Sign up at www.sunrisepublishing.com or scan our QR code.

ACKNOWLEDGMENTS

Thank you for reading *Hunting Justice*. I had so much fun writing Noelle and Jonah. Scars, both physical and emotional are tough as these two find out. Thank you for going on the journey of healing with them.

I'd like to send a special shout out to my agent Tamela Hancock Murray and to my mentor Lynette Eason. You two are the best! I absolutely love working with you. To my partners in crime Kate Angelo and Kelly Underwood. You've made writing this series a lot of fun. We've built a beautiful friendship through this journey. I couldn't imagine this writer's life without you. To Sunrise Publishing for giving me the opportunity to write for you. And thank you to my Suspense Squad girls. Knowing there's a group of writers who I can call at any time for writing help or just to laugh is amazing. Thank you, ladies. You're awesome!

Let's not forget a special thank you to my law enforcement consultant Detective James Williams, Sacramento Internet Crimes Against Children, who answers all my crazy questions. By the way, all mistakes are my own or are author privilege, so please don't complain to him. Lol!

And thank you to my family for their love and support. Love you bunches, Darren, Matthew, and Melissa!

I hope you enjoyed reading Noelle and Jonah's story as much as I did writing it. I'd love to hear from you. You can contact me through my website at samiaabrams.com where you can also sign up for my newsletter to receive exclusive subscriber news and giveaways.

Hugs,

Sami A. Abrams

ABOUT LYNETTE EASON

Lynette Eason is the best-selling, award-winning author of over sixty books. Her books have appeared on the USA TODAY, Publisher's Weekly, CBA, ECPA, and Parable bestseller lists. She has won numerous awares including the Carol, the Selah, the Golden Scroll and more. Her novel, *Her Stolen Past* was made into a movie for the Lifetime Movie Network. Lynette can be found online at www.lynetteeason.com

facebook.com/lynette.eason
instagram.com/lynetteeason
x.com/lynetteeason
bookbub.com/authors/lynette-eason
amazon.com/stores/Lynette-Eason/author/B001TPZ320

ABOUT SAMI A. ABRAMS

Award-winning, bestselling author Sami A. Abrams grew up hating to read. It wasn't until her 30's that she found authors that captured her attention. Now, most evenings, you can find her engrossed in a Romantic Suspense. In her opinion, a crime with a little romance is the recipe for a great story. Sami lives in Northern California, but she will always be a Kansas girl at heart. She has a love of sports, family, and travel. However, a cabin at Lake Tahoe writing her next story is definitely at the top of her list. Visit her at **http://www. samiaabrams.com.**

- f facebook.com/samiaabrams2
- ⊙ instagram.com/samiaabrams
- 𝕏 x.com/samiaabrams
- BB bookbub.com/authors/sami-a-abrams
- g goodreads.com/goodreadscomsamiaabrams
- a amazon.com/stores/Sami-A.-Abrams/author/B094S4WWWX

MORE ELITE GUARDIANS

Elite Guardians: Savannah

Vanishing Legacy

Hunting Justice

Guarding Truth

Elite Guardians Collection

Driving Force

Impending Strike

Defending Honor

Christmas in the Crosshairs

Elite Guardians

Always Watching

Without Warning

Moving Target

Chasing Secrets

9 781953 783967